THE LAST TYRANT

THE LAST TYRANT

Book Six of the Last War Series

Peter Bostrom

www.authorpeterbostrom.com

Summary: Change is coming. Legendary American Admiral Jack Mattis, thrown into an unfamiliar universe, must now confront the impossible and do the unthinkable in a place very different from his home. New alliances must be forged in the face of powerful new enemies. Strange technologies may hold the key to victory, or hasten Earth's demise in all timelines. Change is coming and the howling winds of war at his back will drive Admiral Mattis onward toward a final confrontation. One thing is clear: The future is mutable, changeable, malleable. Or is it? Are Mattis's and Earth's destinies set in stone? Dark secrets will be revealed, terrifying enemies unleashed, and through it all, the true face of Spectre looms ever closer.

Text set in Garamond

Cover art by Tom Edwards

http://tomedwardsdesign.com

ISBN: 9781091619937

Printed in the United States of America

For my three favorite admirals: Kirk, Ackbar, and Adama

Prologue

Computing Core
Warfrigate 66549
Outer edge of the Assault Staging Ground
The Future

One hour after Admiral Jack Mattis's arrival in the future

The signal came through, a pulse that ran through Warfrigate 66549 like an alarm clock, waking Proconsul Michael Robinson from his slumber.

<ACTIVATE EMERGENCY COMMAND PROTOCOL>

Artificial intelligences did not sleep. Not in the traditional sense. They were either active or inactive—Robinson's mind was a synthetic organ, biological, but only in the loosest possible sense. It was a lump of biomatter that had been extruded from a medical printer, infused with nanobots, and spun it into a brain.

Power surged through his systems and his eyes—the

warfrigate's sensor network—lit up, illuminating space around him.

Wreckage. Heat signatures. Distress signals that were slowly dying as their power faded, as the Avenir sending them expired, as the inky black void of space returned everything to its natural state: nothing.

It made no sense to him.

Directive: *introspection.*

Outside provided no answers. The coordinates of their destination were correct . . . the staging ground for the transition into the past timeline. What had gone wrong?

If he could not find any guidance from without, he would search within. Robinson queried his internal sensors, flicking his eyes to the bridge.

The bridge crew was dead. Their air had run out. CO2 levels were well above lethal. The escape pods had either been launched or had malfunctioned.

He moved his vision elsewhere, to engineering. Engineering had totally decompressed and its crew was dead too. The engine room was the same . . . all dead. Reactor room, all dead. Crew quarters, all dead. Infirmary, cryochambers, fire control centers, damage control, fuel storage and management, munitions room, superstructure corridors, brig, cloning bays, maintenance corridors, life support room . . . all had suffered breaches, or life support had failed. Either way, all the crew had either abandoned ship or were dead.

That was why he had been awoken. The ship's computers realized there was nobody alive and had activated the backup program to govern the ship. The emergency backup to take over when all living things were dead.

Directive: *damage report.*

Robinson's sensors flooded with information. The ship was at condition Zebra; it was on war footing. Why had it lost its life support? He cycled through the systems, trying to understand. Every critical system reported functional or with active functional redundancies—and then he found it.

Atmospheric integrity was lost in several sections. Unrepaired hairline fractures had allowed air to spill out, and the atmospheric regulators had tried to replenish the lost oxygen until their supplies were exhausted. There were no crew left to stop the mindless system from slowly venting all the atmosphere into space.

Why? The only thing that could cause such devastation was the collapsing waveform from a time travel portal. However, auto-repair should have taken care of rebuilding the ship. Even with the crew dead, the ship's systems could have recovered from this state. Yet it had not. He queried the automated repair.

Time passed. Nothing. The attempt timed out. Not even an error signal. It must be either completely destroyed or totally out of power.

Either way, when the crew was gone and the auto-repair out of action, protocol was clear.

Directive: *establish communications.*

Thousands of queries flew to every digital system onboard, looking for anything that could send or receive Z-space transmissions. Long range systems, short range systems, battlefield meshes. Nothing was operable. He could not call for help.

Directive: *replenish crew.*

He brought up the ship's DNA storage facility and selected the standard labor kits: strong, simplistic mutants who could survive the harsh conditions, mature quickly, and provide the raw strength required to effect the repairs that 66549 required. They would take months to grow, but an artificial mind had infinite patience. The maturation time was a non-consideration.

<ERROR: CLONING VATS OFFLINE>

The critical systems may well be functional, but cloning was Tier 2. It had no redundancies. With no auto-repair, there was no way to fix it. The exact nature of the damage eluded Robinson, but was irrelevant. He possessed no hands, arms, or limbs.

If it could not be controlled with software or fixed with auto-repair, it could not be fixed.

Directive: *await assistance.*

With nothing to do but return to idle, Proconsul Michael Robinson powered down the reactor, turned off Warfrigate 66549's systems, and let the shift drift through the debris field, its cracked hull a tomb for the crew, its power source cold and its weapons idle, its guns pointing like the frozen fingers of a dead man to the stars. He left only enough power to keep his synthetic brain functional and to jumpstart the reactor when assistance arrived.

And so he waited.

CHAPTER ONE

Meanwhile

Bridge
HMS Caernarvon
Unknown Location
The Future

Captain Jack Mattis had never faced down a full-blown mutiny before.

"I'm sorry, Captain Mattis," said the Chief of the Boat, Chief Petty Officer Andrew Green. He was a giant of a man, his massive hand ever-so-casually resting on his sidearm. Behind him stood a dozen British Marines, and beyond, a sizable portion of the crew. "But I cannot turn over control of this Royal Navy asset to you, sir."

Many crewmembers were against him, especially the enlisted men. This had been expected. He was an American officer who had assumed command of a Royal Navy warship under truly strange circumstances. But, fortunately, a sizable portion of the crew had also thrown in their lot with him, and

Admiral Yim and Special Agent Blair were watching his back.

It just *felt* more alone without the whole crew behind him.

"I understand," said Mattis, cautiously. "The circumstances under which I assumed command of the HMS *Caernarvon*—"

"Illegitimately *seized control*," interjected Green.

Mattis would not be intimidated by verbal bullying and spoke over him.

"—assumed command of the HMS *Caernarvon* are certainly extraordinary, and I cannot honestly say that, if I were standing in your shoes, I wouldn't share your opinion. You are correct to be suspicious and angry, and I don't hold that against you."

Such a blunt confession seemed to steal some of the iron from Green's posture. "Yes sir," he said.

And the circumstances *had* been truly extraordinary. Commander Jemima Blackwood had turned out to be a clone of Spectre and had opened a rift that had consumed Earth. That kind of thing didn't happen every day. What had followed—a rift which had catapulted them into the future—was equally unprecedented. They had arrived in a different place, a different time, surrounded by the still-hot remains of a fleet of ships. Ships which had been preparing to shift into their timeline but were now wrecked.

It had been one hell of a day. He was still processing it.

"However," continued Mattis, his tone firm and even. "I will remind you that our *current* circumstances remain extraordinary and our options limited. Captain Spears is dead. Commander Blackwood . . ." he attempted to keep any kind of venom or anger out of his voice. It wouldn't help to mention Blackwood's true identity. "Is as well. Lieutenant Commander James White, the former Combat Systems Officer, is also dead, as he was on the bridge when—" he chose his words selectively. Commander Blackwood had killed them all. "The bridge incident occurred. This means that the next most senior department head is also gone—excluding Doctor Manda who is, by protocol, unable to assume command as she is the CMO."

"You're telling me things I already know, sir," said Green. He gestured over his shoulder. "Lieutenant Daylin-Rutland is working with the damage control teams, but he is the next most senior officer capable of performing their duties. The chain of command goes to him. But since he's working with engineering, he's nominated me as his proxy until the damage is shored up."

Capable of performing their duties. Mattis knew what Green was referring to. The Ops officer, Lieutenant Alexander Mohammad, had suffered what his training had called an *acute combat stress reaction*. That was to say, after the battle with the Chinese warships, Doctor Manda had sedated him in the infirmary.

With Daylin-Rutland working with engineering, and Mohammad . . . *unavailable*, that left the most senior enlisted person as the CO. Which was Green. Or Admiral Yim. But both Yim and Mattis had agreed—extremely quickly—that a British ship was more likely to follow an American commander than a Chinese one.

The politics of a mutiny had to be dealt with very carefully. Normally under these kinds of extraordinary situations, the only goal of a ship who had lost so many of its senior staff was to finish the mission and get back to port so the brass could decide who to fire and who to promote. But the ship was stranded out of time and this was clearly not an option.

"I understand," Mattis said carefully. "And believe me. What I want to do is respect the chain of command on this ship. I respect your position as Chief of the Boat, as I'm certain you respect my position as a senior Commanding Officer in the United States Navy."

"Of course I do," said Green, his tone overly formal, suggesting otherwise. "Sir."

"Very well." Mattis took a deep breath. "With that in mind, my proposal is as follows. If Lieutenant Mohammad is judged by Doctor Manda to be fit for duty, then I will stand down and yield command to her. If Lieutenant Daylin-Rutland completes the repair work on the ship's systems and is no longer required as a matter of urgency by the engineering department, then I will stand down and yield command to him. At that time, at either CO's discretion, I will transfer aboard the USS *William Harrison* or remain here under an advisory position."

That seemed to take Green aback. "You'd willingly stand down, Captain?" His huge hands twitched slightly by his side. "Without a fuss?"

"Assuming the situation warrants it," said Mattis. He extended his hands, palms up. "That, Chief Petty Officer, is all I can offer you."

"How can I know that you're telling me the truth, Captain?"

Carefully, making no sudden movements, Mattis reached

down to his sidearm, unclipped it, and drew it with two fingers. He turned it over in his hand, then leaned forward and offered the weapon to Green. "Admiral Yim, Special Agent Blair, turn over your sidearms please."

Both of them did so with palpable reluctance.

"You have my word," said Mattis, firmly. "Failing that, you now have all the guns."

Green inspected the weapons, then handed them over to the crewmen behind him. He seemed to digest what Mattis had told him, deliberating on it, then reached a conclusion. "Very well," he said, stiffly bringing his heels together. "What are your orders, Captain?"

His efforts had bought him some time, but what he had to do next would tax that fragile peace. "The very first thing I need to do is have the entire crew's blood examined by Doctor Manda in the infirmary. It's unlikely, but there could be more Spectre agents aboard."

"Aye aye," said Green. "And then?"

"I need… to ask a favor."

He stood straighter, his shoulders squaring. "You can ask, Captain," he said, a clipped edge to his tone.

"Once critical tasks are completed, I need Lieutenant Daylin-Rutland to do one task. I need him to head out with the Reardons and their vessel, the *Aerostar*, and scout the surrounding wrecks for potential salvage. They may be knocked out, but they're all intact. I'm prepared to wager we can get at least *one* of these ships working again, or at the very least find components we can integrate into our systems." He ground his teeth. "There are two of us here, Chief Petty Officer. The *Caernarvon* and the *William Harrison*. Two ships.

We need to even the odds if we're going to have a chance."

Green touched his chin and didn't answer right away. Mattis gave him all the time he needed. The Chief of the Boat spoke for the enlisted crewmen aboard, and right now he needed Green on his side. Without the crew, the ship had no weapons, no engines, and was essentially a floating tube full of air.

"That seems reasonable," Green said. "But in exchange, Captain, I need something from you."

Mattis was in no position to refuse a request. "Proceed."

"The crew wants to know when they might be going home."

Probably the worst possible question to ask.

They had passed through a strange portal to the future of Spectre's making, where the Avenir ruled. Its mechanisms and operation were entirely unknown to him, and while it was clearly possible to return somehow—Avenir ships had traveled to their timeline, after all—he had absolutely no idea how to do that, or if he even should.

Here, he could strike the Avenir where they lived. Where they might be weak.

"The truth is I don't know. The more complete truth is we have a lot of work to do before we can even consider the possibility of returning to our timeline." He wasn't sure how to phrase this, so he just said it. "Furthermore, I'm . . . not sure we want to do that. Earth is gone. I watched it happen."

"Doesn't mean we won't want to go home, Captain," said Green. "Many of us have family offworld. I'm from New London myself, sir."

"Not much left of that, either," said Mattis dryly.

"True enough, sir."

Mattis let the lengthier rough draft in his head slip away, speaking the honest truth directly from the heart. "As I said, I don't know if we can ever go home again. But I promise you that if the opportunity presents itself and our mission is complete—or as complete as we can make it—I will make the attempt."

Green nodded, then turned to the rest of the crew behind him. "Okay," he said, a firmness in his voice Mattis hadn't heard before. "Get back to work! We've got a whole lot of work to do on the *Caern'*, and those wrecks out there are precious bounty. Hell, any one of them could be our ticket out of here. Now go. Get!" Then he turned back to Captain Mattis. "Is there anything else, sir?"

"Not for now," Mattis said, giving a formal nod. "Get me some salvage. Dismissed."

Green saluted, then began herding the crew out of the armored casement hatch and into the ship proper.

One crisis managed, on to the next one. When they were gone Mattis turned to Blair. "Hail the USS *William Harrison* and patch it through to me. I want to talk to Commander Lynch."

Blair fumbled with the radio for a moment, her clear inexperience showing. Seconds ticked by. And then, "Okay Mattis, I think I got it."

He signaled for her to go. The channel opened with a faint hiss of static. "This is *William Harrison* actual," said Lynch's smooth, thick Texan accent. "How did it go with the mutiny and all? Going to assume you chamber-of-commerced it."

Sometimes Lynch could be almost incomprehensible with his Texas-isms and thick accent. "Oh, more or less as I expected," said Mattis, unable to fight back a wide grin. "I have to be honest, I was *not* expecting you to show up when you did. Aren't you meant to be in a coma?"

"I am definitely *meant* to be," Lynch drawled. "But, you know how things are. The Navy needed someone to take the fight to Spectre while you were . . . busy."

Another reminder of Chuck's death. Mattis's chest tightened. His only son… dead. The thought screamed at him in the back of his mind.

Dead . . . and Elroy. What had become of him? Or of baby Jack?

He couldn't let the paralyzing grief crash in right now. He pushed away the thought, the wailing keen in his brain. He had to focus. "Okay. I hope you gave him Hell."

"We hadn't really started," said Lynch, confessionally. "But I did have something I've been meaning to tell you about for a while now."

"Okay," said Mattis. "I'm all ears. Send it."

"Not here. Not over a radio line. I wanna look you in the eye for this one." Lynch paused, as though considering. "Something else though. Admiral, is it true you have one of the backup computers salvaged from the *Stennis* aboard?"

That caused a raised eyebrow. He did, in fact, possess such a system; Harry Reardon had brought it on board. Captain Spears had wanted it badly. "How in God's name did you know about that?"

"I know a lot of things," said Lynch, cryptically. "And that thing is important to . . . well, to everything. I want to discuss that with you as well."

"Come over on a shuttle," he said. "We can chew the fat. Catch up. Just like old times."

Lynch's voice adopted a faintly dour note. "I think old times are gone for good, friend."

The fragile dam holding back the weight of the truth crumbled. Lynch's words hit Mattis like a hammer to the chest.

Earth was gone. Everyone he knew and loved was gone. Billions of people, their lives extinguished in an instant.

"Take your time," said Mattis, voice cracking only slightly. "First, I want to speak to Harry Reardon and find out what's on that computer of his that Captain Spears died for."

CHAPTER TWO

Infirmary
HMS Caernarvon
Unknown Location
The Future

The light of the surgical ward hurt Sammy's eyes as, ever so slowly, he found himself drifting from the strange, dreamless sleep of medically-induced unconsciousness into wakefulness.

Where was he?

"Hey hey," said Reardon, leaning over the bed, a big grin on his face. His eyes were red and puffy, like he'd been crying. "Well, guess who's awake?"

"Is it me?" asked Sammy weakly.

Reardon clapped him on the shoulder. "Never a single doubt in my mind," he said. "I knew you weren't going to die a virgin."

Oh boy. He didn't know. For ages Sammy had wondered if Reardon . . . *knew* . . . about Peter, if he suspected. Apparently not.

"Yeah," said Sammy, hoping that the after-effects of whatever surgical knockout drugs he'd been given would mask the inevitable embarrassment that would creep over his face every time he thought of Pete. "I guess not. At least not today, bro."

"Don't worry, Sammy! Still plenty of time to get you some action." Reardon casually pulled back his bedsheets, revealing his wounded leg—really no more than a huge lump of bandages—and blew out a low whistle. "Daaaaamn, though. They really did a number on the ole' walking pin right there. The whole thing's wrapped up in more bandages than an Egyptian Mummy. It was just a little bullet hole!"

Such a tiny hole indeed, and yet he remembered the blood. So much blood. And how quickly it had come from him, spraying out like water from a leaky hose. That kind of injury couldn't just get patched up. "I think they got me pretty good." With no sensation below the waist since the accident, he had no idea how bad things really were. "Maybe they needed to do some surgery or something. Wouldn't be the first time."

"Yeah," Reardon said, casually dropping the sheet. "Well at least you're okay."

Yeah. That was true. He was okay . . .

Not that it really mattered. A bullet hole in the leg did nothing if the leg itself couldn't move. Having a broken back was good in that respect, no pain, but no gain, either.

For some reason he couldn't explain, Sammy tried to do something he hadn't done in years. He tried to move the limb. Perhaps while they had him under they had found something, some simple thing the Earth doctors had missed. Some subtle yet easily repairable problem that would allow him to walk again. Maybe. Just maybe . . .

Nothing. Nothing happened.

But, well, at least there was no pain.

"So, yeah," said Reardon. "Looks like you and me will be out and about real soon. Once you've recovered, we'll get back on the *Aerostar* and go take a vacation, okay?"

That made him snort. "Vacation? When was the last time you actually did any *real* work, huh? I'm the one who flies the ship, I'm the one who loads the cargo, I'm the one who shoots the guns. You just spend all our money on hookers and drinks."

"Hey," Reardon said, faux-gasping. "I do a lot of stuff on that ship, okay? I . . . I sort out the contacts. I'm the man with the plan. I'm the *ideas guy*."

"Well, here's an idea for you: do more work, bro."

"Work," said Reardon, waggling a finger disapprovingly, "is a four-letter word. Especially for big brothers. That's just how the world works. Little brothers make the money, big brothers spend the money. And drink." He clapped his hand on Sammy's leg in a way which would probably have hurt if he could feel anything.

"You're a dick, bro."

"You're a bro, dick."

"That doesn't make any sense."

Reardon grinned. "*You* don't make any sense!"

They shared a laugh, and then a strange quiet fell over everything.

Reardon switched to Hindi—something he only really did when things got serious. "I thought I almost lost you this time," he said, his voice soft, cracking as he spoke.

"Nah, I couldn't die yet," replied Sammy, also in Hindi. He felt his face dampen. "You'd be totally screwed without me."

"Totally," said Reardon, a single thin tear leaking out of his left eye. "Like I said, who would do all the work?"

Another moment of quiet, but this one seemed less oppressive, less serious. It ended when Reardon's phone rang. Apparently the communications device had patched into the ship's systems—and changed his ringtone to be some kind of Korean music.

"*Caernarvon* morgue!" answered Reardon, in English, his voice chipper. "You kill 'em, we grill 'em!"

"This is Captain Mattis." He sounded unimpressed. "I need to speak to you about an urgent matter."

"Why?" asked Reardon. "Are we at Earth yet?"

"Not exactly," said Mattis, a grim edge to his tone which suggested that something quite dire had taken place. "Meet me at the *Aerostar* in the hangar bay ASAP."

"Uh, sure," said Reardon, then hung up.

"Sounds bad," said Sammy.

Reardon shrugged, casually stuffing his phone into his breast pocket. "How bad could it be?" he said, rolling his eyes. "Mattis always sounds like the damn world is ending."

CHAPTER THREE

Infirmary
HMS Caernarvon
Unknown Location
The Future

Patricia "Guano" Corrick was pretty sure she was going to die this time.

Don't get out of bed, her doctors had told her, yammering in their annoying voices. *It's extremely dangerous for someone who's just had major brain surgery to be wandering around inside the ship.*

Turns out that they were right. For nearly half a day she had see-sawed wildly between unconsciousness, uncontrollable vomiting, and a headache that felt like someone was cracking her skull with a sledge hammer. Even the magical surgical-grade painkillers seemed to do nothing for the agony.

"So," said Doctor Manda, her voice sounding like power tools drilling at the inside of Guano's eyes. She scanned over a clipboard with a worried look on her face. "This is not good."

There was no need to tell *her* that. Guano didn't want to

speak—noise was anathema to her—so she just nodded very gently.

Doctor Manda continued, evenly and calmly. "The postoperative nausea and vomiting is obviously a problem, but our latest scan has shown something much more serious —something in addition to the motor deficit. Since you ripped out your stitches, you've undergone what we call intraoperative bleeding. That's a fancy way of saying massive blood loss. We've given you a transfusion, but we're going to have to prep you for posterior fossa surgery to correct the other issues, and we're concerned that in your weakened state you might be in a lot of trouble."

When doctors said things like that, it was not good. "Might . . . be?" asked Guano, the effort sending fresh shards of pain into the top of her skull.

Doctor Manda's voice was blunt. "I'd give you a fifteen percent chance of a serious complication such as partial brain damage, disability, or death."

Oh. Only that much. That was okay. Not even fifty-fifty. Guano nodded firmly. "Do it," she said, grimacing through the agony. "Give it your best shot."

Blessedly, one of the nurses touched Guano's IV machine and drugs surged into her system. And whatever they gave her to knock her out seemed to, finally, take the edge off. The world faded away, maybe for the last time. She had regrets, she had missed opportunities, she had a thousand things she wanted to do but couldn't, but as she passed out, she could only think of one thing.

Finally, it didn't hurt anymore.

CHAPTER FOUR

Corridor to Cargo Bay
HMS Caernarvon
Unknown Location
The Future

"So," said Mattis, power walking down the corridor with Yim and Blair in tow. He didn't have any Marines—they couldn't spare the manpower—so it was just them. "Where the hell are we? And *when* the hell are we?"

"I can only assume," said Yim, keeping up with only a moderate amount of difficulty. "That we are in the future."

"I know that." Mattis clicked his fingers. "The *year*, Yim. I want to know the year."

"We can calculate that by analyzing the star patterns," he said. "And estimating based on their movement around galactic central point."

Good plan. Definitely a good plan. "But what about the where?"

There was a very brief pause, and Mattis sensed, rather than saw, Yim glance over to Blair.

"Don't ask me," she said, an edge of frustration in her voice. "I'm just a federal agent. I'm not a stellar cartographer."

"But you are an investigator," said Yim. "Perhaps this is something you could . . . investigate."

Blair muttered something darkly under her breath that he didn't catch. "This is my first time going offworld, I literally have no idea what I'm doing."

Then it was Yim's turn to mutter something. In Chinese. That he didn't understand.

"Very well," said Mattis, pressing on farther down the corridor toward the hangar bay. "Yim, find out the when and where. Just do your best. Not asking for anything special. Blair, you're an investigator. I assume you have some applicable training. Including forensics. Yes?"

"I've done some lab work," she said. "And plenty of theoretical courses. Mostly to pad my resume, but it's there. And I was actually quite good at it, if I do say so myself."

"Good," said Mattis. "We'll need someone of your skills with the salvage team. Link up with Lieutenant Daylin-Rutland, work with the salvage team." Anticipating her complaint, he held up a hand. "You shouldn't have to do an EVA unless you need to. I don't want you puking all over whatever we find. Instead, take a look at what they've brought in so far. I'm sure your skills will turn out to be remarkably useful."

"I hope so," said Blair, sincerely. "I'm feeling mighty useless here. I can barely work the radio. It'd be nice to do something I can actually, you know, be good at for a change."

"Okay. Sounds good. Report to Daylin-Rutland. Try to . . ." Mattis had no idea what specific order to give her, so he just went vague. "Find something we can use."

"On it," said Blair, turning and disappearing down a fork in the corridor.

"Kids, huh?" said Yim, moving up to walk beside Mattis. "Were we ever so young and full of energy?"

"I was," said Mattis, managing a little smile. "I think you were born old and crotchety."

Yim laughed as they turned a corner, the airlock to the hangar bay appearing in front of them. They walked through into the large, open space where the *Aerostar* was docked.

Mattis took in the sight of the thing. It was a bright pink, dented, scorched and battered ship, seemingly cobbled together from random spare parts; the main hull seemed to be two different kinds of yacht cut in half and welded together, with various other ship debris attached in a seemingly random fashion, then the whole thing covered in thick slabs of paint. Below the ship, a brown stain had crept across the hangar bay deck, and the soft *drip drip* of fluid emanated from some unseen source.

If he hadn't seen it actually sail, he would be very skeptical that it was space-worthy.

Maybe it wasn't.

"It looks like it might fall apart at any moment," said Yim with a sour glare. "I couldn't believe Captain Spears was searching so hard for this ship, and now that I see it, I can't believe she even let it into her hangar bay." His face fell further as he walked over to pink monstrosity, gingerly extending a finger to the hull. The digit came away covered in dirt. "Don't they ever wash it?"

"Oh, I don't know," Mattis sighed dejectedly. "But you

should see what it looks like on the *inside* ."

"You've been *in* that thing?" Yim's eyes widened. "In *space*?"

There was a loud, rude cough from the other side of the hangar bay. Harry Reardon, his hands on his hips, looked at them with a mixture of indignant anger and quiet frustration. "If you're both finished slagging off my girl," he said, quietly muttering something Mattis couldn't catch. "Or is that why you brought me down here? To insult me?"

"No," said Mattis, awkwardly calling across the hangar bay. "Listen. Spears knew about the computer you salvaged from the *Stennis*. While your ship was getting its new engine . . . well, she broke into the data file."

"Wow." Reardon's expression hardened, becoming a dark glare that intensified as he spoke. "That's gratitude for you. Guess we're done, then." He raised his wrist to his mouth. "Sammy, we're leaving. Get Doctor Whatever to bring you down to the hangar bay and load you aboard. We are fucking out of here." He let his arm fall. "Shame, because I was going to give that to her as a parting gift."

No doubt *sell* would be the correct term, but Mattis couldn't quibble. "You probably don't want to leave right now," he said, sincerely.

"Yeah, no, I do." Reardon raised his wrist again. "Reardon to Captain Spears."

Nothing.

"Hey, Spears. It's Reardon. Is it true? Did you really hack into my ship?"

More nothing.

"She's dead," Mattis said flatly, the words heavy on his

chest. "And we're not in Kansas anymore."

Reardon gaped. "So where the fuck *are* we?" His hand drifted down to his pistol. "I don't like this, Captain Mattis."

Mattis was in no mood to argue with the kid. He gestured around vaguely, then his hands fell limply to his side. "You know? That's what I keep trying to find out."

A brief moment of silence. "Well," Reardon said, "she's not the only one who can get access to computers."

"What's that supposed to mean?"

"I'll show you." With an angry snort, Reardon stomped toward them. Mattis thought he might be attacking, but a subtle change in course belied the truth. He was heading to the *Aerostar*.

Mattis fell into step behind Reardon, up the loading ramp and into the cargo bay. Mattis followed Reardon over to a large screen which lit up, displaying space outside the *Caernarvon*. Reardon had somehow obviously gained access to the ship's cxternal camera feeds.

That would have been useful information to have back when they were walking on the *Caernarvon*'s hull. Hindsight, though, was 20/20.

Slowly, Reardon's anger melted away as he panned across space, revealing drifting, burned-out wreck after drifting burned-out wreck. The more he scrolled, the more destroyed ships appeared—endless amounts, it seemed—and the more his fury faded.

"Wow," Reardon whispered.

"I know this might sound totally crazy," said Mattis, carefully, "but we... are in the future. This is the timeline where the Avenir come from."

"Wow," said Reardon, again. "Shit. *Wow*."

Mattis gave him a second to let it sink in. "I need your help with that computer of yours," he said, softly. "We have to copy it for Sammy and our own techs to work on."

"Why does it have to be him?" asked Reardon, his voice soft.

"The truth is, this is a small frigate. We don't have any spare computer-hacker-geniuses aboard. And we're a long way away from resupply. Believe me, if I had a better option, I would take it."

Reardon nodded. "Sammy's the best shot we got, then. I hope whatever's on it is worth all this effort."

Spears thought so. And she had given her life for it. Another item on the growing pile of grief to sort through later. Mattis went to say more, but as he did so, his communicator chirped. "Mattis here," he said.

"Sir—" it was Blair on the other end. "The salvage team checked in."

About time they did. "Okay," Mattis said. "What did they find?"

Blair's voice held an edge of triumph. "They found a ship."

CHAPTER FIVE

Corridor to Cargo Bay
HMS Caernarvon
Unknown Location
The Future

Blair split off from Mattis, heading toward the cargo bay alone. The promise of a haul of alien artifacts and salvage to sift through was intriguing, as was the potential for her to use her actual skillset for once instead of awkwardly trying to use the radio.

But now she had a purpose and that purpose empowered her. She power walked toward the cargo bay, following the signs, occasionally passing a crew member or small groups of the same. They were giving her the stink eye for the most part.

She was aware she wasn't popular. The near mutiny aboard had seen to that.

Her phone beeped. She would probably have to swap it for a communicator, the military issue hardware, or maybe one of those wrist-mounted computers the British had.

Absently, she pulled it out of her pocket and checked the message. It was a reminder.

ORGANIZE ASHLYNN'S BIRTHDAY + PRESENT

The message made her smile. Her eldest daughter was turning five, and of course, that meant a birthday with all her friends. And presents. She'd been putting it off because of work, but it was time to get down to business.

Blair slid the phone back into her pocket and resolved to make sure that everything was organized when she got off the ship. But after only a couple of steps farther down the corridor, the grim reality of her situation hit her like a hammer to the gut.

Ashlynn and Katey were on Earth. It had been her ex's week with them. Joint custody was a bitch.

The thought barely took a little moment to sink in, to worm its way into her head and process. They had been on Earth. They were gone.

Her girls were dead.

Blair stopped walking, frozen in place in the corridor. Quickly, far too quickly, everything slammed into place. A numb feeling crept up her legs, climbing her body like a creeping vine, wrapping itself around her chest and squeezing her.

Her kids were *dead,* both of them, and she couldn't even give them a funeral. There were no bodies to bury. No place to bury them—the whole Earth was gone. Even if there was something—what, a memorial service for the Earth?—organized by someone somewhere, she wasn't just in a different place. She was in a different *time*. This wasn't some vacation with a pre-planned itinerary for the spaceflight home. There was, to the best of her knowledge, no clear way home at all.

She might never be going home.

Ever.

Blair slumped up against a bulkhead, sliding down until her knees were against her chest, her face in her hands. The party was going to be in a month. Five years old . . . five years old. She remembered Ashlynn's birth like it was yesterday, and now . . .

She cried. That kind of ugly-crying where her cheeks went bright red and snot ran down her face, sobbing loudly in the corridor of a British warship, her chest heaving, not even trying to keep her tears concealed. A billion thoughts ran through her head like stampeding cattle. If she hadn't gone offworld to help with the investigation into the President's assassination, she would have been on Earth, too.

Maybe that would have been for the best.

With eyes misted by tears, she fumbled for her phone, pulling up her pictures and flicking through them. Katey's giggling baby smile. Ashlynn shoving spaghetti into her face. That time she had taken them both to the Police Officer's Ball. Her ex was there in the background, laughing and smiling. They were still together then.

Her marriage hadn't been an easy one. She'd always been focused on her career. Eventually she had got herself married, a house, cute cat, and two kids. Then one day, she'd come home to find her husband with some girl seven years younger than her.

And then she had a house, a cute cat, and two kids.

The house was on Earth. The cat was on Earth. And the kids . . .

"Special Agent Blair?"

At first she barely heard the voice, then, slowly, it filtered through her brain.

Lieutenant Daylin-Rutland, still wearing his space suit. "Hey." He sat down beside her, his back up against the bulkhead. "You didn't show, so . . . I thought I should come find you. You okay?"

It was one of those polite, rhetorical questions. She obviously wasn't. "Nah," said Blair, wiping her cheeks with the back of her hand. "Not okay. Sorry, I just—" her voice cracked. "It's my phone, it just reminded me, my eldest daughter's birthday is coming up and—and she was on Earth, so . . ."

"I'm sorry," said Daylin-Rutland, grimacing sympathetically. "I don't think it's hit me yet. I don't think it's hit most of us yet."

Blair sniffled and looked away. "Yeah. Look, I know you have a lot of work to do. You don't have to say anything."

"I know," he said. "But I want to. If you want to listen."

That would actually be nice. She smiled thankfully. "Here," said Blair, handing him the phone. "See the pictures."

He took it, clumsily scrolling through the images with his fat gloved hand. "They look happy," he said, scrolling left, going through picture after picture.

Then he stopped.

"That's kind of odd," he said, "looks like the rest of the images are still downloading."

"Downloading?" she sniffed. How was that even possible? "From where? We're . . . we're not near Earth anymore."

"Dunno," said Daylin-Rutland. "I think one of these wrecks must be acting like a relay. Downloading a cache of your emails from some server somewhere." He turned the phone around to show her, and it was true. "Those messages must have been floating around in some server farm somewhere all this time. For hundreds of years. And now they're finally getting transmitted to you."

She watched in bewilderment as her phone flashed, signaling a new message. And another and another. The top of her device showed a preview of each as they came in.

Emails from her ex, discussing the upcoming switch, where the girls would be sent to her. Another one asking when the party was going to be organized. Another one mentioned a school trip.

A school trip offworld. To the Tiberius system.

Blair snatched the device back with trembling fingers, opening up her emails and frantically scrolling through them. There she saw the message.

Hi Denelle,

The kids are being sent on a school trip to Los Alamos v2.0 and I'll need $400 for it whenever you have the time; money is still short, so if you could send that it'd be great. I know I haven't had a job in a while, but my friend Joey can spot me if you don't get this in time. I know what your work is like and . . .

The rest of it was totally irrelevant nonsense.

"Wait," said Daylin-Rutland, reading over her shoulder. "So your kids were actually—"

"They were offworld." Blair sniffed, sucking in snot and then disgustingly blowing it back out again. "H-holy shit."

"Definitely," said Daylin-Rutland. "They're definitely okay."

Doubt began to creep in. $400 wasn't a lot of money to someone who had a job these days, but it was a lot if one didn't have it. The kids had once missed a school excursion to some stupid museum because Deadbeat Daddy couldn't pay, but . . . offworld was something else. They had to have made it.

Hadn't they?

She checked all her messages. Nothing from him after the ship had passed through the wormhole. There were plenty of other messages—random stuff, spam mostly. But everyone probably thought she'd died on Earth.

A lot of people would be in the same basket.

"So," she said, her breath trembling. "You're going to tell me that everything's going to be okay now?"

Daylin-Rutland put his hands on his knees. "I'm not here to tell you anything, just that . . . I'm here."

Blair wiped her face with her sleeve, smearing salty tears and snot all over them. "So, uh . . . what's up? How's the salvage going?"

"Great," said Daylin-Rutland. "You should call Mattis. We found him a ship. I wanted to give my report in person, but . . . it's fine. I should get back and help my team into the airlock."

"I'll let him know." She pulled out her phone, tapping into the ship's communications relay, calling up Mattis on his communicator.

Daylin-Rutland stood, clipped his helmet back on, and saluted. "Good luck, Special Agent Blair."

She smiled her thanks as the phone dialed. As Daylin-Rutland disappeared down the corridor, she wondered.

What the hell is happening back in our own timeline?

CHAPTER SIX

Main Street
Los Alamos v2.0
Tiberius System
Main timeline

Elroy Mattis still hadn't processed exactly what had happened over the last few hours. He had been told Earth was destroyed in a cataclysmic ball of energy and light, turning it into some kind of portal. He didn't know what was going to happen. Nobody did.

Except maybe John Smith.

He'd been sent away from Admiral Mattis with Jack to safeguard him. Getting off Earth had apparently been a very wise move. But no sooner had he discovered his homeworld's fate then he'd been approached by a stranger in a bar, a man now leading him to places unknown.

"So," he said, jogging to catch up, holding Jack close to his chest. "Where are we going again?"

"You'll see," said Smith, hurriedly walking toward the spaceport. At least that's where Elroy figured he was going.

"We're close."

Elroy glanced over his shoulder, trying his best to look inconspicuous. What if someone was following them? Or had noticed him slip out of the bar?

"Stop looking around so much," said Smith, his voice soft but judgmental. "Eyes down, just walk like you're in a hurry. With purpose. Like you know where you're going. Making eye contact with people imprints your face into their brain. Just look at the ground in front of you. Constantly looking for a threat makes you look guilty."

Guilty? He hadn't done anything. Still, he did what he was told, keeping his eyes down, trying his best to keep up with Smith.

Smith muttered something to himself, too low to hear, then added, "Your husband was the same."

A surge of anger shot through Elroy. "Hey."

Smith said nothing, and kept walking.

"Hey!" Elroy grabbed Smith's shoulder, stopping him. "Don't talk about Chuck that way."

Smith spun around, his eyes lit up. "You don't understand," he hissed. "I *helped* him. I'm trying to help you too. And your son."

Helpfully dragging him and Jack into some nonsense . . ."You got a strange definition of help, John Smith."

"Right now I'm trying to help you by making sure you aren't identified."

"Identified? But I haven't done anything wrong. All my papers are in order. I'm here legally. Until a few minutes ago I was just some guy sitting in some bar watching the news."

Smith pulled himself away with a jerk. "Nobody's *just some guy anymore*, not after today. Remember how, at the outbreak of the Sino-American war, the whole blasted American people rallied together? People ran to recruiting stations, donated money to the military, you name it. Imagine that, but for the whole human race."

He was too young to remember that war. It was something he'd seen on newscasts and various other things, of course. But not something he remembered personally. He'd been just a kid. "Okay," he shrugged. "So I'm a hero now or whatever. Jack too. Why not? So what are we doing?"

"We're going to find a way to kill Spectre," said Smith. "And to do that, we need the Avenir. Or more specifically, their technology. And then we're going to save Earth."

Elroy only had a fuzzy idea of what the Avenir even were. Future humans come to kill Spectre. He *did* have a good idea about Earth, though, and it looked screwed. Not the kind of damage one could buff out. "You think we can convince the Avenir to help us kill him?" Elroy shook his head. "That won't work. If it were that simple . . ."

"I never said it would be simple," said Smith. "We can't exactly talk to them and convince them that it's in our shared best interests to work together, that's not how they think." He turned a corner, drawing closer to the spaceport. "They have a . . . well, I wouldn't say it's an inferiority *complex*. More of an inferiority *simple*. They think they're better than us. It's that simple."

"You seem to know a lot about them all of a sudden."

"I've been busy," said Smith, somewhat cryptically. "But the point is, I saw Admiral Mattis go through that portal. And that means he's going to get into contact with the Avenir sooner or later. Hopefully he'll come back with some of their tech, but he'll need a way home back to this timeline. That's what we're here for—soon as I confirm the identify of that ship and start getting the things I need."

They were bringing Mattis home. "The ship?" asked Elroy. "Uhh, well, I know what ship he was on last time I saw him."

"What ship?" asked Smith. Something in his tone suggested he *really* wanted to know, but was playing it casual.

Elroy struggled to remember. "The *Caravan* . . . no, wait, the *Caernarvon*."

"*Caernarvon*. Right. That confirms it, then." Smith turned another corner, and there, perched on a landing pad like a resting bird, was a gleaming spaceship. A small transport, with a small turret slung under the chin and a pair of shuttles attached to the sides. Fairly standard for an armed transport, even if they usually only carried one shuttle. But the most curious thing about it was the color.

It was bright pink.

"Why pink?" asked Elroy, staring in confusion at the garish thing. Jack squealed happily, arms outstretched as though to grab it.

"A . . . friend of mine had his ship the same color," said Smith, smiling wryly. Almost sadly. "Salmon, he called it. Or *blood in the water*. Or some nonsense. The catalogue called it Girl Power, though, which is just hilarious." His smile widened. "Or would be if you knew this guy."

"Okay," said Elroy. "What's it called?"

"*Einstein*." Smith walked up to the ship, the loading ramp

lowering obligingly to grant him passage. Elroy followed him, walking up the ramp and inside the ship.

A synthetic voice, male and with a thick Indian accent, rang throughout the ship. "Who is this?"

"A friend," said Smith. "Give him level two access."

"Level two access granted," said the voice. "What about the adult?"

Smith paused, and laughed. "Give him level two access as well."

Elroy chuckled too, but still couldn't help but gape. "You have an AI?"

"I stole it," said Smith, as casual as could be. "Debris from the Battle of Earth. Technically I stole it from people who stole it. You'd be surprised what someone can accomplish with my connections. Its original name was Michael Robinson, but I renamed it." He idly picked his teeth with a fingernail. "I call him Albert."

"Albert. The AI aboard the *Einstein* is called Albert."

"Naturally," said Smith. He clicked his tongue. "Couldn't get the holoprojectors though. What a shame."

Holoprojectors? Holograms were nothing special. "Couldn't you just rig up some of the hologram you showed me?"

"Too small," said Smith. "And I only have a handful of those. They have to be saved for important things."

"Okay," he said, not entirely convinced. "So. Now we're alone. What's the big deal? Why do you need me to bring Mattis home?"

"Because, like I said," said Smith, "you're a Mattis. Not by blood exactly, but you'll do." He rubbed his missing ear, his tone losing its levity. "And no matter what, I'll need a partner to do this, someone I trust. And I trust Mattis. So I trust you."

"Okay," Elroy said, still a bit befuddled.

"So," Smith went on, "we need some things." He ticked off his finger methodically. "First, we need a ship's reactor, which we push to overload. That'll create a portal to the future like the one that destroyed Earth and take a ludicrous amount of energy—energy converted from mass. The whole process is kickstarted by a much smaller, but still vast, release of energy. Like a reactor going pop. Size doesn't really matter; what you'd find in your standard starship will do."

That sounded dangerous. "So… we need to steal a ship?"

"Oh no, that's what *this* ship is for, once we're done using it to get around. Congratulations! Task one complete. On to number two." He waggled his second finger. "We need a wildly complex technological marvel from the future that can open portals. Fortunately, I asked Albert to build one and he did. Sorry. He gets credit for that little effort."

"Uhh, that's great." Elroy didn't really want credit for that. "What else?"

"We also need a planet or big moon to consume, but fortunately, I already have one in mind. Don't worry, it's a rogue planet called Serendipity, and it's totally uninhabited."

Serendipity. Elroy had heard of it. From what Chuck had told him, it had apparently once held an illegal gambling den named the Dark Side which had been recently shut down, or been put out of business, or was in some other way no longer operating.

"We're going to destroy the Dark Side?" Elroy blew out a low whistle. "A lot of Darth Vader fangirls are going to be pretty pissed."

Smith reached over and clapped him on the shoulder. "You're definitely a Mattis. And congratulations on getting that thing crossed off, too. You've been on my ship thirty seconds and you've gotten two things done."

"Yeah. I'm great at this. Super useful. It's all me so far." Elroy clicked his tongue. "I'm guessing the others won't be so easy."

"You're a good guesser." Smith smiled. "The others won't be easy, no. The third thing we need is a Spectre clone who can give us the last piece of the puzzle I need to unlock the portal."

"Okay," said Elroy. "I have no idea where to find one of those."

"Fortunately, I *do*." Smith tilted his head as though listening to a sound only he could hear. "And the best part is, she's just a short walk away. She's why I'm on this world in the first place, but recent . . . *events* . . . have changed my plan. Now I have an assistant."

Elroy immediately thought of Jack and a chill shot down his spine. "There's a Spectre clone here? On this world?"

"Oh yeah." The way Smith said it made the news sound decidedly grim. "We'll pay her a visit when we're done getting ourselves settled in."

Suddenly, it briefly flashed into Elroy's mind that he had only just met this guy. Was this the right thing to do?

"Is there anything else?" Elroy asked, trying to mask his discomfort.

"Yeah, one more thing," said Smith, as casual as anything. "We need a LGM-99 Minuteman XI entry vehicle. Or at least a part from it."

That sounded bad. It sounded like a weapon. "What is that?" he asked, almost dreading the answer.

"It's a MIRV," said Smith, as though he were describing the weather. "A magic wand that turns countries into rubble." A slow smile spread across his face. "We're going to need the isotropic core from a live nuclear warhead."

"I'm sorry," said Elroy, unable to believe what he just heard. "You need a *what now?*"

CHAPTER SEVEN

Hangar Bay
HMS Caernarvon
Unknown Location
The Future

"A ship?" asked Mattis, curiously. "What do you mean?"

"Lieutenant Daylin-Rutland tells me that their sensors have detected one of the frigates out there is drifting at the outer edge of the debris field." Blair sounded like she was reading off a list or report. "It's suffered some kind of massive decompression, but most of its systems are online. There's reactor integrity, although it appears to be in some kind of powered-down state. They say that they're preparing to enter the airlock, and when you give the word, they can go aboard and inspect it to see if the hull breaches can be sealed and the ship returned to action."

"Okay," said Mattis, scowling and scratching his chin. "So this is a potential salvage target? We can take components from it? Weapons, maybe?"

"Actually, Lieutenant Daylin-Rutland's recommendation is

to take the ship itself, assuming we have the crew to do so and it can be repaired." Blair hesitated, a tense note coming into her voice. "Just hurry up. There's no way that this many damaged ships are just going to be ignored by the Avenir. We don't have unlimited time here, and until we get onboard, we won't know if it's a wild goose chase or not. If so, we need to know ASAP."

While she was right, Daylin-Rutland was also correct. The whole ship *would* be better, and probably faster. Large-scale ship-wide decompression was not good—that was the ocean-going equivalent of losing water integrity and sinking—but it was something that was fixable. Metal could be welded, bulkheads shored up, and repairs made.

Still, it was a lot of work. Some weapons would be better . . . but removing weapons systems from a damaged warship and grafting them to their own was also a lot of work. Maybe Daylin-Rutland was right. "There's no other option? Nothing in better shape?"

Blair didn't answer right away. Probably reading. "Lots of the other ships are in a much worse state," she said. "This one only seems to be okay because it was significantly out of place relative to the rest of the fleet. Preliminary analysis suggests that it was some kind of communications ship, or perhaps a rearguard of some description. It was substantially farther out than the others. Even so, despite the distance, it's been very heavily damaged."

That made sense. He had seen the waves of energy blast away a gas giant and also consume Earth. A ship, no matter how well engineered, would have to be a substantial distance away for it to survive at all.

immediately," said Modi. "Once the *Caernarvon*'s teams are similarly retrieved. It's not worth the risk."

He wanted them to rabbit? No way. "Mattis thinks its worth the risk," he said.

Modi bit his lower lip. "Then I have no suggestions for you."

There it was again. The hesitation. The *agreement.*

Lynch had not asked Modi to be his XO because they were friends and always agreed. He'd asked him because they were friends and always *disagreed.* He didn't want yes-men on his bridge; he wanted officers who would challenge him, think outside the box, and provide alternative solutions to problems. Obviously this desire was not imparted on the man. He would have to be more direct. "Modi, I'm thinking we might try a gut punch."

A gut punch, despite its name, was a stalling maneuver. A ship moving through space had to spend as much time decelerating as they did accelerating. Even though the eight incoming ships were coming in faster and faster, they would have to begin to slow down at the halfway point.

Accordingly if the *William Harrison* waited until the incoming hostile ships were at the halfway point, then began accelerating toward them. The incoming ships would not be able to stop fast enough and would zoom past, then they'd turn around and double back, wasting vast amounts of time.

"Is that wise, sir?" asked Modi, cautiously. "Is it not better to enter Z-space and escape?"

"We need that potential salvage prize," said Lynch. "If the *Caernarvon* can seize it, and if both ships contribute crew, being able to field three vessels is better than two. Further,

"Okay," he said. "Instruct Daylin-Rutland to breach the airlock and get a closer look. If we can turn that ship into a prize, I'm all for it." How exactly they would crew the ship would be a separate question.

"Right," said Blair.

Mattis cut the connection.

"So you think we can actually salvage that ship?" asked Yim. Mattis had almost forgotten he was there.

"I hope so," he said. "But I'll settle for some Avenir tech."

Yim's skepticism was clear. "I don't know about this, Captain Mattis. We should focus on restoring order on this ship and examining Reardon's computer."

Reardon coughed. "Yeah, about that. You really don't think you're going to be able to get a whole ship working? Sammy and I have done less-than-legal salvage before, as you know, and we just . . . well. It's an acquired skill."

"Great," said Mattis. "Wanna join the salvage team?"

Reardon snorted derisively. "Only if you do."

"Deal," said Mattis, grinning slightly. "You're on my team."

Reardon's mouth hung open, but then—in what Mattis figured was an attempt to preserve his masculinity—Reardon straightened his back and puffed out his chest. "Will do," he said, giving a sloppy salute. "Lead the way. I'll prep the ship."

Mattis opened his communicator. "Blair, get ready to open the main hangar bay doors. Reardon and I will take the *Aerostar*, pick up the salvage team, then take them over to the damaged ship."

"Got it," said Blair. "Good luck."

Yeah, good luck was something I haven't had in excess for so long I can barely remember living any other way. Mattis nodded to Reardon. "We're heading out. Please make sure—"

"Sir!" said Blair, her voice charged. "The bridge reports that we're picking up a lot of long range radar contacts exiting from Z-space. A *lot* of contacts. And they're heading this way."

Damn. "How far out?" A tense pause.

"Six hours from us," she said. "At their current speed."

It sounded like a lot of time, but wasn't. "Six hours to refloat that ship," he said. "Let's get to it."

CHAPTER EIGHT

Bridge
USS William Harrison
Unknown Location
The Future

"Dang," said Captain Lynch, staring at the main viewscreen which was displaying their long range radar. It was almost impossible to detect the ships through the debris field. The swarm of ships raced toward them, forming up into a V, their speed constantly increasing. "Those bastards are coming in fast."

"Correct, sir," said Commander Oliver Modi, his long-term comrade, friend, and now XO. He was always so . . . *robotic*. Like a machine given human form. "The incoming vessels are moving through the debris field at a rate hitherto unobserved by even experimental military spacecraft. Their rate of acceleration is truly impressive."

Fast little bastards. Busy as a funeral home fan in July. "Suggestions?" asked Lynch.

"We should recall our salvage teams and enter Z-space

"Okay," he said. "Instruct Daylin-Rutland to breach the airlock and get a closer look. If we can turn that ship into a prize, I'm all for it." How exactly they would crew the ship would be a separate question.

"Right," said Blair.

Mattis cut the connection.

"So you think we can actually salvage that ship?" asked Yim. Mattis had almost forgotten he was there.

"I hope so," he said. "But I'll settle for some Avenir tech."

Yim's skepticism was clear. "I don't know about this, Captain Mattis. We should focus on restoring order on this ship and examining Reardon's computer."

Reardon coughed. "Yeah, about that. You really don't think you're going to be able to get a whole ship working? Sammy and I have done less-than-legal salvage before, as you know, and we just . . . well. It's an acquired skill."

"Great," said Mattis. "Wanna join the salvage team?"

Reardon snorted derisively. "Only if you do."

"Deal," said Mattis, grinning slightly. "You're on my team."

Reardon's mouth hung open, but then—in what Mattis figured was an attempt to preserve his masculinity—Reardon straightened his back and puffed out his chest. "Will do," he said, giving a sloppy salute. "Lead the way. I'll prep the ship."

Mattis opened his communicator. "Blair, get ready to open the main hangar bay doors. Reardon and I will take the *Aerostar*, pick up the salvage team, then take them over to the damaged ship."

"Got it," said Blair. "Good luck."

Yeah, good luck was something I haven't had in excess for so long I can barely remember living any other way. Mattis nodded to Reardon. "We're heading out. Please make sure—"

"Sir!" said Blair, her voice charged. "The bridge reports that we're picking up a lot of long range radar contacts exiting from Z-space. A *lot* of contacts. And they're heading this way."

Damn. "How far out?" A tense pause.

"Six hours from us," she said. "At their current speed."

It sounded like a lot of time, but wasn't. "Six hours to refloat that ship," he said. "Let's get to it."

that ship's from a much more advanced timeline than ours. Who knows what surprises it will have in store for us."

"The surprises are what I am worried about, sir," said Modi, sounding vaguely defeated. "But you're right."

"A'right," said Lynch, leaning forward in his command chair. "You just let me know the moment those bastards decide to flip and burn, and we'll burn toward 'em in turn."

"Yes sir," said Modi, straightening his back. "I'll make it happen."

His first battle in command of his own ship, the *William Harrison*. Or rather, his first attempt to *avoid* a battle in his own ship. Despite all his combat experience, Lynch couldn't help but feel a powerful wave of nerves. He cupped his hands together, squeezing them to bring a little pain. Just enough to refocus his mind and bring him into the moment, ready to lead.

"All hands report ready for the gut punch," said Modi. "When the enemy flip and burn, we'll be ready to burn toward them right away."

What would Mattis do in this situation? "Let's make this happen," Lynch said, nodding firmly. "We gotta cover the *Caernarvon*. Have weapons and sensors standing by as well. Might as well see if we can spit in their eye as we fly right past 'em. We'll paint the town and the front porch."

"Aye aye," said Modi. A pause. "Which town?"

"It's a figure of . . . Never mind. Just execute the burn when it's time." Now all Lynch had to do was not die in his first real battle in command, and everything would be peachy.

Easier said than done.

CHAPTER NINE

Command Core
Warfrigate 66549
Outer edge of the Assault Staging Ground
The Future

Proconsul Michael Robinson's slumber was interrupted by a pulse through his biobrain that jolted him out of inactivity.

<LIFE FORM DETECTED>
<INCOMING>

He examined the output, pumping the raw data into his mind, separating it, and analyzing it piece by piece. The ship, his body, had detected life signs approaching them. Life signs in a ship.

Directive: *analyze.*

The newcomers were definitely life signs, but they were not supposed to be there. Perhaps the response team had arrived, a work unit designed to put his body back together. A signal from his chronometer, however, refuted that. He had only been in standby for a few hours.

He scanned the incoming shuttle with his myriad sensors, peering beneath the hull to the people within. They were definitely alive. Heartbeats and oxygen and heat. They wore bulky, ancient protective suits of a model that were not in his memory banks. He could see weapons—or what his systems determined had a high probability of being weapons—but they were at their hips and back, on standby.

Directive: *generate threat matrix.*

The decision came easily to him. This small team of strangely dressed humans and their primitive seeming weapons posed very little threat to him. Harmless. Safe.

Yet something was off. Something in his pattern cognition nagged at him. They might not be a direct threat, but neither should they be trusted completely.

Michael Robinson watched the ship dock with his own, the polymorphic airlock struggling to make contact with whatever their system was, which as far as he could tell possessed no adaptive qualities at all.

More and more curious.

A billion courses of action surged through his biobrain. He trimmed the decision outcome tree, removing those which were nonsensical and passing those which provided favorable outcomes for him, weighing his own survival against his mission objectives, fleet safety, and Avenir Alliance goals. Eventually, he settled on one which satisfied his qualifications and began to execute it.

Directive: *confront intruders.*

CHAPTER TEN

Cargo Bay
Aerostar
Unknown Location
The Future

The last time Mattis had done an EVA he had nearly been killed, frozen to death by a broken crypod salvaged from an Avenir vessel.

Hopefully this time would go differently.

"We're docked," Reardon said, standing beside him, rifle slung comfortably over his back. "The seal failed to lock, so make sure your suits are done up nice and tight. The Brits are in the airlock prepared to go inside, so you can ingress with them. I'll guard the *Aerostar*."

Mattis checked his suit once more, the diagnostic computer flashing up a pleasant green. He had atmospheric integrity, mag-boots were working, and his air intake tube was unblocked.

That last one was important to him, as it had frozen over last time and nearly killed him.

"Decompressing the cargo bay," said Sammy over their comms. He sounded very tired, which made sense, given that he had recently been in surgery. "Hold tight, bro. Hold tight, Mattis."

"At least this thing still works," Reardon muttered . "Pretty sure I patched all the holes in it. *Pretty* sure."

How reassuring. Mattis was glad his own suit was British and hopefully maintained to a higher standard than whatever cobbled-together, fly-by-night model Reardon was wearing.

With a faint hiss, air pumped out of the cargo bay of the *Aerostar* until nothing but vacuum and silence was left. A tense, uneasily stillness filled the room. Reardon didn't die, which was good, but before Mattis could remark on that fact, the loading ramp began to silently lower, revealing the airlock beyond.

Six British Marines stood in the fairly spacious airlock on the other side, their arms full of equipment and tools.

"Admiral Mattis," said Daylin-Rutland. Mattis's suit helpfully projected the guy's name above his head. "Ready to breach the airlock and take this ship?"

Mattis was torn between conflicting desires: risk versus reward. "As fast as safely possible," said Mattis.

Reardon clapped him on the shoulder. "Good luck exploring a dangerous wreck," he said. "I'll stay behind, here where it's safe."

Wonderful. Cautiously, Mattis stepped down the loading ramp of the *Aerostar* and out into the airlock with the rest of the Marines. It was a tight fit, but apparently in the future, airlock space was no longer at a premium. "I'm as eager as you are," he said. "But we should take a look at her first before we decide we're going to claim her."

"Seems prudent, sir," said Daylin-Rutland, shuffling to one side and hitting the airlock cycle button with his hip. "I'm considering this one a bit of a fixer-upper. You know, the kind of ship that will last for decades more with just a little bit of elbow grease."

The airlock began to cycle, sealing off the *Aerostar* behind them and pumping in air. However, only a few seconds into the process, bright red light filled the room. Had there been atmosphere, he presumed there would have also been warning alarms. The doors jerked open just a crack, then strained and vibrated before ominously falling silent.

"Make that a *lot* of elbow grease," said Daylin-Rutland ruefully, pulling out a pry bar and jamming it into the door. With a jerk, the left door fell completely off, and the way into the ship was revealed.

The corridor was cracked and obviously decompressed, although gravity seemed to still work. Bulkhead panels had blown out or simply fallen off, revealing familiar piping, tubing, and three-dimensional circuit boards.

This wasn't the first time Mattis had been aboard a damaged Avenir ship. They had found a ruin in the Pinegar system, but didn't have the time to fully inspect and salvage it. The whole area had been awash with radiation . . . which reminded him.

"Radiation levels?" he asked.

"Nominal," said Daylin-Rutland, waving an instrument around. "Looks like the reactor is fine. There's no sign of the radiation seen on the other Avenir wreck."

That was good news. "A real fixer-upper," said Mattis,

taking the lead, stepping through the hole and into the ship. Just ahead, a body lay facedown on the deck, barely visible in the dim light. "Damn. Got a body."

Daylin-Rutland moved beside him, rifle raised. Mattis signaled for him to halt, then stepped forward, clicking on the light mounted on his suit's shoulder.

It was an Avenir mutant, its pasty green skin paler even than usual. The body had been dead for some time—probably from the moment they had fallen through the wormhole—and its blood was pooling in its extremities, giving them a strange, lurid olive color. Mattis casually poked the corpse with the tip of his boot. It didn't move.

"They don't look so tough," said Daylin-Rutland, but there was a slight tremor in his voice betraying a different opinion entirely.

"They aren't when they're dead," said Mattis, grimly stepping over the body and moving onward. "But you wouldn't like them when they're still kicking."

Daylin-Rutland fell into step beside him. "One day I'll get my chance, sir," he said, a stiff determination in his voice. "I've trained all my life for combat; this is what I was born to do, and there isn't a bigger challenge in the world than knocking off one of these Greenies, sir."

"Greenies?"

"The bigguns. That's what the Royal Navy has taken to calling them in our briefings."

"Is it true," asked one of the other Marines behind them, "that they have no dicks, sir?"

Mattis blinked and, for a moment, considered that his oxygen might be obstructed and he'd misheard. His visor told him the guy's name was Lipham. "To . . . be perfectly honest," he said, "I don't know. I never checked."

"Everyone says that they have no dicks," said Lieutenant Daylin-Rutland. "Nobody's been able to give us a straight answer one way or the other. Also, shut up, Lipham."

Maybe they would have a chance to check out the body—or other bodies—at another date, but Mattis didn't say anything now. "Let's just focus on the mission for now," he said, and turned a corner.

A translucent, glowing figure appeared suddenly in front of them, ethereal and bright, lit up by a green glow from within. It shed light like a lantern, bathing the dark corridors in soft luminescence, the exposed pipes and circuit boards casting sharp, jagged shadows along the bulkheads and deck. It quickly took the form of a man, tall and strong, with dark hair and dark eyes, floating a few inches off the deck.

"I am Procouncil Michael Robinson," it said, its voice cool and artificial. "Identify yourselves immediately and state your purpose for being aboard this vessel."

"Holy shit," said Lipham, squeaking down the radio. "It's . . . it's a bloody *ghost!*"

CHAPTER ELEVEN

Housing District 4
Los Alamos v2.0
Tiberius System
Main timeline

Elroy lidded his eyes in frustration as he took in the building they had been sent to. It was a prefabricated structure dropped in the middle of the housing district, barely bigger than the tiny apartment he and Chuck had shared back on Earth. It was rust red just like every building on the block, and apart from the number 304 spray-painted on the side he would have had no idea how to find this place.

That, he was forced to concede, was probably the point of having a house like this.

Elroy took a breath. Normally, he would *never* leave Jack alone in such a place, but given what they were coming here to do, it was probably for the best. The kid was big enough to grab something and choke on it . . . but Albert had promised to keep him safe. How, exactly, he would do that was unclear, and Elroy fretted as he walked. "Okay," he said, inhaling deeply. "So. The Spectre clone is in there. What's the plan?"

"Plan's simple," said Smith, striding boldly up to the door. "Follow me."

Confused, but very glad they'd left Jack back at the ship—the hologram could "take care of him," apparently—Elroy followed Smith to the door.

Smith's foot flashed bright orange.With a swift kick, he broke the door in as some powerful technological effect gave him additional strength. The door shattered into a million pieces, dangerous shards of metal flying all over the inside of the otherwise neat and tidy dwelling .

As though it was just another day at the office, Smith strode into the room, drawing his pistol. Elroy followed behind, suddenly aware he had . . . fists. What the hell was he even doing here?

No time to think about it. A yell from within—feminine, raw and full of anger—tore him away from those thoughts. "Hey, get the FUCK OUT OF MY HOUSE!" A woman, young and with a completely shaved head, stood behind a computer desk, angrily waving her hands around. She wore a bright orange maintenance worker's overalls. "OUT!"

"Not a chance," shouted Elroy. "You're a Spectre clone!"

A flicker of something in the woman's eyes—recognition? Fear?—vindicated him.

"Way to put all our cards on the table from the get-go," growled Smith, moving with surprising speed over to her, his hand flying to her throat, cutting off any further complaints. He jammed his pistol against her stomach. "Close the door."

How? It was laying in a billion pieces. Elroy awkwardly picked up a far-too-small coffee table and, with a grunt and some clumsy maneuvering, placed it in front of the entranceway as a makeshift door. His effort looked pathetic, barely chest-high, and easily able to be tipped over by anyone determined enough to force their way in.

"Nice work," said Smith, his spare hand still around the woman's throat, his other on his pistol. He kept his grip tight. "We just want to talk."

She kicked and struggled, then finally held up her hands. Smith let her go and she stumbled back, gasping and wheezing.

"Okay," said Elroy, moving up beside Smith. "Now we've broken about a dozen laws and committed a handful of felonies, what next?"

"That," Smith said ominously, "depends on this one."

"What do you want?" she hissed.

"You're a Spectre clone," Elroy repeated, once again glad Jack wasn't there. "And we need information. We can do it the easy way or the hard way."

The woman spat on the ground. "I'll die before I tell you anything. If you know what I am, you must at least know that."

"Okay," said Smith. "The hard way it is."

Well now, that was a dark sentiment if ever there was one. Elroy was not about to be party to torture. "Wait, hold up," he said, waving his arms around like some kind of trainee traffic conductor. "We can't just—"

Smith shot her in the face.

Elroy staggered back. The gunshot was extraordinarily loud in the confined space and conjured a profound ringing in his ears. Blood splattered over the back of the apartment, dripping down the walls like happy little Bob Ross trees. Elroy stared in mute horror as the body slumped over, the top of its head missing.

"What happened to *we just want to talk*, huh?" he shrieked, taking a step back.

"Calm down," said Smith, waving his hand dismissively. He stepped over to the body, crouching beside it, and raised up the head—it looked like an upside down salsa bowl complete with chunks—and he tilted the thing from side to side, as though studying it curiously. "Hmm. Check out this mark on the inner skull; a Type 4."

Elroy averted his gaze, feeling bile burn throat. "I'm not looking at that."

"You'll get used to it," Smith said. There was a wet squelching, snapping noise. "Okay, I've retrieved the neural implant." Retrieved? From where? "That's all we needed. Let's get out of here and see what we can learn from this thing."

There was nothing Elroy wanted to do more than to leave that place and get as far away from it as he could. "Can you believe I came here on *vacation?*" he muttered, shoving the table out of the way and clearing the door.

Smith followed him out. Elroy deliberately went first so he didn't have to look at him.

"Elroy," Smith said. "Take us back to the ship."

Not a problem at all. It wasn't that far away. "You're *sure*," Elroy asked, "that that woman was a clone?"

"Unless you think it's common for natural-born humans in this timeline to have computer chips in their heads," he said. "And I'm not talking about what I have. My dinky little implant. I mean *this* thing—my hardware is basically a glorified calculator, but *this* . . ." he laughed. "This is something else. It's a database, cognition engine, and repository of almost unlimited knowledge. It has more storage than a small datacenter, and more processing power than a warship's data engine. All in a package small enough to fit inside someone's skull."

"I—" Elroy could not contest that. "Fine." He would have to work through the moral implications of this later. "I guess shooting a clone is fine."

"It is," said Smith casually.

A surge of anger and confusion shot through Elroy. "Why did you bring me here?" he demanded. "I don't have a gun. I don't know how to fight. I don't even know the full details of the plan. I should be on the ship with my son!"

"You should," said Smith, "but I needed you here. I needed you to see what we're up against with your own eyes. It's one thing to be *told* that there is a clone, but another thing to experience it entirely."

Elroy gave a confused, annoyed grunt.

Smith sighed behind him. "Look, if there was a way to get the chip out without killing them, and without letting them live so they report us to any other Spectre assets or even local law enforcement—or go on to hurt someone else—then I'm all ears." They walked for a moment in silence, slipping between buildings away from the residential area and toward the spaceport. "I'm CIA. I'm used to this sort of stuff . . . or at least, I'm supposed to be. Allegedly."

Allegedly, the CIA had a long, storied history of murdering people. Of course, one person's assassination was another person's extra-judicial targeting killing. Regardless,

Elroy suspected that, given Smith's hardware, he was some kind of soldier or government employee, but hearing it was another thing entirely.

But one other thought jumped into his head too. "My husband was CIA?"

Smith laughed mirthlessly. "I'm afraid not. Chuck Mattis would have made a great agent, I must say, but the truth is he was just . . . helping us. Helping me."

"Oh." Elroy hesitated. "But I mean, it would have explained a lot. Chuck did . . . a lot of things."

Smith let out a long, low sigh, and then chuckled again. "You know how I met him, right? He was breaking into some Senator's office. And he was a total *idiot.* Threw a brick through the window, totally missing that there was a silent alarm on the building. Got himself arrested."

Elroy knew the story well. "It really affected our income," he said. "He lost his job. Couldn't find a new one with his record. Which definitely means he wasn't CIA, now that I think about it. I figured if he pulled a stunt like that while working for you guys, you would have at least kept him on the payroll." A thought jumped into his head. "Hey, by the way, if I'm helping you, is there any money in this for me? I got a kid to look out for."

He could hear the smile on Smith's face. "Already been taken care of. You'll get a weekly stipend, plus expenses, and I've already transferred your first advance."

Cautiously, Elroy pulled out his phone and checked his balance.

+$43,944.91

"Whoa."

"Saving the world pays well," said Smith. "Plus you'll need it where we're going."

Elroy couldn't help but continue to stare at the number on his phone in disbelief. Forty-four grand . . . even in this economy, it was a year's rent. Per *month*. "Where's that?" he asked. "Where are we going?"

"Oh, nowhere fancy," said Smith. "Just, you know. A place."

Elroy blinked. "What kind of place?"

"History lesson: Los Alamos National Laboratory was where they tested nuclear weapons for the Manhattan Project. That was nukes, by the way. Los Alamos v2.0 is no different. They test nukes here too, just modern ones." Smith smiled grimly. "I wouldn't drink the water here."

Elroy awkwardly wiped his mouth. "Well, uhh, too late for that. Fortunately Jack still has bottles."

They walked the rest of the way back to the ship without saying a word. When it s came into view, Smith broke the silence.

"You did good today."

Yeah. That may have been true. But still, he couldn't feel good about it. His thoughts were drawn to Jack on the ship, with Albert. "Mmm."

Smith offered him a gentle pat on the shoulder. "You'll get used to it."

"I kind of don't want to."

Smith stepped out in front of him, and for the first time since they had left the residential district, Elroy saw his face. It was stony and expressionless. "You're going to have to," he said. "Earth may be gone, but the war hasn't even really begun yet."

CHAPTER TWELVE

Corridor
Unknown Avenir Warship
Unknown Location
The Future

"It's not a ghost," said Mattis, staring in bewilderment at the translucent man floating in the middle of the hallway. "It's a hologram."

"Never seen a hologram like *that*," said Daylin-Rutland. "That's so much more advanced than . . . anything I've even *heard* about."

Mattis vaguely wished Lynch was here to analyze this thing. He stepped forward. "My name is Captain Jack Mattis of the United States Navy."

The holographic man's eyes flickered. It was difficult to make out, but Mattis could see text scrolling past his pupils at a dramatic rate. It seemed as though he was checking some kind of database at a frightening speed.

Mattis waited. Michael Robinson, it had said its name was.

The flickering abruptly stopped. "That isn't possible,"

said Robinson, shaking his head. "Facial recognition places your age at nearly six hundred and forty years old. That is beyond even the most augmented human life span by a significant margin."

I may be a grandpa, but I'm not THAT old. Mattis made a careful note of the year. At least they knew *when* they were now. One question answered. "I understand this might be difficult for you to understand," he began, "but we have come here from the past, and—"

A ghostly tendril darted toward him, stabbing through his suit and into his shoulder. Pain and surprise caused him to cry out. His suit began wailing in alarm.

The Marines behind him raised their rifles and all began shouting at once.

"Let him go!"

"Release Captain Mattis!"

"Put down the tentacle!"

Mattis grabbed hold of the appendage—somehow able to touch it even though it was ghostly and translucent—and tried to pull it free, but it was stuck fast. He watched in mute horror as bright red fluid trickled out from his shoulder, into the long thin tube. His blood. It was taking a sample of his blood.

Daylin-Rutland fired a spray from his rifle. A dozen rounds passed harmlessly through the ghostly creature, flying down the corridor and throwing up sparks as they bounced off the bulkheads and debris.

"Cease fire!" shouted Mattis. There was no point shooting it.

Slowly, the thing sucked his blood. Little drops, really, but enough to be concerning. The other Marines stood or knelt, weapons trained on the threat.

"*Put down the tentacle?*" whispered Daylin-Rutland to Lipham, incredulously. "Dammit, Lipham, *really?*"

With a lurch, the creature tore its tentacle away from him. His suit sealed the gap, chirping in complaint and demanding a service at his next opportunity.

"Identity confirmed," said Robinson. "No trace of mitochondrial interference detected. You are not a clone. You are a normal unmodified human being. But that is not possible."

"Like I said," said Mattis, rubbing his shoulder ruefully, "we are not from this time. It's complicated. Just go with it for now."

The briefest of pauses. "Then I am at your service," said Robinson, straightening his holographic shoulders.

Mattis cocked an eyebrow. "Explain."

"The United States Navy has not existed as an institution for four hundred and eighty-six years, five days, one hour. Its assets—including vessels, equipment, and personnel—were absorbed into the Earth Diaspora Coalition, which one hundred and fifty years ago became the Diaspora Collective and six years ago formally dissolved and rebranded itself as the Avenir Alliance. At each step, active-duty servicemen were grandfathered into the new institution at their existing ranks and authority. Accordingly, you are my commanding officer."

It was difficult for him to process, but he wasn't about to look a gift horse in the mouth. "Great," he said. "So . . . uhh, okay. I'm in charge. If that's the case, tell me where we are and give me a sit-rep. Who are you? Where are we?"

Robinson waved his hand. A holographic map of space floated into existence in front of him. "I am Proconsul Michael Robinson, the ship-board synthetic intelligence. You may consider me a backup system for this warship, in the event the crew are incapacitated. As to the *where*, you are aboard the Warfrigate 66549, currently positioned at the outer edge of the Assault Staging Ground in the Sol sector."

Sol sector. That was Earth, their home system. "You must be mistaken," said Mattis. "Our systems detected no planets."

"Of course they did not," said Robinson, as though Mattis was talking nonsense. "Earth has been destroyed for five hundred, sixty-two years, two hundred and one days, sixteen hours."

That made even *less* sense. "Earth was destroyed in *our* timeline," said Mattis, patiently, "but Spectre was very clear: timelines don't cross. Besides, there's a . . ." he did a quick mental calculus. "Five year difference between the two."

"Correct," said Robinson. "Earth was destroyed by an attacking force from timeline ZZ-1014589."

So Earth had been destroyed in this future timeline too. But five years later. Five years . . .

A dark feeling began to grow in Mattis's gut. On some level—some unknowable level—he suspected which timeline ZZ-1014589 was.

"The details," Mattis demanded, grimacing slightly despite himself. "Give me details. The attack that destroyed your Earth—what happened?"

If recalling the details of the attack disturbed Robinson, he gave no clear sign of it. He might not have even had the potential to feel such emotions. "At 0124 hours, a single ship appeared through a wormhole in the Sol System. It was commanded by a man who identified himself as Spectre, but our databases know as Christopher Skye. The US and Chinese Navy attempted communications, yet the ship did not respond. After only a few moments, it activated a time rift weapon and consumed Earth. Thirteen billion humans perished in the attack, and the resultant shockwave destroyed Luna and altered the pathway of Sol around the Milky Way."

An experience that was all too fresh to Mattis. Seeing the tendrils of the Avenir weapon wrap themselves around Earth and crush it, consuming it . . . already, within him, a fiery anger burned at knowing his homeworld was destroyed. Was this how the Avenir had felt?

But more importantly, Robinson had revealed a very important, even crucial, piece of information.

Spectre had attacked the Avenir first.

But before he could consider this, his suit chirped. "Captain Mattis," said Lynch, "this is *William Harrison* actual. We got a problem over here."

CHAPTER THIRTEEN

Infirmary
HMS Caernarvon
Former Sol System
The Future

Guano woke up with what felt like a five alarm hangover, but the pain in her head was different than before; this was farther back toward the rear and top of her head, and while throbbing, it wasn't so piercing. Her neck felt stiff as a board, as though turning her head might cause it to snap.

But overall . . . better.

"How are you feeling?" asked Doctor Manda, concern on her face. A very genuine concern that, in turn, concerned Guano. The good doctor usually smiled.

"I'm . . . feeling a bit better," she said. "Was the operation a success? Did you fix the . . . head . . . issue?"

"Yes and no," Doctor Manda said, folding her hands in front of her. "We managed to stop the bleeding. However, we detected an advanced, undetected viral infection in your cerebrospinal fluid. We did a lumbar puncture and confirmed it. You have a form of viral meningitis."

She'd heard of it. An infection didn't sound so bad. "That's treatable, isn't it? Just kinda soak me in antibiotics and carpet bomb my immune system?"

Doctor Manda didn't answer right away, and when she did, her tone was slow and measured. "Normally yes. Normally, advanced treatment can bring the survival rate to eighty-five percent. However . . ." She obviously struggled with the news, trying to find a way to phrase it. "The infection has spread far and is dug in deep. It's not responding to anti-viral medication. It presents in its advanced stages despite being only a few hours old. At this stage, less than five percent of cases result in survival, and those are in cases where the anti-virals have an effect."

Less than five percent? No way. She felt better. She felt *better* . . . how was it that she was now doing *worse?* "This is some kind of joke, right?"

Doctor Manda said nothing and her stony, despondent expression didn't change. Slowly, very slowly, the truth began to dawn on Guano's drug-fogged brain.

This was bad.

This was real bad.

"How come you didn't notice it before?" she demanded.

"We think the viral infection might have been caused by the nanobots emitting some kind of chemical kill switch when they detected that they were being removed. A failsafe of sorts. These kinds of things take a little while to get going, so that's probably why it works the way it does."

"Okay," said Guano, taking a shallow breath. Her neck hurt, her head hurt, but she focused through it, calling on her warrior's instincts. She'd fought battles in space, she'd fought fist-fights and gun-fights on the ground, she had been captured by Spectre and tormented . . . she would get through this. Patricia Corrick was not going to die from some tiny weak-ass virus. "So what's the next step here?" she asked. "What can we do?"

"We can make you comfortable," said Doctor Manda, her voice soft but unyielding. "We can make sure you're not in any pain."

That was the kind of thing doctors said when things were truly dire.

Oh yeah. This was real, *real* bad.

"I want to talk to Captain Mattis," she said. "I want to see if there's—there's anything more we can do."

"Captain Mattis is not aboard the *Caernarvon*," she said gently. "He is away on a mission. Even then, he is merely a Naval officer. He is not a doctor."

"I still want to talk to him," said Guano, heat rising to her temples. "Gimme a radio."

"When he's available," said Doctor Manda, "I'll see what I can do. In the meantime, I have to get back to testing the crew's mitochondrial DNA to verify that they are not . . . working against us."

Guano lay back onto her rubbery hospital bed, staring up at the ceiling. Anger welled up inside her. Rage. It seemed so unfair to have to suffer multiple brain surgeries, to survive them, and then just—and then just die in a bed like a wounded pig. The injustice of it all. It wounded her.

There had to be something she could do. Some hope she could cling to.

Mattis would have the answer, she just had to hang on that long.

She just had to.

CHAPTER FOURTEEN

Corridor
Unknown Avenir Warship
Former Sol System
The Future

"Problem?" asked Mattis, torn away from his discussion with the hologram.

"Yeah," said Lynch, his voice charged. "The Avenir aren't slowing down for the flip and burn. They just keep accelerating like they're doing a land-office business. And they're altering course. It might have been a feint."

Odd. Very odd. "I can't imagine that's good," said Mattis, eyes flicking to Robinson. "Stand by." He muted the channel. "If I'm in charge here, tell me: what are those incoming ships doing? Why are they overshooting the USS *William Harrison*?"

"Analysis," said Robinson, and once more code flew in front of his eyes. There was a brief pause. "The incoming ships are not vectoring toward the USS *William Harrison*. They are instead vectoring toward this vessel."

Well, shit. "We need to get out of here," Mattis said.

"Back to the *Caernarvon*, via the *Aerostar*. If they aren't decelerating, then that *dramatically* decreases the amount of time we have."

Bizarrely, Robinson seemed to acknowledge that order as well. "Very good, sir," he said. "My recommendation is that you utilize this vessel to cover your retreat. Do you wish me to proceed?"

That stopped him. He took in a breath of his suit's recycled air. "How can you help us, especially with this ship crippled and drifting in space?"

Robinson's answer was immediate. "Auto-repair is nonfunctional because its power connector to the reactor has been severed. However, a preliminary analysis of your attached vessel suggests that if its main power was diverted to the auto-repair mechanism and utilized as auxiliary power, then rudimentary auto-repair functionality could be restored; the system could re-link itself to the reactor, and then proceed with repairs all over the ship. By the time the hostile ships arrive, combat capability can be adequately restored, if only partially."

Mattis tried to translate it all. Robinson seemed to speak in long, complex, detailed sentences that were at odds with how his brain processed information. So many questions. No time to ask them. "Do it," he said, adjusting his radio. "Sammy, Reardon, you're going to see a little drain on the *Aerostar*'s power. Don't worry."

"I'm worried," said Reardon. "Don't tell me not to worry. I'm worrying. What are you doing to my ship?"

Sammy cut in. "Holy smokes! You said it would be a little drain, but the lights just went out here! Life support and radios are on emergency battery backup, and we are draining power like a goon bag with a hole in it!"

"What's a goon bag?" asked Mattis.

"Cheap alcohol. In an aluminum flask. *Duh.*"

"Hey!" Reardon pissed voice blared over the comms. "What would *you* know about alcohol, huh, kid?"

"Nothing, bro. Nothing!"

"Have you been drinking at some point, ever?" Reardon demanded. "You better tell me!"

Mattis talked over them. "Guys, guys. The power!"

"Yeah," said Sammy, obviously eager to change the subject. "It seems like *something* is draining all the power out of the *Aerostar*'s reactor. I've pushed it to redline to try and give us some back, but it seems like whatever's draining our power is just drinking that up too!"

"Power down the reactor," said Reardon.

"Belay that." Mattis inhaled sharply. "The derelict ship is using the *Aerostar*'s power to repair itself. We need to give it all the juice it's got."

"But it's a *new engine*," whined Reardon. "I just got it installed a few days ago!"

Spears had given him that thing. It seemed appropriate now that her actions would help them, even though she herself was gone. "We need this ship operational, and if we want it to be operational, it needs auxiliary power."

"Fiiine," Reardon moaned. "But if you break my ship . . ."

Mattis sighed into his radio. "We'll deal with that *if* it happens. Mattis out." He refocused on the hologram in front of him. "Let's get to the bridge," he said.

"This way," Robinson replied, gesturing mechanically with his hand.

Cautiously, Mattis led the team of suit-clad Marines down the corridor, passing blown-out bulkheads and cracked deck plating, revealing more circuitry beneath. The ship was in ruins. How could this 'auto-repair' system bring it back to functionality before the enemy ships arrived? And how long were they talking—days, hours, minutes?

As he watched, the exposed circuits began to glow with the same green light as the Robinson hologram, and the tiny fractures in the metal slowly sealed themselves up, as though they were being stitched together with tiny, microscopic sewing needles.

Corrick's—Mattis's pilot's—brain was swarming with nanobots. It was obvious that the Avenir used them as part of their repair process . . . but he'd never even *heard* of nanobots that moved as fast as he was now witnessing. With every step they seemed to get closer to closing up the cracks in the bulkheads. Disturbingly, they also seemed to consume the bodies laying on the deck as though they were some kind of powerful, invisible acid breaking down the corpses into pieces too tiny to see, and then evaporating them to . . . somewhere.

"Look," said Daylin-Rutland, pointing to the metal slugs from his shots that were lodged in the walls. As Mattis watched, the slugs disintegrated, disassembled, and—most likely—were recycled. A glance over his shoulder revealed that the spent brass casings from Daylin-Rutland's shots were also gone.

By the time Mattis had arrived at the bridge in front of a room labeled COMMAND CORE, the corridors were looking almost brand new. Granted, the damage could not have been that bad *inside* the ship, but even so . . .

"Blasted fast workers, aren't they?" said Daylin-Rutland.

"Sure are." Mattis stepped up to the door and it immediately slid open to grant him passage.

The bridge was unlike any other he'd ever seen. The low roof was in the shape of an oval, seemingly carved into the metal of the ship rather than being made out of shaped, forged metal. There were no consoles, no screen upon which to view anything. Just an empty ovular room.

Robinson glided into the center of the room and almost immediately lights flicked on all around him, highlighting the hologram and surrounding him with similarly-colored glowing screens. "Warfrigate 66549 is ready for your command," Michael Robinson said in his cool, artificial voice. "Step into the bridge when you are ready."

Mattis was no hologram and definitely couldn't fly like Robinson could, but there was no time to figure that out. Mattis cautiously stepped through the doorway, suit-clad foot hovering in the air. Was this really the right thing to do?

Steeling himself, Mattis put his weight onto his foot. For a moment he thought he would fall forward and smash his face on the inside of the curved surface, but instead, some invisible force kept him aloft.

He pushed off from the surface, floating into the void, some gravitational force lifting him up and gently propelling him into the center of the ovaloid room. He tumbled over, ending up upside down relative to Robinson, who drifted to one side to make room.

Screens lit up all around, holograms winking into

existence in front of Mattis's face. But with his orientation inverted, he couldn't understand them.

"Uhh," said Mattis, spinning his arms awkwardly. "Is it meant to be this way?"

"No," said Robinson, rotating himself to match. "The system is damaged and cannot orientate itself."

Good thing it worked at all, then, Mattis thought.

"Sir?" ventured Daylin-Rutland, "did you want us to come in there with you?"

"Is that necessary?" Mattis asked Robinson. They were Marines, not crew.

"You may operate this ship entirely on your own if you wish, although a crew of five is recommended. I can fill in for any role you wish in the short term."

"Okay," said Mattis, holding out his hands. "Marines, get back to your shuttle and back to the *Caernarvon.* Give them a full debrief while I try to figure out this ship."

"Aye aye, sir." Daylin-Rutland saluted, then turned back to the rest of the Marines. "Okay, shitheads! Let's file out—Lipham, don't trip over your own feet this time, okay? C'mon! Back to the shuttle!"

They left, and Mattis tried to refocus his attention on the various screens around him.

"Uhh, Mattis?" Sammy's voice piped up over the communication system. It was painted with worry. "I'm bleeding again."

Dammit. "How bad?"

Sammy paused just a moment. "Bad. I think I tore some stitches or something."

There was nothing more Sammy could do to help, and if

he died, Reardon would be completely unmanageable. "Okay," said Mattis. "Undock and return to the *Caernarvon*. Check into medical. Inform Doctor Manda that I'm giving you a priority pass."

"Thanks," Sammy said weakly.

The line cut out and Mattis went back to trying to make sense of the screens. Helpfully, one of them flickered and inverted. It displayed a myriad of readouts—mostly error messages—overlaying a wide multi-system sensor readout.

Eighteen dots raced toward the ship, long red exhaust trails following behind them. They were aggressive, mad even, and Mattis knew he'd be soon in for a fight.

"So," he asked Robinson, "what kind of weapons does this ship have?"

"At the present?" asked Robinson. "Nothing. The reactor core is still powering up."

"Okay, how long until I can shoot something?"

"Twelve minutes."

Great. He was totally defenseless for twelve minutes. Nothing to worry about.

Hope Lynch is doing better than I am . . .

CHAPTER FIFTEEN

Bridge
USS William Harrison
Former Sol System
The Future

"I hope Mattis is doing better than we are," said Lynch, growling in frustration as he looked at the monitors. The Avenir ships had not taken the bait. They were rushing toward the *Caernarvon*, despite all the efforts of the *William Harrison* to steal their attention. They'd painted them with targeting lasers, pinged their ships with the radar, and were now using the radio like a searchlight, beaming a hailing signal directly at them.

And all for nothing.

"Revising our interdiction position once again," droned Modi. "When are they going to start slowing down?"

He didn't have any answers. "If they overshoot . . . that's a good thing, right?"

"I don't know if it is," said Modi, frowning slightly. "They wouldn't do it if it didn't make sense for them or give them some kind of advantage."

"We gotta figure out what they're fixing to do." Lynch drummed his fingers on the command chair. "How's the *Caernarvon* doing?"

"Admiral Yim reports he is bringing the ship to General Quarters, but due to the loss of crew and the situation aboard, it is taking some time to ready the ship for combat."

At least they still had one functioning ship. "Guess it's up to us, then. Screw interdiction; get ready to execute a Z-space micro-translation. Take us directly in front of *Caernarvon*."

Modi stared at Lynch like he'd ordered him to slit his own throat. "You can't possibly be serious," he said, a confused stammer creeping into his voice. "W-we haven't mapped this section of space, and even if we had, micro-translations are incredibly risky—the slightest miscalculation could mean we appear *inside* our ally, or overshoot them by light-years. Assuming we even emerge at all, or don't burn out our Z-space engine, or . . . or any number of horrible calamities."

"But you've done it before, right?"

"In a *simulation*," stressed Modi. "At the academy. *Ten years ago*."

"That's what simulations are for. Practice for the real world. Right?"

"The simulation failed."

Lynch smiled. "You've got plenty of arrows in your quiver, so this time you'll know what to do."

"I do not own a quiver." Modi hesitated for a moment, and then straightened his back. "I guess we're doing this, then," he muttered, tapping at his keyboard furiously. "Okay. Preparing to execute a Z-space translation. Plotting out a micro-translation. Aiming for one hundred thousand kilometers in front of the *Caernarvon*, uh, just to be safe."

Good. Lynch took a shallow breath. If they messed this up, it would be an inglorious end to the *William Harrison*. But he knew Modi. And Modi wouldn't screw up.

"Captain, there is something very odd about these ships." Modi frowned, perplexed, at his console. "Something very odd indeed."

"You're going to have to give me more than that," said Lynch. "C'mon. Don't rile the wagon master. Talk to me in people-speak. Gimme words. What's happening?"

"*You* want me to use people-speak? You?" Modi grunted in frustration, saying nothing for a moment. "The incoming ships. They are not moving as they should."

Just gotta be patient. Modi was obviously still working on the Z-space translation, or letting the computers do it. "Explain."

"A normal military strike force moves in a well-disciplined formation, with the thickest armor pointed toward the greatest threat, and with its arcs of fire arranged so that the maximum number of guns can fire at the target at once. It positions itself so that its point-defense can cover one another with overlapping arcs. Yet these ships . . . they seem to be just moving at maximum speed in an ungainly formation with no pattern or evident plan. They duck and weave amongst each other, crossing one another's lines of fire and risking collision. They—" he struggled to continue. "Well, it is similar to how German aircraft in the First World War flew: just a—a blob, sir."

A blob. A strange description, but more importantly, what did it *mean?* "Okay," said Lynch. "So they're a great big ole' blob of Avenir coming directly at the *Caernarvon*. Fascinating. How do we use that?"

"Unclear," responded Modi. "Just that they seem to be moving more like scavs than anything else."

Scavs. Illegal salvagers operating in Earth's orbit. But there was no way they had come through the portal with them, or they would have been seen and identified long ago. And they would certainly not have appeared from Z-space.

"How did they get here?"

"Unclear, but one thing is obvious—these ships are not of any uniform military design."

"Spectre, then?"

"Again, unclear. Perhaps they are mercenaries or hirelings."

Unlikely. Spectre tended to use technology and weapons from this time period, and preferred to either crew them with clones or with duped and deceived friendlies. It was not his style to employ scavengers and outlaws. Then again, he was always shifting his tactics, and nothing seemed beneath or beyond him. Spectre was colder than a well-digger's knee.

Decisions, decisions. His gut instinct was probably the best. "I don't think so," said Lynch, leaning forward in his command chair and studying the radar readouts intently. "I think we're dealing with a third party here."

"I concur," said Modi. His console beeped. "Z-space micro-translation ready to execute, Captain."

"Do it," Lynch said immediately.

Modi punched a key. The ship shuddered from stem to stern, and just as it slipped into Z-space, a warning light flashed.

Lynch's eyes flicked to the glowing red alarm. "*ENGINE FAILURE.*"

"Oh shit—"

CHAPTER SIXTEEN

Einstein
Los Alamos v2.0
Tiberius System
Main timeline

Elroy followed Smith aboard the ship in a daze. It only now began to sink in—he'd just watched a total stranger kill someone and take a chip from their brain. He hadn't imagined there could be so much blood.

"Is this what we do now?" he asked, almost as much to himself as to Smith. "Just kick in doors and shoot people?"

Smith slipped into the cargo hold and plugged the chip into a socket in a computer panel. The device lit up, flashing a series of green and orange lights.

"Only when I have to. I'm a subtle man, Mister Mattis. The problem is… subtle doesn't work too well on Spectre clones." He waved a finger idly at the chip. "You know these things control nanobots, right? And they can release a chemical that kills the host—slow or quick, whatever they choose—to make prolonged interrogations ineffective. The only solution is to stop them activating it, and the best way to do that is to disable the brain attached." Smith sounded almost wistful. "We got lucky here. Only five percent of clones have these chips. The ones they don't expect to get X-rayed or scanned or analyzed. Just a bit of good luck."

"Just lucky I guess," echoed Elroy, not even disguising his bitterness.

Smith tapped on some keys. "The download is coming now," he said, eyes flicking to Elroy, scowling disapprovingly. "Okay. Time to spend some of that money. And I know the perfect place to get you some new threads."

Elroy pulled on his collar. "What's wrong with my clothes?"

"You're dressed like a normal," said Smith, that critical eye roaming over Elroy's body. "Not like the person we need."

"And what exactly is that?"

Smith touched a key, and the far wall lit up. It was some kind of screen. It showed a grainy out-of-focus image taken of a military facility out in the middle of the desert. It was comprised of a dozen small, white structures dotted over the sand, seemingly placed without pattern or rhyme, each structure connected by simple dirt roads. A wire mesh ran around the facility and a bright red sign with stark white lettering read:

HICKAM AIR FORCE BASE

PROPERTY OF THE UNITED STATES ARMED FORCES

NO ENTRY. AUTHORIZED PERSONNEL ONLY

INTRUDERS WILL BE SUBJECT TO LETHAL FORCE

"Lethal force?" said Elroy, his heart beating faster in his chest. He could just picture a squad of armed goons filling his body with sharp, fast-moving bits of tungsten. "Hey, no, c'mon buddy, wait—"

"Rela*aa*x," said Smith, dragging out the word. "You aren't going in there properly this time. I am. I just need you to drive the getaway car."

Oh. Well. That significantly helped matters. "So why do I need to dress fancy?"

"Because my 'character' isn't going to be driven around by just *anyone*. You need to look like a driver, not just any old guy."

Only one question remained. "They wouldn't shoot me for driving the car, would they?"

"Just don't get caught," said Smith, "and it won't be a problem."

Elroy rubbed his back, a sudden ache developing there. Once more he imagined a legion of soldiers filling his car with bullets, and him inside. "You know, that doesn't make me feel better."

CHAPTER SEVENTEEN

Command Core
Warfrigate 66549
Former Sol system
The Future

Mattis considered his options. "Open a channel to the *William Harrison*," he asked Robinson. "Lynch, what's going on over there?"

Nobody answered. That was extremely odd. He resolved to try again in a moment, returning his focus to the battle.

"How long until those weapons are operational?" asked Mattis, one eye on the sensor readout, watching the incoming ships getting closer and closer.

"Two seconds," said Robinson. "One. "

Typical. A system chimed, and a new holographic window popped up at the side of his vision, labeled *Weapons Control.*

Only one question remained. "How do I shoot things?"

"Select targets by pointing at them," said Robinson. "Then select your weapons and engage."

Operating a US Navy warship from *his* timeline was an

extremely complicated, challenging process that required years of specialist training and practice, taking the best and training them to operate the most complicated machines man could build.

It seemed ludicrously easy to him to just *point,* and he felt foolish as he extended a gloved hand, prodding at one of the ships. A golden circle appeared around it, as well as a series of holographic buttons off to the side.

PARTICLE GUNS

FUSION TORPEDOES

MASS DRIVER

This ship had a mass driver? Even seeing the name of it made his chest tighten. He had seen that weapon in action, tearing apart Friendship Station and other places. A weapon terrifying in its potential.

And now he had one.

"Is that thing loaded?" Mattis asked. Every time the Avenir had used it in action, the weapon had required a substantial loading and charging cycle.

"Insufficient mass has been loaded to fire the mass driver," said Robinson. "And insufficient power to charge it."

Well that settled that. "Particle guns? I'm guessing those are the red laser things that the Avenir have. We were never able to figure out how to get them working—doesn't help when you're trying to rebuild technology centuries ahead of your own time using parts salvaged from blown-up spaceships."

Robinson nodded. "Yes, they are red. And yes, I can imagine that would make integration and salvage difficult."

No kidding. "Okay. Status on particle guns?"

"Two aft guns are functional, but their targeting systems are degraded and they can only be used in close quarters."

Not helpful. "What about these things—fusion torpedoes?"

"Fusion torpedo launcher tubes one-through-five and seven-through-eight are offline." That left only tube six.

"Okay," Mattis said, trying to keep his voice even. "Guess that makes the choice easy. Load fusion torpedoes." He corrected himself. "Fusion torpedo. Singular. Tube six."

"Very good choice, Captain."

He glanced sideways at the hologram. Was it capable of sarcasm? "Right. Get ready to fire when it's loaded." Mattis touched the button labelled "*PARTICLE GUNS*." A red button floated hear him: "*FIRE*."

"Loading complete, warhead armed."

The button was still red. "Is it ready?"

"Red means it's out of effective range," Robinson said, helpfully. "When the button turns green it's ready to engage."

Mattis's finger hovered over the holographically rendered object. He hesitated, even though it was still red. "Is that wise?"

Robinson's holographic head jerked to one side, as though looking at something 'off-camera'. "My analysis concludes that it is. We are fortunate. The combat capability of the incoming ships is minimal compared to this vessel, even with our damage and their considerable numerical advantage."

"Why would they be at a disadvantage?" asked Mattis. "They're ships like this one, right?"

"No," said Robinson, his holographic expression difficult

to read. "These ships are not Avenir."

Mattis's finger twitched as the button flickered, then turned green. He knew the smart play was to fire; he had no idea what kind of weapons those incoming ships had, what kind of defenses. But his ship was not in fighting condition, and he was still learning the controls. Maybe opening up with all guns was a bad idea.

He glanced to Robinson. "Put me through to the *Caernarvon*."

"This is the *Caernarvon*," said Yim, almost instantly. "We're ready—sort of. Guns are *finally* loaded. Locked on. Just waiting for the signal to engage."

And engage they could. At any moment. And they should . . . but why?

"Wait. Who *are* they?" asked Mattis, finger still hovering over the fire key. "Robinson, who are they?"

CHAPTER EIGHTEEN

Bridge
USS William Harrison
Former Sol System
The Future

Lynch was thrown out of the command chair as the *William Harrison* appeared back out of Z-space, twisted and warped and on fire. He landed hard on the deck as alarms and warning chimes rang all around him.

"Report," he said, dragging himself off the deck and stumbling woozily to his feet. "What the goddamn hell happened?"

"The Z-space micro-translation failed," said Modi, similarly sprawled out. Blood streamed from his nose which was cracked and squashed. "The ship is damaged."

That much he could figure out on his own. Settling back into his chair, Lynch tried to make sense of what had happened. The various monitors and screens that displayed views of the outside world were bathed in an ominous, fiery glow. "That doesn't look good," he said, trying to keep his composure. Fire. Fire was never a friend in a ship.

But fire on the *outside* of the ship? Fire in *space?*

"The failed Z-space micro-translation has caused a spacial anomaly of unknown origin," said Modi, staring in concern at the monitors. "It appears as though fragments of Z-space have been torn from that reality and have consequently been converted into a material similar in composition and effect to anti-matter."

Lynch stared at the roaring flames. Out of the corner of his eye, his radar screen blinked, trying to get his attention. The enemy ships were getting close. "I thought anti-matter was a mite . . . theoretical."

"Theoretically, what we're seeing shouldn't be happening *at all.*"

Lynch couldn't even begin to contest that. What to do, what to do . . . slowly, fortunately, the flames began to die down.

"The anomaly is consuming itself," said Modi, no small amount of relief in his voice. "It should be disappearing momentarily."

Momentarily was still a worry. And some space-fire-stuff was the least of Lynch's concerns. "Where did we come out?" he asked. "And I want a sitrep on those incoming a ships."

Modi checked his instruments. "We have arrived approximately at our destination," he said. "Apart from some buckling of the outer hull and the anomaly, everything was a rousing success."

". . . *Ish,*" said Lynch.

"Ish," agreed Modi.

The flames died out. There was damage—how could

there *not* be?—but there were fires on the inside of the ship, too, and Lynch had no time to consider it. "Away damage control teams. Get them there in a New York minute. Commander Modi, lock up those incoming ships. I want to at least spit at them as they fly on by."

"Confirmed," said Modi. "Preparing to kill skunks with guns. Locking in a fire solution on skunks Alpha through Lima. Loading DE shots; we're going to need the densest material we can get, since they're moving so extraordinarily fast."

The radar flashed another warning. The ships were almost atop them now and showed no signs of slowing down. They must be missing a few buttons off their shirt. Lynch switched to external cameras.

The ships were small, fast hunks of scrap crudely welded to engines that spluttered and spat silver and red exhaust trails. No two of them were the same, seemingly hand-crafted, hand-painted, hand-decorated. But they all had one thing in common, and that was plenty of weaponry.

"*William Harrison* to *Caernarvon*'s away team," said Lynch, scowling slightly as he regarded the ships. "This is *William Harrison* actual. Mattis, I don't think these skunks are with the Avenir."

"They are not," replied a voice belonging to a stranger, one which carried with it the unmistakable aura of the synthetic.

The presence of that voice sent a faint shiver up Lynch's spine. "Who is speaking?"

"I am Proconsul Michael Robinson, the intelligence unit aboard Warfrigate 66549. You are conversing with a fork of my personality, as the primary unit is currently engaged directing Captain Jack Mattis and instructing him on the command of this vessel."

Proconsul? Warfrigate? Intelligence unit? Lynch had so many questions, but Modi asked them first. "Are—are you an artificial intelligence?"

"That is an accurate way of describing me," said Robinson.

"Fascinating," Modi whispered, his eyes wide. He had a look on his face;—the look of a child desperately asking for permission to play with a brand new toy. "Wonderful. *Amazing.*"

Lynch couldn't help but think of those ships bearing down on the *Caernarvon* and the away team. "Survive now, be amazed later," he said, returning his attention to the incoming ships. He wasn't sure exactly what to call Mattis's prize. "We are ready to engage, away team." Pointedly, Lynch leaned forward slightly in his chair. "I'd like to speak to Mattis to confirm."

"Ending the fork and terminating my processes, restoring connection to the primary unit." There was a tiny squeak of static followed by a brief pause, then Robinson's voice returned. "The line is open."

"We'll fire together on your mark," said Lynch.

"Who *are* they?" asked Mattis, the hesitance in his voice clear. "Robinson, who are they?"

"The attacking ships," said Robinson, his artificial voice lathered with contempt, "are the Human Resistance."

Lynch thought he must have wax in his ears. "The human *what?*"

"The Human Resistance," said Robinson, seeming to almost spit the words. "Vultures and parasites on our culture, insects that pick the bones of the dead, steal pieces of ruined ships, smuggle contraband and food and weapons."

Smuggling food seemed like an odd crime to engender such hatred in an artificial being. The problems of basic sustenance had long been solved for humanity, a combination of robotics and genetic engineering that provided enough for all; the Universal Food Program provided baseline nutrition, required for every human being to exist, and although there were plenty of disparities between rich and poor, nobody starved.

"If that's so, do we really want to engage?" asked Mattis. "We don't know *anyone* in this timeline. And we don't know how the Avenir truly feel regarding Spectre, but we can at least presume they aren't friends. Any enemy of theirs probably has to, at least, want to talk to us."

"Probably," said Lynch, muting the channel and turning to Modi. "I wanna talk to them."

"On it," said Modi, typing furiously. He touched his ear. "This is the USS *William Harrison*, calling approaching vessels. Please be advised: we are not Avenir. We have been thrown forward in time, and we are not your enemies. Please respond."

Nothing. The ships continued to advance. Maybe the Avenir of this timeline didn't even use that phrase. It was possible. Still, if they were in the weapons range of the *William Harrison*, then it was difficult to believe that they couldn't shoot back.

"They're still accelerating," said Modi, eyes widening with

alarm. "And they're coming right for us. Faster and faster, with no sign of stopping. They'll be on us in minutes."

Why? What kind of plan were they trying to pull? "Are they . . . going to ram us?" Lynch asked.

"Looks like it," said Modi.

"Status on our engines?"

Modi gave a helpless shrug.

"Fix them," said Lynch, staring at the radar monitor as it displayed the incoming ships roaring toward them. "*Quickly.*"

CHAPTER NINETEEN

Command Core
Warfrigate 66549
Former Sol system
The Future

Mattis watched the incoming ships. A swarm of angry hornets speeding toward them, so fast that the doppler effect gave them a faint blue tint.

"Thirty seconds until they're on is," said Robinson. "Twenty-nine, twenty-eight—"

Lynch's voice came over the line. Mattis could hear wailing klaxons in the background. "Captain Mattis, we've experienced a *technical glitch* that's made the outside of the ship look like it got whipped with the ugly stick, and we have a situation with our engines. We won't be able to engage right away. Stand by, will advise." His voice got quieter, as though his head was moving away from the microphone. "Modi! Modi, put out that fire *now!* I don't *care* whose fault it is!"

Sounded like he had his hands full. "Not being able to shoot might be a blessing," said Mattis. "Hold fire, regardless, until I say otherwise."

"That," said Lynch, sounding slightly relieved, "will be the easiest order you've ever given."

Good . . . ish. He closed the link.

The enemy ships were coming in hard. "Get ready to engage evasive maneuver," said Mattis to Robinson. "Probably best if you take the helm on this one. If you can avoid them, do it. At the rate they're moving toward us a ram would be more like an incoming missile."

"Significantly more powerful," clarified Robinson. "They are moving at a considerable pace, and their mass is substantial despite their small size; an impact would be more akin to a nuclear detonation, but focused at a single point."

"Then make sure they miss."

"Confirmed," said Robinson. "Statistically, there is a high probability the Warfrigate's engines can outperform theirs, even with their considerable size advantage."

Mattis hoped that would be enough. "You can do it, right? We can outmaneuver them?"

"Seventy-seven percent probability," returned Robinson. "Based on standard Resistance designs."

So about a quarter chance they would die instantly. Better odds than some of the battles in the Sino-American war.

Maybe this time would be it. Maybe the odds wouldn't play out this time, and the last thing he would see would be those blue-tinged ships ploughing into his. Blowing him up. Ending him like all the ships he'd ever ended.

"Ten seconds," said Robinson. "Commencing evasive maneuvers."

The Warfrigate lurched, throwing him across the ovular

room into the edge. Gravity pulled him back, drifting him back toward the center, in front of the holographic viewscreens.

He was still alive, so they hadn't collided. Small mercies. "Report," he said. "Show me those ships."

The screens flashed, showing the incoming ships: no longer blue, no longer darting around like wild fish, and completely stationary.

"How did they do *that?*" asked Mattis, bewildered. "They just came to a dead stop. *Instantly.*"

"They must have an Inertia Redirection Device," said Robinson, as though this was something that a ship would, naturally, be equipped with.

"What the hell just happened?" asked Yim. "Mattis, are you seeing this?"

"Sure am." The incoming ships's ability to stop on a dime certainly made things interesting again. "Put me through to them," said Mattis. "If they aren't shooting at us yet, they probably aren't going to.

"Channel open," said Robinson.

"This is Captain Jack Mattis of the United States Navy," he said, firmly. "I want to talk to whoever's in charge over there."

There was a brief pause—nothing unusual—and then a voice came through, thick and raspy and feminine. "This is Slag. We saw this salvage first, and it's ours. So y'all can kindly make like a tree and fuck off."

Sounds like I should have Lynch talk to her, Mattis thought, but he held his tongue. "I understand. Please know we have no quarrel with you. This ship is the only prize we seek to claim from this debris. The remainder of its treasures are yours. And there's plenty to go around. There's no need to fight."

"Yer there is," said Slag, hissing faintly down the line. "See, if what you take doesn't go to us, it'll get turned over to the Avenir. And believe me, that ain't in our best interests."

"Nor is it in ours," said Mattis, genuinely. "We are not directly enemies of the Avenir, though their enemies are our enemies. But they do not consider us" it felt vaguely insulting to say. "Worthy of alliance or consideration."

A pause over the line. "What enemy are you talking about?"

"Spectre," said Mattis.

"No idea who that is." Slag hocked and spat, hopefully not directly into the microphone. "He rich?"

"His resources are considerable," said Mattis, diplomatically.

"Then sure. Let's go fuck him up, if yer okay with a thirty-sixty split of the loot."

Things were suddenly moving in a confusing direction. Loot? Thirty-*sixty?* "Uhh, sure," said Mattis. "Thirty-sixty split is fine."

"Great." Slag coughed wetly down the like, hacking like a dying bird. "Gimme coordinates and let's go."

What the hell had he suddenly agreed to? "Well, it's uh, it's not that simple," said Mattis, trying to think of a way of explaining the complex situation he and his ships had found themselves in. "We—we don't know where he is."

"Oh, that's fine," said Slag, unconcerned. One of the ships broke away from the pack—a bright orange construction vehicle with dozens of guns welded all over it and extra armor plates bolted on at random. "Let's head to Yggdrasil. We'll be able to find anyone you're looking for there, no matter who they are."

Yggdrasil… the tree of life in Norse mythology. "That's the name of your base?" Mattis ventured.

"It's my *home*," said Slag, offended. "And the home of all free humans. The last one standing. The Avenir don't know about it, but . . . well. We can see by your ships that you ain't them, so I figure, eh. What's the harm?" She coughed again. "Worst case scenario, you're stringing me out, and if that's the case, well, we cook your crew and eat 'em."

"Sounds good," Mattis said drily. "Lead the way." He tapped the *close link* button.

"We are receiving coordinates," said Robinson. "Auto-repair has completed enough work to travel. Do you want me to follow the Human Resistance ships?"

"Sure," said Mattis. "Punch it. Coordinate with the *Caernarvon* and the *William Harrison*, and make sure they're with us." He paused. "They don't really eat people, do they?"

Robinson stared at him with holographic eyes. "According to our intelligence, on Yggdrasil, meat is extremely rare and cannibalism is not unheard of."

Great.

"I'm sure it'll be fine," said Mattis, as the ship's Z-space engine charged up. "*Pretty* sure."

CHAPTER TWENTY

Command Core
Warfrigate 66549
Z-Space
The Future

Warfrigate 66549 drifted through Z-space, the tip of the spear, with the *Caernarvon* and *William Harris* following.

Mattis had one of the Warfrigate's cameras pointed toward the *Caernarvon*, watching the British warship trail them. It was scarred from its battle with the Chinese frigates, but much of the damage appeared to be resolved. It was space-worthy and combat ready . . . assuming the crew didn't mutiny again.

A chime rang, the *Caernarvon* was highlighted with bright blue lines, and an *open line* box appeared beside it.

"We are receiving a signal," said Robinson.

Mattis touched the *open line* box.

"This is *Caernarvon* actual," said Yim. "We have a problem, Mattis. Specifically three problems. But first I wanted to talk to you about this Yggdrasil that we're going toward. It could be a trap."

Of course there were problems. That was the nature of the job. "It could very well be a trap," said Mattis. "In fact, it's *likely* to be. Good things just don't seem to happen to us, do they?"

"I suppose not, but—well, I agree with you. We should go. Things can't get worse."

"Don't say that," groaned Mattis.

"Regardless, I think we should be cautious."

"I wasn't exactly considering going in there like it was Disneyland Luna," he said. "Don't worry. We'll be careful." Mattis backtracked mentally. "Okay. Problems. What are they?"

Yim seemed to be reading off a list. "First, the *Caernarvon* crew has lodged a formal complaint over your transfer to this Warfrigate. They said they barely agreed to sign up under your command, let alone mine."

He knew why they were complaining. The idea of a British crew serving under an American captain would have been galling enough, but a Chinese captain? The people they had, within memory, fought a hot war against? It wasn't racism. It was pragmatic distrust.

"I know," said Mattis, trying to think of a way out of this one. "But I don't have a good solution for you, unless you want to trade."

"Honestly? That might be best."

It would be, too, and although Mattis was now starting to get used to the ship, Yim was right. "Very well. When we get to this trap of theirs, we'll switch out." He clicked his tongue. "Next problem."

"The morgue's refrigerators have failed. The bodies we have are starting to deteriorate."

Definitely a big problem. "This ship is big," he said. "We can store them here. Make sure that transfer happens. Third problem?"

"Lieutenant Patricia Corrick has taken a turn for the worst," said Yim, his voice softening. "Doctor Manda is giving her twelve, twenty-four hours at the most. Corrick is asking to speak to you."

"Can't it be done by communicator?"

"In person. She is . . . quite insistent." Something in her tone suggested he should give her what she wanted.

Mattis swore quietly. "Okay, I'll make time. Bring her over with the bodies—" he realized how that sounded. "But separately."

An awkward silence filled the radio.

"I'll make sure the transfer is completed," said Yim, formally, obviously trying to move on to the next order of business as quickly as possible. "As soon as we arrive at this mysterious base."

"Right." Three problems, and all with one solution: an exchange of items between ships. Something they could not do in Z-space, but hopefully would be able to do when they alighted. Something else clicked in Mattis's head. "How goes checking the crew for Spectre-clones?"

"All done," said Yim. "Everyone got the jab. Nobody was detected."

"Test them again," said Mattis, firmly. "I want to be sure."

"The crew won't like that." Yim's hesitance was clear. "Are you sure you want to push them on this?"

He was very sure. "I want to distract them from more mutiny talk," he said, "and also foil the attempts of anyone who might have slipped under the radar. Break." He thought for a moment. "We're going to a strange, potentially hostile location. Tell the crew that they will need to get their immunizations updated—and honestly, definitely *really* do that. We can't afford to have anyone get sick—but while they're there, test them for Spectre's mitochondrial DNA again on the down-low."

"That is actually a good idea."

Mattis smiled grimly. "Despite appearances, I sometimes do have them."

"Okay. I'll get right on it. *Caernarvon* out."

Mattis closed the connection.

"I couldn't help but overhear," said Robinson, his synthetic voice almost demure. "My analysis of your ship's medical capabilities suggests that this vessel's systems are much more advanced and are almost certainly more capable of caring for your injured crewmen. I recommend you transfer any injured you have along with the bodies of your fallen. I can divert the auto-repair to ensure that the morgue and medbay are active by the time the transfer is complete."

"Do it," said Mattis, without any deliberation.

They couldn't afford for anyone else to die.

"Working," said Robinson.

Good. "How far away are we from the coordinates we were given?" asked Mattis.

"Six hours."

Six hours. "Okay," said Mattis. He squirmed around in the strange ungravity of the command core. "Report on combat system status?"

"With repair resources diverted to medical and mortuary systems, reconstruction of combat capabilities has been halted. System report as follows: two aft particle guns are operational, as are two forward guns. Fusion torpedo launchers six-through-eight are functional, all three of them port broadside. Mass driver remains offline."

That was better than what he had before in terms of weapons. "How are the hull fractures?"

"Forty percent of the decompressions have been repaired," Robinson reported. "Auto-repair has been prioritizing the innermost bulkheads, and life support has been restored. However, you should be advised: the ship's supplies of oxygen and nitrogen have been depleted, so despite the fact that the systems are functional, life support remains offline."

His suit was surprisingly comfortable, but Mattis was still uneasy after the near-death experience in his last spacewalk. And being surrounded by vacuum was disconcerting. The sooner he had air to breathe that wasn't coming out of a tiny tank on his back, the happier he would be.

Just another fine day in the Navy.

"Okay," said Mattis. "Let me know if there's anything happening that I should know about."

The hours ticked away. Mattis watched the ship repair itself, regrowing like a damaged tree before his eyes. It was fascinating to observe; the ship seemed almost to be a living thing, attended by uncountable numbers of nanobots, the microscopic machines dutifully rebuilding the ship to its original specifications.

Finally, the silence of the work was broken.

"Attention, Captain," Robinson's cool voice sounded, "we will be arriving at the provided coordinates momentarily."

CHAPTER TWENTY-ONE

Near Hickam Air Force Base, home of the 6,774th Missile Wing
Los Alamos v2.0
Tiberius System
Main timeline

Elroy pulled the Stylecar off the main road toward the Air Force Base, the wheels whining in complaint as they touched dirt. Probably for the first time in the vehicle's entire lifetime. They had waited until night to leave, and Smith had made him leave his electronics back on the ship so they couldn't be tracked, all sitting in a neat pile beside the crib Albert had built for Jack. The artificial intelligence was apparently very apt at keeping him entertained.

For now, he had to focus on the mission ahead. The military base. It had been hard to navigate there in the dark without the aid of computers but, somehow, he'd managed it.

Elroy had never driven anything like the Stylecar. It was exactly as its name implied; the seats were genuine leather, the interior black, chrome, and wood, and there was even a minibar. He slowly drove toward the main boom gate, tires crunching the raw dirt underneath the car. They passed the big red sign warning them to stay away, the last line echoing in his mind. *Lethal force…*

"We're almost there," said Elroy, adjusting his driver's cap. Suits and formal wear never really sat well on him—pretentious and gaudy, he always said—but it was necessary to play the part. And even he had to admit he looked good. He pushed away a small pang at wishing Chuck could see him.

"Great," said Smith in the back of the car. He was dressed as flamboyantly as Elroy had ever seen anyone dress. And Elroy was *gay*. The guy had purchased a bright pink suit, bespeckled with sequins and complete with a wide brimmed hat that more resembled a crown than anything else, dotted with gems and semiprecious stones. "Now remember, the main thing is for you to stay with the car no matter what. And just act natural. And do what I tell you."

Elroy sighed, deep and long. "Yeah. Okay, so you wanna tell me the plan now that we're almost here? Or is this another *shoot-our-way-in-and-tell-the-civilian-nothing* plan?"

"It's better you didn't know," said Smith. "Just tell the guard what I told you. "

He ground his teeth together.. Elroy had to remind himself that Smith was a CIA agent and was probably versed with all this spy movie protocol. Still, it sounded crazy to him.

Elroy turned on the music—loud and obnoxious, some Korean pop-jazz playing at a ludicrous beats-per-minute, and clicked on his high beams just as he had been told. The car's headlights sent bright beams of light right at the guard station and the airman manning it, who instinctively raised his hand to shield his eyes. Elroy saw him mutter something darkly to himself.

"Are we *trying* to piss them off?" he asked, having to shout over the music. "Because they certainly look pissed off."

"Yes," Smith shouted in return. Elroy sighed.

The guard, squinting, held up his hand to stop them. In other hand he held a glowing tablet.

Obligingly, Elroy pulled to a stop right in front of the boom gates. And he sat there, music pounding, just as he'd been told.

The guard tapped on the window, a dark scowl on his face.

Elroy lowered the window. "Yes, Lieutenant?" he said.

"Turn off the music, sir," said the guy. "And I'm not a Lieutenant. My name is Private Weyer."

Elroy hit the *mute* button. "No worries. Just visiting the base."

Private Weyer looked like he was trying to give Elroy cancer with his hateful gaze alone. "Do you have a permit?" he asked, voice edged in righteous indignation. "And ID?"

"I do." Elroy took the card out of the cup holder and held it up. It was a fake, of course, but it had his face on it and *looked* convincing. To his untrained eye, at least.

Weyer took the ID, scanned it against the tablet, and then nodded firmly. "Okay." A slight smile came over the guard's face, his eyes lighting up. "With that out of the way . . . sir, you've been randomly selected for a Random Vehicle Inspection, or Bravo Sierra search. We're going to be searching your vehicle for contraband, weapons, and explosives. I understand this may be a frustrating process, but I do need you to comply or you may be arrested."

B.S search? Elroy knew, just as everyone did, that 'randomly selected' was total bullshit, as searches were conducted at an officer's discretion. A lightbulb went on in his head. Of course . . . that's why Smith was pissing them off. He *wanted* to be searched.

"Okay," Elroy said, smiling pleasantly. "Go right ahead."

Weyer seemed to take a particular relish in opening the side door.

Smith—looking *utterly* ridiculous in his wide brim hat—sucked in air through his teeth. "Oh, honey, you cannot be serious! Searching lil-ole-me?"

"That is correct, sir," said Weyer, as guards descended on the vehicle, checking underneath with mirrors and waving sensors near the engine block. "Even lil-ole-you."

Smith made an extremely effeminate sound and, with almost comic exaggeration, rolled his eyes. "Will there be a cavity search involved?"

Elroy glared at Smith in the review mirror and gave a hearty eye roll.

"No sir," said Weyer, "but we will need to check both of you. Please turn off and exit the vehicle so we can give you both a pat down.

"O*oooo*," said Smith.

Jesus Christ, what the hell is he playing at?

Elroy opened the door, carefully stepped out, and raised his hands like a scarecrow. "Sorry about my passenger," he said. *He's a goddamn idiot,* he wanted to say. "He's . . . working late and the stress gets to him."

"No comment, sir," said Weyer as he patted Elroy down, shoulders, torso, hip and legs. He then moved on to Smith, doing the same.

"Vehicle is clear," said one of the guards.

"And we're clear here too." Weyer nodded to Elroy, handing him back his ID. "Okay, on your way then, sir. Welcome to Hickam Air Force Base."

"You too," said Elroy, then groaned softly as he realized what he had said. "Uhh . . . yeah." *Well, guess I can't come back here ever again. Not that I would.*

He got back into the car, started the engine, and drove onto the base.

"Well," said Smith, all business, ripping off his hat. Any vestiges of the personality he'd been affecting only moments ago were completely gone. "Stage one complete."

Elroy drove toward what he presumed to be the barracks. "What the hell was that back there?"

"Social engineering," said Smith. "One that serves a dual purpose. Your average guard is not expecting spies to be dressed like lispy male escorts, nor to rock up in a limo. Basically a glorified confidence trick."

"But . . . *why?*" asked Elroy. "We had IDs. We could just have driven in."

"It means they wouldn't check our fake IDs too closely. Also . . . " Smith held up an ID card. It was Weyers's. "I needed this. And to get it, I needed him to get close enough to me for me to swipe it."

Elroy gaped.

Smith slid the ID card back into his pocket. "In the glove box is an earpiece. Put it on so we'll have communications. I'll talk to you while I'm inside. Keep the motor running, we might have to get out of here in a hurry."

"Okay," said Elroy. He reached over to the glove box, awkwardly opening it. Inside was the earpiece. He clipped it on.

Smith waggled his fingers. "See you soon," he said, pushing open the side door of the limo. "Don't get shot."

"You too," said Elroy as the door slammed shut.

CHAPTER TWENTY-TWO

Bridge
HMS Caernarvon
Z-Space near Yggdrasil
The Future

"I don't like this," said FBI Special Agent Denelle Blair, staring in frustration at the multi-hued pattern that covered the various monitors, showing the strange, otherworldly dimension known as Z-space. A place she knew jack shit about except that it allowed ships to go really far in short spaces of time and instant communication basically anywhere, through some strange method she had vaguely studied in high school. "I don't like this at all."

"There does not appear to be any reason to be concerned," Yim reassured her. "Initial contact with this *Human Resistance* has proven quite amicable."

"They threatened to eat us," said Blair, scowling. "That isn't exactly amicable where I'm from."

"Obviously," said Yim, with a playful smirk, "you've never been to San Diego."

She blinked in surprise. "*That's* where I'm from. I promise you, global warming might have done a number on the West Coast, but we're not *eating each other* in San Diego. Not yet, anyway."

Yim smiled an apology. "Last time I was there, a homeless man tried to stab me with a fork. Said my face looked like a bucket of iced cream."

Blair felt vaguely humorless. "Homelessness is a big problem." *Lighten up!* She managed a little smile. "Also, the last time your clone was there, he shot the President of the United States."

"Maybe the homeless ate him afterward," he said.

The thought actually brought her down again. She had watched Earth blow up. Yim's clone, along with everyone she had ever known for more than a week, had just died in front of her eyes. Their end had been so swift, so brutal, the vast majority of them had seen nothing, felt nothing . . . they had been in coffee shops, sleeping, at work . . . and then nothing. Annihilated by a gravity force so powerful that it shredded the planet; the effect must have torn Earth's inhabitants to pieces almost instantly, so swiftly they didn't even have time to cry out before . . .

She felt like crying again, overwhelmed with thoughts of billions of people, millions of years of history, all wiped out in the blink of an eye. And for what?

Nothing.

Her eyes drifted to the blood stain on the deck, scrubbed but not removed, where Captain Spears had died. Blair had only known her for a brief time, but her loss had been keenly felt. Now Yim and Mattis had command of her ship, and they were hopelessly lost in a weird future timeline. She would never see San Diego again.

Ever.

Not even a joke about the zombie homeless eating Yim's clone-assassin could cheer her up after that.

A chime sounded on her console. She wiped her nose with the back of her sleeve, sniffled, and then tried to find her resolve. She could cry later. "Sir," she said, checking out the readings. "The computer says we're coming up on the coordinates."

"Very good," said Yim. Open communications to the *William Harrison* and the . . ." Mattis's ship hadn't gotten a proper name yet. "The *Warfrigate.* Make sure that we're in touch with each other when we drop out."

"Right." She tapped at some keys, using the mnemonic that she had taught herself. *TACCIO.* Turn on console. Activate radio. Check current frequency. Change frequency if needed. Initiate hail. Open channel. Blair had settled into the role of using the communications equipment fairly well. The manual had helped. She'd flipped through it while waiting in the hangar bay for salvage that had never come. She was a quick study.

Fortunately, all the right lights blinked on in all the right places, and the very faint hissing of static—an artificial noise, she had learnt, not an innate part of the digital communications line, but a cue for the radio operator—told her that it was working. "Channel open, Captain."

"Confirmed," said Yim. Blair was grateful for the reassurance that she hadn't screwed up. "*Caernarvon* to *William Harrison*, away team. Radio check and sitrep."

"*William Harrison* here," said Lynch. "We are all ready to go."

"Away team here," said Mattis. "Green light across the board. I presume."

It must really suck for him, having to figure out a futuristic ship all on his own, but Blair had watched the blasted thing slowly repair itself on the viewscreen. A ship that could almost put itself completely back together without human help or even knowledge. It seemed like magic, but she had read enough Asimov to know that was just a matter of perception. The ship wasn't a mystical artifact growing itself back together. Everything behind the vessel's regenerative abilities was based in science.

Still. Even knowing otherwise, it sure looked magical.

The *Caernarvon* slid out of Z-space, translating into the real world, the multispectral hues being replaced with the flat blackness of space. Directly in front of them, floating in the endless ocean of nothing, was a space station completely unlike any Blair had ever seen or heard about.

Yggdrasil was a giant crystalline bubble, semi-translucent and filled with atmosphere. Inside were buildings, floating, attached to cables and guide wires, each structure seemingly suspended in mid air. The cables grew out from the bubble, forming giant, rooty tendrils that stretched out into space, seeking—something.

"What is that thing?" asked Yim, obviously trying to make sense of it as well. "It cannot be natural, can it?"

It took Blair a moment to realize that her console was beeping, trying to tell her something. "Uhh, sir? We're receiving a communication from Slag." What kind of a name was *Slag* anyway? "Audio only."

"Put it through," said Yim. She did so.

"This is Slag, second stationmaster of Yggdrasil," Slag said, her voice charged with pride. "Welcome to our home. The only place in the galaxy where humans still live free."

CHAPTER TWENTY-THREE

Command Core
Warfrigate 66549
Open space near Yggdrasil
The Future

Mattis stared at the holographic screen, at the spherical, crystalline space station and its long metal tendrils floating through space. He could see how it had earned its name—the drifting cables indeed resembled the roots of an uprooted tree floating in the void—but the station's appearance seemed far more sinister than he had imagined. It looked to him more like a fat, bloated, headless octopus, its long, spindly tentacles reaching out to strangle them. The structures floating inside seemed like the iris of an eye staring at him.

But what it *looked* like didn't matter. He opened a channel to their escort. "Warfrigate 66549, Slag. How do we dock?"

"Just fly toward anywhere," said Slag, almost contemptuously. "It's easy as shit'n. Just steer and go. The grav-drive will do the rest."

"Probably best to do what she says," said Mattis. "Plot in

a course. Nice and slow, nice and easy. Don't want to alarm them."

Robinson waved his hand and the Warfrigate's nose turned toward the space station. It began to advance, slow and steady, with the *Caernarvon* and the *William Harrison* in formation behind them, following in a tight V.

"I don't like this," muttered Robinson.

Seeing worry in an artificial life form caused, in turn, worry in Mattis. "What do you mean?"

"I'm reading a substantial buildup of power from those appendages," said Robinson, his artificial forehead creasing. "And the energy signature does not match any gravity-drive in my database."

Well, now, that wasn't very good. Right as he was about to order a halt, a wailing alarm—high pitched and keen—rang out in the command core.

"Detecting weapons lock," said Robinson. "We are being painted!"

"Haha, oops!" said Slag, and then the alarm went away. She burped rudely down the line. "Sorry, just, uhh . . . forgot to turn off the turrets. Of course they see your ship as an Avenir ship; they don't realize that it's been captured, because computers are fucking *dumb*. Am I right?"

If Robinson was offended by this, he showed no sign of it.

"I'm glad the turrets are off," Mattis said diplomatically.

"Yeah, yeah. Sorry, I get kinda forgetful."

Forgetful. "Just make sure you don't forget anything *else* important, okay?"

Slag just laughed, which stole away whatever shreds of

confidence Mattis had in her answer.

Slowly, surely, the space station drew closer. As the station began to fill his holographic monitor, the crystalline structure of the place parted, opening up like a blooming flower and permitting them entry. Weirdly enough, the atmosphere didn't rush out; it somehow remained inside the opened sphere, as though some invisible force were keeping it within.

The Warfrigate shuddered as it passed the open petals of the space station and into the atmosphere. The ship shook as the air rushed over it.

"Everything okay?" asked Mattis, trying not to worry.

"Certainly," said Robinson. "Warfrigates are atmosphere-capable. The damage we've sustained has disrupted the aerodynamics of the ship. It will be discomforting, but not damaging." He smiled slightly. "In fact, this is a good opportunity to restock the ship's oxygen supply."

"Make sure that happens," said Mattis, adjusting his suit's gloves. "I'm sick of having my head stuck in this fishbowl."

"Deploying intakes and drawing in atmosphere," said Robinson. "Filling the Warfrigate's reserves should be completed within four hours."

Well that was one thing they had solved. Now he hopefully wouldn't run out of air and suffocate inside this salvaged, yet still damaged, ship. Getting shot by Slag "forgetting" something important, or being killed by any number of hazards he hadn't even anticipated in this future timeline . . . now those possibilities—those were all still on the cards.

No time to conjecture. A long cable reached out to the Warfrigate, searching, feeling, sensing, and doing nothing to dispel Mattis's impression of the space station as an octopus.

The wires wrapped around the Warfrigate and pulled it into a beak-like airlock. Mattis heard a faint hiss and felt air moving across the outside of his suit.

"Seal established," said Robinson. "Atmosphere is entering Warfrigate 66549. You should be able to remove your suit presently."

Sure enough, the atmospheric indicator on his wrist changed red to green, and his visor indicated an Earth-like atmosphere. 78% nitrogen, 21% oxygen, 1% carbon dioxide. Air pressure 0.7 PSI. 0.75 PSI. 0.79 PSI.

Mattis carefully unclipped and depressurized his helmet, fresh air blessedly rushing into his suit. Fresh air that stank like rotten fish, stinking bodies, and rusted metal.

"It does have a unique smell, doesn't it?" Robinson asked pleasantly.

"How do you know that? You got a nose?"

"I have a database," said Robinson, "and the database says that the number two complaint of Avenir spies visiting this location is the smell."

Number two. "And what is the first one?"

"According to the database—" Robinson paused, consulting his systems. "Violence. Threats of violence."

"Great," said Mattis, unclipping his gloves and peeling off his suit. "Sounds like a lovely place."

"That is inaccurate," said Robinson. With a flick of his wrist he unlocked the door to the command core. "Enjoy your visit."

CHAPTER TWENTY-FOUR

Primary Airlock
HMS Caernarvon
Inside Yggdrasil
The Future

Blair thought she was going to be happy getting off the *Caernarvon* and onto solid land. She had adjusted to her space-sickness reasonable well—certainly with regard to being on the bridge of the warship, which was reasonably steady and stable—but the promise of solid ground beneath her feet was one she was eager to enjoy.

So when the airlock breached and the rancid stench of the place wafted toward her—like someone had thrown week-old prawns into a blender, drank them, and then vomited them all over—she withered.

Everyone grabbed their noses.

"*Tā wén qǐlái xiàng gǒu de gāngmén!*" hissed Yim, his words distorted by the pinch on his nose. Blair's Mandarin was rusty, but there was definitely something in there about the inside of a dog's anus.

She couldn't disagree. Her eyes watered so much that she could barely see anything. "When I said there was something fishy about this place, *holy shit*, I didn't mean *literally!*"

Slowly, the water in her eyes faded, and Blair was able to look out into the stinking place.

The airlock had opened to reveal a long bridge jutting out from the central floating structure, like an old fashioned wooden pier, leading straight to the *Caernarvon*. Beside it were dozens of other piers with other ships docked, including their recently captured Warfrigate and the *William Harrison*. Beyond the docking platforms, a collection of buildings all emanated out from the central point of the station. Buildings—buildings like old skyscrapers. Concrete and steel, windows made of glass, even streetlights.

The inner heart of the station looked like a tiny Earth with giant buildings covering every inch of its surface. People walked around, wearing chaotic mismatches of clothing: yellow construction vests with yellow beanies instead of hard hats, orange life preservers with combat armor pieces thrown into the mix, and other things even more bizarre—some guy wearing the lower half a chicken suit. A woman wearing a cat costume, complete with long tail. Someone dressed as a hard shell taco, including actual lettuce leaves and a splatter of spicy-smelling sauce on the meat.

What the fuck.

A blonde woman approached them, wearing a space suit minus a helmet, except the whole thing was spray-painted bright pink. A brown teddy bear hung around her neck, mounted on a thick neck chain. Her boots were mismatched, one green and one red. Her skin was pale, ghostly almost, as though she had never seen the sun. And her smile was absolutely massive.

"Sorry about the turrets!" she boomed, giving a wet cough into her hand, then sticking out that same hand for Blair to shake.

Blair looked to Yim, then—with palpable reluctance—took the slimy hand, squeezed it, and pushed through. "It's fine. I'm Special Agent Denelle Blair. It's a pleasure to meet you."

"Lovely to meet you, Special!" Slag shook her hand violently enough to hurt her wrist. "Fuck me, though, *four names*. That's pretty sweet."

"No, no, Special Agent is a . . ." Not this again. "Just call me Blair."

"And I am—" began Yim, but Slag talked over him.

"You serious?" asked Slag, squinting. "What the fuck kind of name is Blair?"

Blair cocked her head, regarding the bizarre creature before her named *Slag*. "Just a weird old name," she said, smiling politely.

"Right," said Slag, sticking her hand out toward Yim. "And what kind of name do you have?"

"I'm Admiral Yim," he said, reluctant to touch Slag's gross hand, but he did it anyway. "And before you ask, my name is Yim."

"Good, I don't know what an Admiral is either. But it sounds admirable."

Blair had no idea if that was a joke or not, and was uncertain enough about the customs of this timeline to laugh, so she nervously tittered, then folded her hands behind her back. "Anyway, yes. Thank you for providing us with safe harbor."

"No worries," said Slag with a loud, open-mouthed burp. "We got ourselves a target, this Spectre fucker, so don't worry. If he's as rich as you say, you'll have plenty of opportunity to pay me and mine back."

Blair would let Mattis handle that.

"If you don't mind," said Yim, obviously trying for diplomatic, although his face scrunched up and he looked a little green, "What's the source of that odor?"

"Well," said Slag, "we farm fish for protein." She jabbed her thumb over her shoulder. "And because space is pretty tight here, the smell gets fuckin' *everywhere*. You get used to it after a while, but it definitely gives the place a . . . brisk ambiance." Slag grinned like a jackal. "And believe me, it's good for you that you're so shocked."

"Why—why's that?" asked Yim, holding back his gag reflex.

"Because the Avenir prep their spies to infiltrate this place. The first thing they tell them is about the smell, so they're prepared for it. The fact that you aren't prepared for it tells us that you're not a spy."

"Or just not a well-prepared spy," said Blair without thinking.

Slag laughed, then stopped, enormous mouth bending instantly into a deep frown. Then it went back to laughing. "Yeah, you're okay, Special Blair."

Yim smiled diplomatically. "Anyway. Slag, is it? We're very grateful. And, as agreed, we'll provide you with all the information on our—uh—target as soon as some transfers between ships have been completed."

"Transfers?" asked Slag.

"Mostly injured and dead crew, from our old ships to the new."

Slag whistled lowly. "That sucks. Shiiiit…"

From the airlock behind Blair, medical staff wheeled out stretcher after stretcher—a convoy of the dead, all of them covered in ominous white sheets. She counted a dozen of them, including the bridge crew Spectre had killed. And others . . . crewmembers killed during the battle with the Chinese frigates. Each one had a label with their name.

Last came Spears.

"Sorry," whispered Blair as Spears's body passed by.

The injured came next. Corrick, pale and gaunt as a ghost, her head swathed in bandages. Then Sammy, Reardon's brother, his legs elevated—apparently he'd hurt himself again—followed by various crewmembers she didn't recognize. Ten wounded, all in all, carried across from the *Caernarvon* to the captured Warfrigate.

After a brief discussion that Blair didn't catch, Manda moved Spears's body to the front of the queue—to honor her, perhaps—and the procession disappeared into the Warfrigate.

"Okay," said Slag. "With that macabre shit out of the way . . . let's go get fucked up on fish juice and figure out how we're going to rob this Spectre guy, shall I?"

Blair forced a smile. "Sure. When Captain Mattis and Captain Lynch get here, we'll go. But first we have to find him."

"Yeah," said Slag, picking her teeth and dislodging a

fingernail full of plaque. “I know a guy in the Hole. He’ll know how to find *anyone*.”

CHAPTER TWENTY-FIVE

Docketing Port
Inside Yggdrasil
The Future

Captain Mattis couldn't stand the smell of the place, but the more he walked, the easier it got. He spotted Yim, Blair, and odd woman he presumed to be Slag and approached them.

Putting on his most diplomatic voice, Mattis stepped up to the group. "Evening, folks. Slag."

She screwed up her face. "What the fuck is 'evening'?"

"It's—" it struck him that Yggdrasil may not have a day-night cycle. "Just a greeting."

She looked dubious. He started to say more, but a familiar face—two of them, actually—walked around from the other side of the pier. Mattis couldn't help but smile warmly, genuinely, as Modi and Lynch approached. Lynch was wearing a huge, broad-rimmed cowboy hat that somehow looked pretty good on him. Typical.

Mattis wanted to greet them, to congratulate them on

their new command, but it was the third face behind them that truly stole his attention.

Martha Ramirez.

"Hello, Admiral Mattis," she said, looking almost as nervous and awkward as he felt.

"Hello, Martha." The words coming out of his mouth felt so forced. Suddenly he felt fifteen again, asking a girl to the prom and having his voice break halfway through. "I . . . was not expecting to see you here."

Ramirez reached up and brushed back a strand of her hair. "I, uh . . . my team and I were covering the construction of the *William Harrison*, first of its class, and we, uh, we were aboard . . . when it got sucked through."

Lynch leaned forward, grinning like a kid who had arranged an expensive gift for his parents. "I was hoping to surprise you, Mattis, but guess that's out of the bag now."

"I see," Mattis said lamely, truly unable to think of anything else. So he turned his attention to the others. "It's great to see you again—" He offered Lynch his hand. "*Captain*."

"Couldn't have done it without you." Lynch grinned, taking the extended hand and squeezing it firmly. "You taught me everything I know. And for whatever else there is that I don't quite get a handle on, well, that's what Commander Modi is for. He's a right smart windmill fixer."

Mattis held the shake for a moment, then released it and smiled to Modi. "And it's good to see you again too, Commander."

"The pleasure," said Modi, his face implacable and emotionless as ever, "is all mine. It is intensely agreeable to see you again."

Mattis clapped him on the shoulder, smiling in spite of himself, then locked eyes with Ramirez again.

"Hey," she said, shuffling nervously—so very unlike her. "When we get a moment, we need to have a chat, yeah?"

"Okay," he said.

"I mean it. An important chat."

"Okay. Okay, we will, Ramirez. Promise."

An awkward silence fell, which ended with Slag spitting onto the ground. "Anything else you fuckers need to do before we get going?"

"Actually," said Mattis, "there is one thing. One of my crew is hurt. Lieutenant Corrick. I have to see her before I do anything else."

Slag scowled. "You're joking, aren't you? You brought me fucking all the way down here, quick as you please, to talk about a job. Now you're asking me to *wait for you?*" She folded her arms. "Do you have a job or not? You playing games with me?"

Mattis knew it was bad form to put her off. Very bad form. "She's part of my crew," he said again. "And she isn't going to last much longer. Before she, uh, goes . . . I would like to speak with her." His tone became firm. "She's on my crew. I owe her that much. I promise you: no games."

Another moment of awkward silence. Slag's visage softened. "Fine," she said. "Go. You got yourself four minutes." She jabbed a finger toward the Warfrigate. "They went that way."

Mattis smiled his thanks and, without another word, jogged back toward his ship.

"What a shit-show," Slag muttered behind him, spitting again.

CHAPTER TWENTY-SIX

Hickam Air Force Base, home of the 6,774th Missile Wing
Los Alamos v2.0
Tiberius System
Main timeline

John Smith adjusted his ridiculous fedora and strode through the base like he owned the place. His prosthetic eye switched to thermal, helpfully highlighting the outlines of figures moving around the facility and inside the various buildings. When he felt he was in the clear—well aware that security cameras would be watching him, but that was what the wide-brimmed hat was for—Smith sent it a mental impulse to look instead for radioactive leaks.

His vision in the artificial eye went from blue and red to green and black. It was always unsettling when that happened. The human brain was just not designed to cope with this kind of rapid change in vision. But after a moment's adjustment, he could see the twinkling green stars that were the silos and their buried missiles.

They were well guarded, of course, but that was only to

be expected. Plus, the personnel were only air jockeys, and Los Alamos v2.0 had never experienced war. The staff at Hickam must have been bored out of their minds. The missiles were there only as a relic of the Sino-American war. Most of them probably didn't even work.

Slowly Smith turned his head, looking at each little twinkling green star. Each was faint, as though buried, but there was one brighter than the rest. And it was above ground.

Jackpot.

He strode down a sidewalk by the main road, vaguely following the direction of the green twinkle, unafraid of the street light shining down from above. After a minute or two, the twinkle's source was revealed—a large aircraft hangar. Smith casually turned off the road and walked into the darkness, then abandoned all pretense of 'fitting in'.

Smith surveyed the hangar with his biological eye. The doors were closed and two airmen stood guard out front, rifles comfortably held in their hands. They looked alert, eyes scanning the gloom as best they could. *Okay, maybe not just air jockeys after all.* Some part of Smith was glad to see the airmen taking their jobs seriously, no matter the boredom, but it was still a problem for him. An obstacle he had to overcome.

Eh. It was nice to have a challenge.

Smith plucked one of the gems from the side of his hat and rubbed it, the heat from his fingers activating the thing. It sprouted six legs like a bug. He linked into it with his hand and issued it his standard set of instructions. Immediately the robotic creature sprung to life, leaping off his hand and sprinting away.

A few seconds passed as the tiny robot moved from

streetlight to streetlight, making a beeline toward the hangar bay. When it got close, the thing let out an ear-piercing screech, running in a circle and emitting a thin trail of green smoke, darting around like crazy.

The two guards, shocked at the appearance of the creature, both shifted their stance into a ready shooting position. *Any moment,* mused Smith, *they'll abandon their post to chase the thing, giving me an opening.* And sure enough, one of them stepped forward, rifle raised, taking two steps toward the screeching robo-insect.

"Don't," said the other guard, his rifle raised as well. "It's clearly a distraction." He touched his radio. "Hangar 61, Bravo, Bravo, Bravo. Intruder alert."

Aw, shit.

Time to use a little trick that Reardon had taught him back in the day, during the . . . incident. Smith took a deep breath, held onto his hat, and started running out of the shadows at full speed, looking over his shoulder and pointing. "Oh my god!" he said, inflecting his voice up, making it shrill and panicked. "There's more of them! It's those horrible robots, there's more of those things—and they're coming this way!"

The guards raised their rifles as he got close but, obviously dressed like a civilian—or possibly just flat out confused by his outlandish appearance they didn't shoot. "Who are you?" they demanded. "Stop, or—"

No time for that. Smith let his fist lead the way, catching the first guard in the gut. He bodily lifted the guy off his feet, holding him up as a shield, then drew his shockstick and slammed it into the second guard.

Subtlety was now completely out the window. Smith snatched up the radio, depressing the talk key. "False alarm," he said, doing his best to imitate the voice of the guard. He glanced down at the guy's uniform. It bore the name *SANDERS*. "This is Sanders. Hangar 61. Sorry, false alarm, nothing going on here."

"Negative, we have a rapid response team en route," said the voice. "Stand by to be relieved."

All around the airbase, red alarm lights began flashing and a low, wailing siren started its mournful cry. He'd never been more proud of a pair of guards. Never again would he underestimate the skill and professionalism of the United States Air Force.

Too bad it was likely going to end in his and Elroy's deaths.

CHAPTER TWENTY-SEVEN

Near Warfrigate 66549
Docketing Port
Yggdrasil
The Future

Mattis jogged to catch up to the convoy of sick and dead. "Doctor Manda!" he called out as he got close. "Wait just a moment, please."

The poor doctor seemed to be carrying the weight of the galaxy on her shoulders, almost slumped over the gurney she was pushing, thick bags under her eyes. Her hair was a mess. As Mattis got close, he could see she the gurney contained Spears's body. Damn.

Still, his call seemed to raise her spirits somewhat. Or at least cause her to hide her misery better. "Admiral Mattis," she said, straightening her back. "I am performing the transfer as requested. How can I help you?"

"I want to speak to Lieutenant Corrick before..." he chose his words carefully. "While there's still some time. I barely knew her, mostly by reputation, but . . . "

The ghost of a genuine smile—some trace of happiness—graced Doctor Manda's face, and she dipped her head. "Certainly. Go right ahead."

When it came to medical staff, rank and position didn't matter so much as with almost any other subordinate. Doctor Manda, technically, had the right to remove him of command if she deemed him—in common vernacular—crazy as balls. So while he didn't have to ask her permission, it was polite.

Mattis jogged over to Corrick's gurney, steeling himself for what she was going to look like, but as he got closer he still found himself shocked.

Corrick's shoulders, arms, and face were puffy and bruised, black like thunderclouds, giving her body a lopsided, asymmetrical look. Her eyes were sunken and depressed, dull and lifeless, and the bandages covering her head made her look like some kind of alien with a huge puffy brain. Her lips were dry and chapped, her bruise-free skin pale and clammy, and she seemed to have aged five years. She was waiting on Death's doorstep, passing the time until the grim reaper opened it a crack so she could slump inside.

Mattis barely recognized her.

"How are you doing, Lieutenant?" he asked quietly.

Upon seeing him, Corrick seemed to recover some of herself, even managing a smile. "Admiral." She coughed wetly. Weakly. "Not—not too great, gotta say. Had another round of surgery, but . . . now they say that . . . something in my brain-thingie is going to cause the—" She struggled to speak. "—Death."

"I'm—I'm sorry," he managed quietly.

"It's fine. Don't . . . need my brain anyway. Lasted this

long . . . without it. I'm fine." She absolutely did not look fine. "You're gonna fix this, right?"

Mattis had one simple rule: don't lie to your crew.

"I'm afraid," he said, "that this one is beyond even me."

Corrick snorted dismissively, then coughed again. "Nah. This is nothing. This is . . . just a little setback. I'm far too latina to die."

"Latinas die," said Mattis, though he just smiled a little, too. "But maybe less than most."

If he was helping her in any way, it wasn't easy to see. Corrick coughed again, raising her bruised hands to shield her mouth. "Anyway," she said. "I'm kinda . . . hoping you have a rabbit to pull out of your hat to get me through this one."

"I wish I did," he said, quietly. "I wish I had something to get you through this, but I don't. No rabbits. No magic tricks. I'm sorry, Lieutenant. I truly am."

Whatever was left of the light in Corrick's eyes slowly faded as his words sank in. "But . . ." she struggled to articulate, stammering slightly. "B-but sir, I thought . . . I thought you could solve anything."

Anything but death. Mattis's eyes guiltily flicked to the gurney that held Spears's body. He hadn't been able to save her. He hadn't been able to save Chuck, or Earth, or even his damn ship. He'd lost everything piece by piece by piece, and lying to Corrick wouldn't help her.

But seeing her like that, he just couldn't help himself.

"I said no tricks," he said, straightening his shoulders and returning her gaze. "Because tricks are what a hooker does for money. We've got something a lot better: science. And a warship from the future. And we are standing on a space station with unknown potential, perhaps unlimited potential, to do things that we could only ever dream about." He smiled grimly. "I don't think Spears dragged you out of a cell to die like this, Lieutenant Corrick. So now hear this: we have a plan, and we're going to make this right. You just stay strong for me, and that's an order. You hear me?"

She seemed to. Some measure of the fire and determination he had expected in her came back, and her voice found more strength. "Yessir."

He knew he had to get moving. "I might be busy for a while," he said. "As soon as I'm available, we can chat again. But for now, duty calls."

"Duty calls," echoed Corrick.

Mattis gave a swift salute. "Your primary mission is to recover from this. I'll debrief you when it's done."

Corrick, slowly and weakly, returned the salute. It was an obvious effort for her but she managed it. "Aye aye, sir. I'll have it written up ASAP."

"Very good. I'll talk to you then." With one last smile, Mattis turned and walked back the way he'd came.

The farther away he got from her, the stronger the feeling grew that he had just seen Corrick for the last time.

CHAPTER TWENTY-EIGHT

Docketing Port
Yggdrasil
The Future

Mattis's head was in a dozen places when he walked back to the docking port at Yggdrasil. Thinking of Corrick. Thinking of Ramirez. Thinking of everything except the mission at hand. He tried to keep his head as he approached the rest of the group.

"All right, now that shit's done with, this way." Slag turned and began walking down the pier, shoving her hands into her pockets and whistling some tune Mattis didn't recognize. If she was mad he'd stepped away, she didn't seem to give much indication of it at all.

There wasn't anything he could say to her odd response, and so with a shrug, Mattis fell into step beside her. He glanced over his shoulder. "You should be filming this," he said.

She tapped her broach. It had a lens on it. "I am. Believe me, I am. My crew has every camera we have pointed out every window we can find on the *William Harrison*."

Classic Ramirez. He had no idea what kind of recording hardware the Warfrigate possessed, but the *Caernarvon* had a full electronic suite onboard, and the *William Harrison* was probably no slouch either. Acquiring data from this timeline would no doubt prove invaluable.

Mattis's attention kept returning to Ramirez. She kept looking at him. She seemed . . . happy. And sad. And nervous. And relieved. A complex, crazy mixture of emotions that he struggled to understand. It was more than just seeing him again—there was something else going on here, but he didn't have the bandwidth to comprehend it fully.

Blair slid up to him, her voice a low murmur, obviously trying to avoid Slag overhearing. "This place gives me the heebies," she said. "And a few jeebies as well. Slag said they eat people, right?"

She sure had. "I'm sure that's just a joke."

"I hope so," said Blair. "I don't wanna get turned into soup." Her face hardened. "I swear to God, I'll stab anyone who tries to turn me into soup."

Mattis gave her a firm look. "I promise you, it's just a bluff."

She paused. "I have a question—why?"

"What?"

"Why would they bluff about that?"

"Probably because they don't know us, and they want us to respect them. Fear is the easiest way to give manners to strangers."

Lynch coughed behind them. "Maybe they need to learn a little southern hospitality," he muttered, loud enough for them to hear, but hopefully drowned out by Slag's whistling. "I don't mind people who just fell off the tater truck, but these people might have landed so hard that if Spectre put their brains in a bumblebee, it'd fly backwards."

Was that a compliment or an insult? Either way, Mattis knew they were desperately short on allies and this "Human Resistance" was the best and only thing they had going on that front. A warship could not normally survive without logistical support. No matter how careful and conservative they were with their resources, the *William Harrison* and the *Caernarvon* would both eventually run out of ammunition, parts, food, and fuel. They needed a base.

The Warfrigate, however, was a whole other story. It had brought itself back from the brink of near-total annihilation and although many systems had yet to be brought back online, the ship had gone from wreck to warship in just under an hour. Something Mattis would have thought impossible only days ago.

Now the rules of the game had changed, but both of the conventional ships in their fleet would require resupply. Yggdrasil may be a stinkhole, but it would have to do.

Yet the more Mattis considered, the more his thoughts drew themselves back to Ramirez and away from their mission.

He shook his head, forcing himself to focus. He kept his eyes on Slag as she led them down the pier toward the cluster of buildings nearby. The structures seemed to possess the same haphazard, DIY feel that the Human Resistance had, but with a twist.

The structures were built out of and nestled in amongst

the station itself, which looked far from homegrown. It was as though the station had been built, and then the Human Resistance had built over the top of it. They had added their own buildings, modified pretty much anything and everything within reach, and taken things apart to turn them into ships—

"You guys like fish juice?" Slag asked, then let out a loud, open-mouthed guffaw. "Aw, bet you don't even fucking know what it is!"

Mattis didn't. But if it tasted like the air smelled . . . "Maybe we should just have water," he said. "Shouldn't drink on duty and all that."

"Life's a mean drunk," said Slag, "only way to beat it is to be meaner."

She walked up to one of the buildings, something that looked it had once been a slick, advanced refrigerated shipping container, but now had holes cut in the windows and cables crudely attached to the walls to provide power. From within, the throbbing sound of some kind of music could be heard, a strange, otherworldly fusion between what sounded to Mattis like traditional throat singing and banjo music. "In here," said Slag, shoving open the unevenly cut door with her shoulder and stepping inside.

Mattis was first inside. He was expecting some kind of office, or maybe a home. But instead, all he found was a refrigeration unit with two holes cut at either end. The music was coming from one of them.

Slag ducked inside, waving them onward. "C'mon, weirdos! This way!" She disappeared into the passage.

Picking up the pace, Mattis ushered everyone into the room, then into the tunnel Slag had gone through.

"Holy shit," grumbled Blair as she passed. "I hear *banjos*. What the fuck is this? *Deliverance* in space?"

"They won't eat you," said Mattis, pushing her onward. "Besides, what happened in *Deliverance* was a lot worse than eating people."

"Is that supposed to make me feel better?"

Mattis only smirked.

"I like their taste in music though," Lynch said, craning his neck thoughtfully. "It's actually not bad, if you just give it a moment to get used to it . . ."

Mattis pushed him on too, then Modi, and then ducked in behind them.

They were on the top level of some kind of underground bar. The loud banjo-throat-singing music pounded on every wall, hurting their ears. Below them, through a transparent railing, hundreds of people seemed to be engaged in some kind of rave, complete with clouds of drugs, copulating couples, and glowing body paint. On the other side of the room was an expansive bar.

"I'll be back," said Slag. "Gotta go find our contact. Find us a booth, I won't be long." She scurried away from them down a ramp and disappeared into the mass of intoxicated dancers.

"Definitely not *Deliverance* in space," said Mattis, watching the cavorting crowd below.

CHAPTER TWENTY-NINE

Airlock 7
Warfrigate 66549
Inside Yggdrasil
The Future

Doctor Sunila Manda wheeled Spears's trolley into the airlock with practiced, solemn forlornness.

It wasn't the first time she had dealt with the dead, either patients she had lost or corpses at the morgue. But dealing with a cadaver was different when she had known the person in life.

Spears had been the first CO Manda had ever served under. The *Caernarvon* had been her first posting. For six years she'd served on the same ship with the same CO, same XO, and in the same infirmary, same operating room, most of the same nursing staff—and often in the same section of space—patrolling Royal territory.

Consistency. Stable, reliable consistency.

Now Blackwood was some kind of clone, Spears was dead, and they were so far away from their patrol route—in terms of distance and time—that it was impossible for Manda to ever get back to how things were. Even with a new CO, even if they got back to their timeline . . .

Doctor Manda knew that there was only one thing to do. Soldier on. Her remaining patients needed her. Corrick would soon be joining Spears in death, and Doctor Manda would have to be strong for her, too. There was no time for weakness.

She led the medical techs wheeling the dead, moving through the airlock into Warfrigate 66549. Taking the bodies over to the much more advanced ship was a good choice. Relocating the injured was much better. Medical technology had advanced so much since the Sino-American war. What technological wonders must be present on a ship from hundreds of years in the future?

Whatever it was, it still wasn't worth Spears's life.

The airlock cycled and Manda was let inside. The inner bulkheads of the Warfrigate was not too dissimilar to the inside of the *Caernarvon*, nor from any other other ship she had been in. Steel, square, long, and empty.

With a bright pulse of light, a ghostly, translucent man flickered into existence in the middle of the corridor. Doctor Manda had been forewarned about the hologram, but seeing it in person was another thing.

"My name is Doctor Sunila Manda," she said, staring at the holographic man. "I'm here with the injured and the bodies of our fallen. Please direct me to the infirmary."

"This way," he said, floating down the corridor. "I am Proconsul Michael Robinson. The infirmary has been powered and prepared for your arrival, as has the morgue."

Doctor Manda pushed the cart after the apparition. Her medical team followed, mute and morose. This was the worst part of the job. "Thank you," she said. "But I hope I'm not distracting you from your work—running the ship and all."

"Do not be concerned," Robinson said, drifting a foot or so off the ground. "I am a process fork, a copy of the version of me that is inside the command core. When my task is completed, my thread will be terminated."

Doctor Manda's cart wheels squeaked as she pushed it along the deck. "You seem remarkably calm about that."

"The human obsession with death is not one shared by most who live in this time, a value the Avenir impart onto the artificial intelligences they create. We all understand that life begins and eventually life ends. This is not to be contested. Resisting it is not good for the soul."

Soul? "I'm just glad you can help. I am a medical doctor, but I'm eager to learn more, especially from a ship from the future—my time's future, that is. Is that a possibility?"

"My databases have various instructional medical books and holograms. We may peruse them at your leisure when time presents itself."

Knowledge and medical sciences… advances she could study and learn from. "That would be ideal."

Robinson drifted through a doorway. Above it was a label. *INFIRMARY.* Manda pushed the trolley up to the doorway. As she got close, the door swung open.

The room within was tiny.

It was barely ten meters cubed and totally empty. No tables. No surgical wards. No equipment. Just empty, featureless walls, with Robinson floating inside them. "As promised, this is the infirmary."

"You mean the morgue?" Manda asked. "I assume that's what this is?"

"No, this is the infirmary. Its purpose is to treat injured personnel. It is capable of healing humans."

Doctor Manda frowned, casting a critical eye around the empty cubic room. "Please explain. It looks empty to me."

Robinson smiled. "Please insert the gurney containing your patient, and I will demonstrate."

He wanted Spears? "This isn't a patient," Doctor Manda said. "Captain Spears has been deceased for almost a full day."

"Please insert the gurney," Robinson repeated patiently.

This was some kind of crazy. Some kind of malfunction in the artificial mind of the hologram. "Why?"

"So treatment may begin."

She almost almost yanked back the gurney, but some part of her knew that the limits of science could advance beyond what any "sane" person could think possible.

And there wasn't any harm in trying. Spears wasn't going to get *more* dead.

Slowly, carefully, Doctor Manda pushed her gurney into the room.

Nothing happened.

"This is crazy," muttered Doctor Manda, reaching for the trolley handle.

The white sheet lifted, pulled up and away by some kind of unseen energy, revealing the body. Spears looked so peaceful, calm. Happy even.

A bright yellow light washed over Spears's body, settling on her head. Robinson reached down and touched her, extracting a thimbleful of blood. Must be a preliminary diagnostic tool.

The hologram withdrew his hand, and the light continued to spread over Spears's body. A holographic image of a brain —her brain, presumably—drifted out her body, then vanished. The lights winked out, the white sheet dropped to the floor, and everything went silent.

Captain Spears's body started to disintegrate, as though being dissolved by some kind of acid. Doctor Manda stared, wild-eyed, as the remains vanished before her eyes.

"What did you do?" she shrieked.

"I'm healing her," said Robinson, sounding confused.

"Hey!" shouted someone from behind her. One of her patients. Sammy Reardon. "What's going on up there?"

She honestly had no idea how to answer.

CHAPTER THIRTY

The Hole
Yggdrasil
The Future

Mattis had not been to a rave since the academy, and had never been to one playing anything like this bizarre groaning banjo music. Though there was that one time during the Sino-American war that they had had a forty-eight hour rec leave in Sandalwood base and had listened to Indian Bollywood-Regge fusion . . .

"Reminds me of the war!" he said to Lynch. He was shouting to let his voice carry over the music.

"The war?" Lynch gave a little snort, shouting as well. "Must have been different from how the history books depicted it, sir. Nobody mentioned drugs and banjos."

It was difficult to explain. He was suddenly acutely aware of Ramirez listening into what he was saying, along with her recording hardware. "I just meant this one time at Sandalwood base, that's all. There was a party like this one. I had a good night."

Lynch looked at him like he had confessed to having two heads. "I can't imagine you're the kind of guy who would drop tabs and slide onto the dance floor to do the worm."

Do the *worm?* How old did Lynch think he was? "Okay, okay, enough."

Modi stared down at the dancing, writhing people with something akin to horror on his face. "Th-they are ingesting pharmaceutical substances," he said, briefly stammering as though he was witnessing an extremely serious crime. "I cannot help but think that the manufacturing and quality control employed by these people must be worryingly lax . . ."

A quick glance from Lynch brought back Modi's diplomatic side.

Mattis thought it best to move on from that. "Modi, we don't know that there's anything wrong with the substances these fine people are ingesting." He smiled politely. "How about you and Lynch go and get us some drinks? Don't forget some for Slag. Blair, take Ramirez, find us a booth and make sure it's as private as possible. Yim, we'll wait here for Slag, and when she comes back, take her to the booth."

"Aye sir," said Lynch, grinning widely. "Drinks for the table. I wonder if they have whisky?"

"Every bar we end up in has whisky," grumbled Modi, and the two of them slipped off.

"Table, got it," said Blair. She and Ramirez slipped off, with Ramirez giving him a little playful wave. Playful and nervous.

What the hell was going on with her?

It didn't matter. She was back and that was all that mattered. For some time—hours, longer really—Mattis had thought she was most likely dead on Earth. Now she was back and that was good. Maybe that was just how she felt too.

Yim moved beside him. "Lots of people with weapons here," he said, the corners of his mouth turned down.

"I know. But they're almost all melee weapons. Don't bring a knife to a gun fight. Like the Chinese learned at Tiananmen, if you stand in front of tanks, the tanks are going to win."

"Huh?" asked Yim. "What tanks?"

Oh. Right. The Chinese, to this day, hid that little *facet* of their history from their own people. "Never mind," said Mattis.

Yim scowled and muttered something under his breath. Mattis's Chinese was pretty rusty, but he was certain he caught the word *xuānchuán*. It meant *propaganda*.

Neither of them said anything for a bit.

"Okay," said Yim, "so, how are we doing this?"

"Pretty simple," said Mattis. "Just try to blend in. Play nice. Talk to her and this 'Human Resistance'. See if we can find out any information about Spectre and figure out how to take him down."

"Sounds good." Yim leaned in, shouting over the music. "Do you think this might be a waste of time?"

Mattis raised an eyebrow.

"I mean," said Yim, "that this Slag person. She doesn't seem to know Spectre at all, even by reputation. Maybe nobody does."

"I doubt that," Mattis said. "The Avenir sent whole fleets back into the past to change it, just to undermine his power in this timeline. He's got to be *someone* important."

"Makes sense to me," said Yim, nodding down toward the dance floor. Mattis followed his gaze.

Slag shoved her way through the crowd of dancers, most of them oblivious to her presence, towing a massive ape of a man behind her. The guy was blond like her, and almost as tall as he was wide, with arms like tree trunks and legs like fire hydrants. The ramp up to their level creaked as he walked up, the metal groaning with the strain of his bulk. Mattis felt his mouth drop open.

"This is Blip," said Slag, jabbing a thumb over her shoulder, a cheeky grin on her face. "He might be a fucking giant, but don't worry, it ain't just his muscles that are big, if you know what I mean."

Yim seemed confused. "His brain, too?"

"Yeah," said Slag, cackling. "Brain. Right."

Blip stepped forward, boldly sticking out his massive hand. It looked like a block of ham with sausages for fingers. "I'm Blip," he said, smiling politely. "Pleasure to meet you, Mister Mattis."

Mattis was not short, but he felt like a dwarf before the massive titan. He shook the hand, feeling the vice-like grip of Blip's fingers squeeze his. "Pleasure's all mine."

"And you, Mister Yim," said Blip, shaking Yim's hands too. "I looked you both up in the archives. You look just like your profile pictures." He suddenly began to speak very fast. "I couldn't believe it at first. I wasn't sure it was real. But here you are! And the initial scan of your hair says you don't have mitochondrial infusions either, so you're as human as could be. This really is fascinating, you know, simply fascinating."

He tried to keep up. "Wait, you scanned our hair?"

"When you walked through the door." Slag casually wiped her mouth. "Just a security precaution, nothing more. Finds Avenir spies."

They seemed pretty paranoid about Avenir spies, but perhaps the caution was warranted. "Okay," Mattis said, shouting over the weird music. "Our people have found us a booth."

He looked over across the bar to where Ramirez and Blair were seated. Ramirez gave him a 'come here' wave. There was no sign of Lynch or Modi yet, but they'd find them.

"Here we go," muttered Yim, following Mattis over.

CHAPTER THIRTY-ONE

Infirmary
Warfrigate 66549
Inside Yggdrasil
The Future

"What just happened?" asked Doctor Manda, staring in bewilderment at Robinson. "What did you do to Spears?"

"I'm treating her," said Robinson, an edge of confusion in his voice. "Captain Spears will be restored at the conclusion of her treatment."

The body was completely gone, and the white sheet that had covered it lay on the ground. "Restored? Her body, it's—it's completely bloody vanished!"

"Oh," said Robinson, as though considering some forgotten detail. "Yes, the body was reclaimed by the nanobots."

She knew that. Could see that. It was as clear as day. Doctor Manda stammered, trying to find a fitting response to this insanity.

"What's going on?" demanded Sammy behind her.

"Good question," she said over her shoulder, turning back to Robinson. "Tell me. Now. What did you do with Spears?"

Robinson seemed unable to answer her question properly. "I initiated medical rejuvenation procedure 677-Bravo. My sensor readings indicate that so far the early stages of this process have been completed successfully."

"Describe these stages," Doctor Manda hissed. "Tell me everything about rejuvenation procedure 66-whatever."

"Very well," said Robinson, his voice suddenly changing, as though the artificial man was reading from some kind of document she couldn't see. "Medical rejuvenation procedure 667-Bravo is an advanced form of procedure 659-Yankee, allowing the imaging of tissue which has suffered significant decay, which in turn is a modification of procedure 599-Golf, which originally allowed imaging from necrotic tissue. The process takes place in four distinct stages. In the first stage, the cognition of the patient is imaged and stored as a default neural-network in the database of the attending program. Imaging includes mental state and memories approximately ten seconds before brain death.

"In the second stage, the body of the patient is disposed of in an appropriate manner; disposal by incineration is recommended if nanobot decomposition engines are unavailable, alternatively, burial is a suitable, if archaic, option.

"In the third stage, a new body is grown in a standard issue cloning vat. In a situation where the new body needs to be aged in order to match the original, artificial DNA oxidation is employed to artificially advance the age of the new body to an approximate level of the original, along with mitochondrial infusions taken from the standard sample. If mitochondrial material is not available, the process is halted. A medical laser approximates any detected scarring or injuries except those that caused the fatality of course, although the default setting is to avoid recreating any damage, reflecting cosmetic changes only—especially if one wishes to create the deception of surviving a serious wound that was, in reality, lethal. Accordingly, user discretion is advised. Further, the default selection is for accelerated growth times, but standard or delayed times can be selected if desired, up to a maximum of one hundred and forty years."

Manda blinked. Behind her, the medical team watched as well, clearly uncertain what to say. Robinson continued robotically.

"In the fourth stage, the imaged cognition is implanted into the cloned body. Patient aftercare is an incredibly important part of this process, as they are typically confused, frustrated, and alarmed when awoken. Typical patient responses include panic attacks, confusion, lethargy, hopelessness, and in some rare cases, psychosis. These symptoms are particularly common when the patient is not aware they are undergoing this procedure. If variant process 679-Sierra is employed, a separate cognition may be employed at one's discretion."

Robinson's voice returned to normal. "Do you have any questions?"

Doctor Manda tried to process what she had been told. "So you're telling me," she said slowly, "that Captain Spears's mind has been *imaged* and is currently being put into a *new body*?"

"In simplified terms," said Robinson, "yes."

Her chest tightened, heart beating wildly. "Are . . . are you saying that, right now, Captain Spears is being brought back from the dead?"

CHAPTER THIRTY-TWO

Hickam Air Force Base, home of the 6,774th Missile Wing
Los Alamos v2.0
Tiberius System
Main timeline

Elroy drummed his fingers on the steering wheel, waiting for Smith to come back. His eyes continually flicked to the clock on the car's dash. Every time he did it scarcely seemed to move. 22:40. He waited an eternity, keeping up the drumming, playing a song in his head. 22:41. Another eternity. Still 22:41. 22:42, finally. And so he waited.

And waited.

And *waited.*

Was there always so much doing *nothing* on these kinds of operations? The raid on the residential unit had at least been exciting. His blood had been pumping and although he hated the implications of it, it had been . . . focusing. It had a certain movement to it. This, though, was tedious, almost torturous. Elroy knew consciously that Smith had only been gone ten minutes at most, but it seemed to be an eternity. The AI was fine with Jack. Right?

Right?

So consumed was he with his thoughts that when a pair of knuckles rapped on the door, he almost jumped out of his skin.

There was someone outside the car. Someone in a neatly pressed uniform. Someone who looked a lot more senior than the gate guard.

With shaking hand, Elroy pressed the button to lower the window, putting on his best smile.

"Can I help you?" he asked, as politely as he could, fighting to keep his tone even and jovial.

"Maybe you can," said the man, a distinct edge of—was that nervousness?—in his voice. Strange and out of place. His uniform was speckled in medals and decorations and patches and cords and ribbons, yet he was alone. At night. "I heard from Private Weyer that a visitor with a pass was coming onto the base, and I just wanted to check it out for myself."

Something seemed odd. Out of place. Why was such a highly-decorated officer coming up to a limo? And most importantly, why was he doing so alone? Didn't senior officers go with guards almost everywhere they went?

Smith's voice came through the earpiece. "Hey, who are you talking to?"

He had no way of directly responding, so he tried his best to be subtle, to talk to Smith without actually talking to him. "My ID's in order, officer," said Elroy, "I can show you if you like."

"No, no," said the officer, chuckling nervously. "Nothing like that is necessary. I just . . ." he coughed. "Can I inquire as to your business on the base?"

It took Elroy a second to put the pieces together. Smith's flamboyant appearance had obviously not gone unnoticed, and it had clearly been passed up the chain of command, eventually arriving at this guy. And the personal interest in the two of them could only mean one thing.

The officer was propositioning him. More specifically, propositioning *Smith*.

"Our line of work very clearly understands discretion, unfortunately . . ." Elroy forced the words out as normally as they could come. "I'm very sorry."

"Flirt with him a bit," hissed Smith. "Just make him upset and uncomfortable. Make him go away."

The stranger smiled approvingly. "Yes? Well, discretion is my middle name."

"Oh," said Elroy, "I bet you say that to all the tourists."

"I will from now on." The guy was obviously not going to be scared away by a little flirting. "Heard you were visiting the base with a companion. I'm . . . in the market, you could say. To hire someone."

Oh boy.

"Well, we do night work," said Elroy, hoping that the evasive edge to his voice would say more than his words did. "You know. Visiting confirmed bachelors late at night. As a friend. A good friend. Maybe have a few drinks, maybe dance, maybe have a little fun, you know?" He repeated the phrase for emphasis. "My boss likes having fun."

Smith snorted faintly down the line.

"Right, right," said the man, a palpable wave of relief coming over him. He looked over the car, trying to peer through the heavily-tinted windows. "Is he here right now?"

"No sir," said Elroy. "He's, uh, working."

"Ah." The officer fished around inside a pocket, producing a business card. "Next time he's here, ask him to look up Major Woody Cocker. I can arrange a base pass and all."

Major. Woody. *Cocker.* If Elroy had thought John Smith was a fake name, this one took the cake of fake names. "Are you serious?" asked Elroy, incredulously.

The major suddenly tensed. "I thought the gentleman was —"

"No, no," Elroy reassured him, forcing down his laughter. "It's not that. It's not. I just—I'm sorry, I was just surprised at your name. Given the circumstances."

"Yeah," said Cocker, humorlessly, "haven't heard that one before."

Elroy bit his tongue. "Uh, don't mind me." He chuckled awkwardly. "I'm just the driver." He extended his hand for the business card. "I'll make sure he gets it. We're back here in three days, haven't got any appointments lined up, so we can probably—" he twisted the words, trying to add a flirtatious edge to them, something he was terrible at even at the best of times. "—Slot you in."

Cocker hesitated, and then handed the card over. "Okay. I just want you to know that, again, discretion is a very important thing for me."

"And for us too."

A faint squeal of static filtered down through the line, then nothing. Was Smith okay?

Elroy tucked the business card into the cup holder. "I'll

sort everything out from here, don't you worry."

Cocker smiled. Elroy smiled back. And for just a moment, he thought he'd actually gotten away with it.

Then, from somewhere on the base, sirens and lights began to flash and wail, and it didn't take a military genius to understand what an intruder alarm looked like.

And then he was in big trouble. Fortunately, Cocker looked almost as scared as Elroy felt. He started frantically looking over his shoulder as though the alarms might be for him.

"What's going on?" asked Elroy, trying to sound as innocent as he could. "Does that mean they're launching the missiles?"

"No—no." Cocker gave a nervous laugh, running his hand against the back of his head. "If that happened, you would *definitely* know it."

"Well, that's one hell of a relief!" Elroy faked the fakest-sounding laugh in the history of fake laughs. "So, hey, Major Cocker . . . what's going on exactly?'

"Intruder alarm," said Cocker. "Listen, hey, thanks for the chat but you have to get off the base. Now."

Elroy couldn't do that. Not while Smith was still out in the field. "I haven't picked up my man yet," he said lamely.

Suddenly a shadow flickered across Cocker's face. The pieces seemed to fall into place. His hand went to his gun. "Sir, step out of the vehicle right now!"

CHAPTER THIRTY-THREE

The Hole
Yggdrasil
The Future

Mattis slid into the booth alongside Ramirez, Blair practically smooshed up against the wall. Everyone squeezed in to make room for Yim. Slag and Blip took the other side of the table, which was remarkably spacious by comparison. How Lynch and Modi were going to fit in was a mystery best solved in the future.

The booth was cozy, with a pile of napkins on one side and a twin pair of salt and pepper shakers on the other. Civilized, almost. It reminded Mattis of a classic 2090's Earth diner.

"Right," said Slag. "So. This guy ya'll want to rob. Let's hear it."

Ramirez looked at Mattis. "Rob?"

He wanted to say *It's complicated*, but he knew that the last thing this meeting needed was for everyone to start arguing after only a single sentence. "He's a person from our . . where we come from," said Mattis, speaking loudly again over the music. "We're unclear exactly how he came here—this place—but we know that his resources are considerable and the level of technology he is able to acquire suggests that he sources it from here. The Avenir were so concerned about this individual that they sent fleets of ships through portals to our place to destroy him and his . . . stuff. And, well, they kind of shot at us, too, which made things a bit difficult."

"A-ven-ir," said Slag, curiously, testing the word out as though it were odd. "Haven't heard that word in a long time . . . *real* long time. I know who you mean, but still. Odd way of saying it."

Maybe they didn't use that word in this timeline. It was difficult to know. "What word would you prefer me to use?"

"We just call them *them*, but Avenir is fine, if archaic." She picked at her teeth. "So these portals, huh? They wouldn't happen to go through *time*, would they?"

The cat was out of the bag. "Matter of fact, they do," said Mattis, cautiously.

"Forward or backward?"

He thought for a·moment. Lying might give them the advantage. "Backward," he said, truthfully. "We're from what you would consider the past."

"'Kay," said Slag. "Sounds like a guy with a fairly standard nanobot reprogrammer unit and access to enough mass to take a trip down memory lane." She looked to Blip. "You ever heard of time traveling portals before?"

"Actually," said Blip, casually tapping on the table, "I *have* heard about that. The Avenir use them to deal with existential threats to their existence."

The man's appearance—that of a brawny doofus—belied his true nature. Mattis was suddenly unclear about which one of them was the brains and which one the muscle. "I'm guessing," he said, "that Spectre somehow acquired that technology and has put it to good use."

"How would we ever know?" asked Slag, and that was a good point. How would someone even *know* if the timeline had been interfered with?

Yim spoke up. "Assuming he *did* acquire it, the question is . . . how? How could someone like him, from our timeline, even *come* to the future in the first place? We came here through a portal opened on the other side. It took the destruction of Earth in order to fuel that. How did Spectre *get* here before?"

Both Slag and Blip shot him an incredulous stare.

Blair muttered something under her breath that the loud music completely swallowed.

"Wait," said Slag, her voice filled with wonder. "Earth was around in your time? As in . . . you've *seen it?*"

"Yes," said Mattis. "I have." The notion that someone might not have seen Earth at all was not unusual—plenty of people in the Tiberius system and other settled colonies had not—but most of them, at least, *could* if they wanted to. Before the stars were settled, the destruction of an entire country was an unthinkable disaster. And yet life would go on.

That sudden thought made him smile, more so than it probably should have given the context. Despite that, Slag and Blip both smiled in return, the corners of their mouths stretching to the edges of their faces.

"What was it like?" asked Slag, but then she immediately

jumped to another train of thought. "You know what? No. Let's talk business now. We can talk ancient history later."

"So stoked, though," said Blip. He awkwardly pulled out a tablet from behind him—was it stuffed into the back of his pants?—and then laid it out, quickly turning it around to face Mattis's side of the table. "Anyway. This Spectre. If he has access to Avenir technology but is a human, he's almost certainly a collab."

"Collab?" asked Blair.

"Collaborator," said Blip, practically spitting the word. "Honestly it's a slur, but its meaning is obvious. Some humans work with the Avenir. Mostly as Judas-guys, betraying their own kind in exchange for meaningless baubles and the approval of evil monsters who hate them. They're the only ones who don't live in places like Yggdrasil, and they're the only ones with any fucking money these days. The rest of us have to feed off the scraps."

Yim shot Blip a look. "That sounds plausible. Spectre could be one of these collabs."

"Yeah," said Blair. "He's the kind of person who would sell out his own kind for a buck."

Sounded like the collabs were, for good reason, quite hated. "Definitely," said Mattis. "But how do we find them?"

Both Blip and Slag snorted with laughter.

"What?" asked Mattis. His side of the table exchanged confused stares.

"Collabs are only in one place," said Slag, casually scratching herself under the table. Mattis was glad he could not see exactly where and how. "They used to be everywhere, you know? They were allowed to go anywhere the Avenir went. But then—" she made an exploding bomb noise with her mouth. "Terrorism. That's what happens when you let an oppressed minority wander around among the rich majority. So they corralled them. Rounded 'em up like tasty, tasty mice. The Avenir keep their pets on a short leash."

That would make their task much easier. All in one place . . . "So," asked Mattis, "where is this place?"

"Chrysalis," said Blip. The moment he said that word, Mattis's heart sank. "It's a little rock out in the middle of nowhere. Fiercely independent, but that's why the Avenir took it."

"*I hate that place*," Blair said.

"They—they took over Chrysalis?" Mattis stared at Blip. "Why?"

"Took over it?" echoed Blip, bitterly. "That's one way of describing it. They had one of their Avenir spies flood the air ventilation system with a deadly neurotoxin. Then their mutants cleared out the bodies and turned them into compost. Now it's a colony for the collabs and under heavy Avenir guard."

It seemed like no matter what timeline they were in, Chrysalis was a place for outcasts and outlaws. However, in this timeline or any timeline, from what he had seen, the people who lived there didn't deserve to be gassed and turned into worm food.

"Okay," said Mattis, "so how do we get in there, if it's so heavily guarded?"

"Oh," said Slag, a mischievous smile spreading on her face. "That's going to be the easy part. You have an Avenir ship. You can just sail right on through and the computers will do the rest." Well, that was something at least. Slag put her finger to her lip in thought. "Unless they blacklisted that ship, in which case you'll be destroyed instantly once you approach within weapons range."

"Helpful," said Mattis. But another thought occurred. "Actually, there's something else we should mention."

"Great," said Slag. "Don't leave me hanging, here."

"His name," said Mattis, the words flashing back into his head. "Spectre's *real* name. Or at least what we have reason to believe is his real name."

"That'll help," Blip said, his massive hands coming together eagerly. "What is it?"

"Christopher Skye."

Blip's mouth fell open. For a moment no one moved or spoke, the only noise the pounding of music around them.

Then both Slag and Blip burst into wild, raucous laughter. Mattis and his side of the table exchanged another round of bewildered stares.

"That's some funny shit," said Blip, slapping the table enough to cause it to rattle and shake, his massive hands pounding on the surface. "You want to rob Christopher Skye! Hah—you actually—you actually . . . " his voice trailed off and became serious. "You *actually* want to rob Christopher Skye?"

"*Actually*," Yim piped up, "to put our cards fully on the table: we want to kill him. You can have whatever he owns. We're not here to steal from him, that's for you. We just want him to die."

Slowly but surely, the mirth on both Blip and Slag's faces completely drifted away.

"What?" asked Mattis, holding up his hands. "What did I say?"

CHAPTER THIRTY-FOUR

Cockpit
Aerostar
Inside the Caernarvon*'s Hangar Bay*
The Future

Reardon laid back in his chair, propping his feet up on the damaged computer from the *Stennis*. It seemed vaguely disrespectful, even to him, to use the valuable salvage as a footstool, but it was dented and scorched and broken anyway. There couldn't be harm in it, and while Sammy was unavailable, there was no way they could analyze it. It was to all the world an inert lump of scorched and broken metal.

Nothing he could do. So, with his feet propped up on the salvaged computer, Reardon played video games.

He tapped absently at the screen of his device, piloting his little dude around and right to the door of Miyu Matsui. He had run through the game a few times and always picked a different girl to romance.

"Reardon-kun!" said Ooba-chan, her voice coming through the speaker. "What are you doing here? It-it's not like

I like you anyway, *baka!*"

The game presented him with dialog choices.

(A) I love you, Ooba-chan!

(B) I don't know how to feel about you, Ooba-chan.

(C) Ooba-chan, I'm breaking up with you. I love Kasai-kun instead.

(D) I forgot what I'm doing here.

He'd never really been fond of the *tsundere*-types, but he'd dated Shimizu-chan, Haru-chan, Kasai-kun . . . he'd seen all the other endings, and this time he wanted to see the *tsundere* ending. It wasn't his favorite, but it was a new experience in his favorite game, *Love Love Extreme!*.

He selected *A*.

"R-Reardon-kun," stammered the tiny character on his screen. Her anime face flushed. "I-I don't know what to say, *baka* . . ."

His phone beeped. *Dammit.* Reardon tapped pause. "Go away," he demanded. "I'm busy."

"Hey, bro." It was Sammy. He was speaking Hindi, and there was *something* in his voice. A mixture of hope and sadness. And being out of breath? "I--I just wanted to talk to you before I do it, and—and get out of your hair for good."

Do it? Do *what*? He tossed his game onto the console, jumping out of his chair. "What the fuck are you talking about, dickhead?" A thought jumped into his head. "Are you drinking? I will kick your crippled ass if you are drinking, *bhai chod!*"

Sammy laughed. Weakly. Sadly. He puffed, and Reardon

heard dragging. "You idiot, *bhai chod* means 'brother fucker'. I'm the only brother you've got. What the fuck? don't you think through *anything* you say?"

Reardon swung his feet off the salvaged computer and settled them onto the floor. "Talk to me. Okay? Talk to me now. What are you doing?"

"I'm on the Warfrigate—the ship Mattis recovered. Doctor Manda took off running." Sammy grunted quietly. Was he crawling somewhere? "And she took most of the medical staff with her, leaving me laying in a corridor by myself, so . . . so I'm fixing the . . . *me* problem. Once and for all." He swallowed, obviously nervous. "I saw Spears's body get pushed into a machine and disintegrated, and—"

Disintegrated.

Reardon dropped the phone, barely hearing it shatter into a hundred pieces. His little brother . . .

He took off running, out of the cockpit, heading for the door. He sprinted out of the *Caernarvon*'s hangar bay and into the ship. He pushed past crewmen, past boxes and obstacles. He sprinted through the airlock and out into the light, into the weird space station he'd been monitoring before he'd grown bored.

Which way to the Warfrigate? He looked around frantically.

"Hang on, Sammy!" he shouted. "I'm coming! Just hang on!"

If only he had any clue which way he should go.

CHAPTER THIRTY-FIVE

Infirmary
Warfrigate 66549
Inside Yggdrasil
The Future

Doctor Manda ran down the corridor as fast as she could, following Robinson to the cloning bay.

Spears . . . Spears was being rejuvenated. *This* she had to see for herself.

"This way," Robinson said with his unshakeable calm. He floated through another doorway. It vanished as she approached, sinking into the floor.

Beyond it were rows and rows of green tanks, full of a strange fluid and lit up from within by an soft, ominous glow. Each one had a number above it. 1, 2, 3, etc. Almost all of them were empty, except for the first one, which glowed more brightly than the others. A tiny bead floated within, no more than a millimeter across. It sat there, suspended by some kind of unseen force, barely big enough to see.

"What's going on?" Manda panted to Robinson, though

she already suspected the answer. The little speck . . . it was about the size of an embryo.

"This," said Robinson, pointing to the tank labeled 1, "is the third stage of medical rejuvenation procedure 677-Bravo. A new body is being created for the patient, grown from her genetic code, and dispensed into the tank."

Manda stared in bewilderment through the green-tinged water, pressing her face up against the glass. "This is Captain Spears?"

"It will be," said Robinson. "The body has yet to be imprinted with her neural pattern, but according to the default settings, this embryo will grow at an accelerated rate, artificially aged, and a precision medical laser will apply scarification to match any repaired injuries detected on the body at the moment of its disposal."

Doctor Manda tore her eyes away from the glowing tank. "Grown at an accelerated rate, you say? How long will this take?"

"The standard growth rate is six weeks until ejection and processing."

Such a clinical way of describing the resurrection of a woman who'd been dead for hours now. But even more fascinating was the time involved. "A fully grown Captain Spears will be created in just *six weeks?* How is that possible?"

"I can provide you with the technical information about this procedure if you desire," said Robinson.

Manda felt nearly giddy with excitement, but tried to keep her doctorly reserve. "Put it on my device. I'll read it as soon as I have a moment to spare."

"Very well, Doctor."

Doctor Manda returned her gaze to the tank, staring in wonder. "So I guess I'm a necromancer now, huh? That's fun."

A bright flash from tank 2 stole her attention. Then the same thing happened above tank 3. "Robinson?" she asked. "What's happening?"

"Other tanks are being prepared," he said. "For the next patients."

"Next patients?" Doctor Manda's fingers scraped against tank 1. "What do you mean *next patients?*"

CHAPTER THIRTY-SIX

The Hole
Yggdrasil
The Future

Mattis couldn't help but shake the feeling that things were about to get really bad, really quickly. Blip and Slag were staring at him with a mixture of anger and betrayal on their faces. They didn't say anything. They just stared.

"Look," he said, trying to bring things back. "If there's something about this that I don't know—"

"I don't know," said Slag, hissing faintly as she spoke, the noise almost swallowed by the music. "Do you? Do you seriously not know who Christopher Skye is?"

"We came to the future through a portal," said Blair, stressed. "We don't know anything about this timeline, no."

"Well," said Slag, straightening her back, "ya'll fucked up, I can tell you that much. Christopher Skye is a collab all right —the *most powerful of them all.* They call him The Last Tyrant… the one who fucking *runs* Chrysalis. And who recruits the collabs. And who runs the spy network that constantly seeks to infiltrate this place and kill us all, and the only reason he doesn't have his bosses—the Avenir—come and wipe us all out is because we never, ever, ever, not once, even *talk* about making a move against him." She wrinkled her nose, as though she was trying to pull the thing back into her face, nostrils flaring. "But now you just did."

"I didn't mean—"

"Of course you didn't," said Blip, almost good-naturedly. "But you *did* talk about going after Christopher Skye. And that's a huge no-no."

The music shifted. Tension rose at the table. Suddenly, Mattis was aware that they were surrounded by people who would likely turn on him the moment Slag told them to.

"How about this," said Mattis, painting his voice in conciliatory tones. "We'll just leave. We'll leave this place, we'll leave this *station*, and we'll make our own way in this lovely, totally normal and sane future. Forget you ever met us. Okay?"

Slag looked at Blip.

Blip looked at Slag.

"Nah," said Slag, settling back in the couch in their booth, a slow, smug smile creeping over her face. "I don't think so. If word got out that me and my man here were plotting against Christopher Skye, even with some randos from out of town, we'd be thrown into the cooking pot and turned into lunch."

"Okay," said Mattis, slowly. In the corner of his eye, he could see Blair growing more uncomfortable. "We're just going to leave now, if you don't mind."

"I do mind," said Slag, her hand sliding down to rest comfortably on the grip of her knife.

Nobody said anything.

"So," said Yim, eyes flicking to meet Mattis's. "Are we doing this? Really? Right here? Right now? With all these people?"

Apparently so. Mattis's hand drifted down to his gun.

The music continued to pound away. Everyone sat there until Lynch's voice carried through the din.

" . . . so what I'm saying is, you shouldn't just drink something because everyone else is drinking it." Lynch navigated through the crowd, carrying a tray full of glasses of a brown alcohol. "Make up your own mind!" He rolled his eyes, groaning loudly like a man in pain. "If all your dang friends jumped off a bridge, would you?"

Modi put his hand to his chin, following close behind him, narrowing his eyes in thought. "Tell me more about this bridge," he said. "How high is it? Is it over water, or land? A footbridge or for vehicular traffic or rail? Is there any way I could climb down without jumping?"

"Jesus, Modi, it's just—"

"My ultimate decision would depend on innumerable factors. I can't make a snap decision with such limited information."

"Of course you can't." Lynch looked them all over. "Jeez, who died and made this into a funeral? Looks like I bought the hooch just in—"

With a roar, Mattis flipped the table over, sending Slag and Blip sprawling onto their backs. Salt and pepper shakers shattered against the ground, spilling salt and pepper everywhere. Napkins flew in a flurry.

He drew his pistol, hoping the music would cover the

sound of the fracas. "Run!" he shouted to everyone. "Back to the ship!"

Slag and Blip took cover behind the table, peering over the top. Mattis did *not* want to discharge a firearm in a crowded nightclub, but he had to make them think he might. He waved his gun around like a lunatic, sweeping it over the rim of the table.

There was a mad scramble to get out of the crowded booth, with Ramirez and Blair climbing out over the rear. Mattis and Yim, pistols out, covered the table. Blair joined them, her own gun out, with Modi and Lynch taking out their pieces as well.

"What the hell happened?" asked Lynch, balancing the whisky on one hand, pistol in the other. "We leave you alone for a few minutes, and the moment we come back everyone starts pointing guns at each other?"

"It's complicated," said Mattis through clenched teeth. "And technically, I think *we* have the guns. They just have knives."

"You know we can't be letting you leave, meatsticks!" shouted Slag. "Drop those antiques, or we're going to pop ya'll so hard they'll be scraping you off the floor with a trowel . . . and that'll ruin your meat!"

"Five guns to a pair of knives," shouted Mattis. "I'm pretty confident!"

The music shut off. A low groan of complaint echoed throughout the suddenly-almost-silent nightclub, and slowly, all eyes turned on them.

"Is that what you think?" asked Slag, grinning cheekily over the top of the table.

CHAPTER THIRTY-SEVEN

Infirmary
Warfrigate 66549
Inside Yggdrasil
The Future

Guano could feel, somewhere in her body—in her *soul*—that she was dying.

Speaking with Mattis had given her confidence, and in some way the will to go on, but she knew the grim reality as well as anyone. Hope could not stop her body from breaking down. Hope could not stop the infection in her brain from killing her. Hope could not make her get out of the gurney and jump in a fighter and fly.

Her mind was scattered. Foggy. All she could do was play Mattis's words over and over in her head, using them to ground her, focus her.

So she barely noticed when someone crawled up to her gurney and, with a low, pained groan, began to climb up it.

"Hello?" she asked, shaking her head to clear out the dustiness. "*Hello*?"

An arm appeared over the side of her bed, and then another, and then a face to match it. "Hi."

Well. Maybe it was because she'd had the top of her head recently cut off, but she couldn't discount the possibility that the guy was some kind of freaky hallucination. So she just stared at him. It. Whatever.

"I'm Sammy Reardon. Lieutenant Corrick, is it?" The kid smiled. "I overheard Admiral Mattis call you that."

"Yeah," she said. He was probably real, then, although now Guano was somewhat worried about how much else he had overheard. "That's me."

"Can I pick your brain for a moment?"

"They already did that," said Guano.

"Huh?"

She pointed to the bandages on her head. "Brain surgery."

"Oh."

"What are you in for?"

Sammy smiled. "Got shot in the legs. Can't walk anymore. But I couldn't before either, so . . ." He coughed, eyes flicking to the strange room at the end of the hallway. Empty. Nothing inside it. "Anyway, uh, so Captain Spears's body got pushed into that thing and . . . *regenerated*."

Regenerated? She must have dozed off for that part. "What do you mean?"

"I mean," said Sammy, "that this device of theirs can regenerate injured people. I don't know how it does it exactly, but that Robinson guy? The hologram? He said it could bring Spears back to life. And that it would grow her a new body." Sammy grimaced, jabbing a finger down at his non-functional legs. "I dunno about you, but I could really use one of those right now."

"I could definitely use a new *body*—this one's kind of broken."

Sammy flashed a wide smile. "Okay," he said, "so we're going to have to work together on this one. We're a team. You drag me into that machine, then go in yourself."

She squinted through her blurred vision to look him over. Seemed like a smart kid. "Is that thing safe?"

"Oh god, no. . . . yes. No. Maybe? I have no idea." Sammy's face hardened. "All I know is that I'm sick of being a burden. Of being useless. I hate my wheelchair and I hate that I make my brother look after me. I want to walk again. And I don't give a shit if this thing doesn't pan out. The hologram seemed to believe it would work, and I trust computers more than I trust people."

It wasn't exactly a compelling argument but Guano felt, *knew*, that if she didn't do something soon, she wasn't going to make it at all. "Sure," she said. "Let's go get ourselves disintegrated. Why the hell not? But we'll have to go in together. I can barely stand as it is."

"Better than I can do," said Sammy.

Groaning softly and fighting a sudden wave of dizziness, Guano propped herself up on her elbows, then slowly slid her legs off the edge of the gurney. Her legs felt like they were made of spaghetti—weak and soft and thin—but there was still some strength there. Not enough. But it would do.

Sammy offered her his hand. She took it, squeezing tightly.

"Okay," said Guano, teetering unsteadily on her feet, one hand on the gurney rail, the other holding Sammy's as tightly as she could. Slowly, she turned her gaze toward the disintegration room. This was probably one of her top ten worst ideas ever, but she was out of options. "Let's do this."

CHAPTER THIRTY-EIGHT

Hickam Air Force Base, home of the 6,774th Missile Wing
Los Alamos v2.0
Tiberius System
Main timeline

With sirens and alarms ringing around him, John Smith picked up one of the fallen guard's rifles, along with a pair of spare magazines, then advanced toward the wall of the hangar. He closed his biological eye, letting his prosthetic eye go to work, scanning through the thin sheet metal with the radiation detector.

The US Air Force secured their nukes against various mishaps. The fusible cores were kept separated from the triggering mechanism to prevent accidental detonation or theft. Fortunately, he didn't need the detonator. Just the core. And the core was radioactive, which meant it could be tracked.

Every nuclear missile needed regular, periodic maintenance where its core was removed. To maintain operational readiness, not every nuke could be down for maintenance at once; while the schedule was classified top secret, there was a high probability there was, at any given time, a missile being worked on.

Smith hated making plans based on probabilities, but that was just how this would have to play out.

Using his prosthetic eye he scanned the area, searching for the telltale signs of the minuscule amounts of radiation it would emit, even through shielding. It presented as a winking green light on the other side of the hangar doors. A giant steel wall might be intimidating to most folks, but not to John Smith. He plucked another jewel off his hat, pressed it against the wall, then scurried back.

With a dull roar the gem combusted, blasting that section of the wall to shreds and sending smoke billowing out in all directions.

Well, if they didn't know exactly where I was before, they do now.

He stepped through the smoke, switching his eye to thermal vision. Plenty of heat signatures. Mostly debris from the blast. No humans—that was good. He didn't want to have to hurt anyone.

There, right at the center of the hangar, was exactly what he was looking for. A conical nuclear warhead on a bench, the interior wires and circuits exposed. The detonator had been removed, as he anticipated, but the core . . . the core was still there, encased in its heavy radiation shield. Just big enough to fit into his backpack. He shrugged it off and unzipped it.

No sign of any more guards. That was odd. Not entirely unexpected—there were guards on the *outside*, which made sense—but he had anticipated better security.

Not one to press his luck, he quickly strode up to the box

containing the radioactive core. But the moment he got close, another wailing alarm broke out, joining the background chorus of wailing klaxons. Not that it mattered much; the thick plume of smoke from the detonation would give the military folks here all the guidance they needed.

Still, it nagged at him. Only more alarms? No guards on the inside? No other defenses?

"Well, okay then," he said to himself. "Looks like the budget cuts have really hit the Air Force hard, so—"

With a faint hum, six robotic, spider-like creatures appeared seemingly from thin air, clinging to the walls and ceiling, their thin, spindly legs seeming to hook into the framework of the hangar. Each one had a huge, bulbous head with a dozen eyes, all looking straight at him.

Of course. It had to be robots.

"Hello, creepyass robot spiders with active camouflage," he said, casually drawing his pistol. "What brings lovely pieces of expensive hardware like you to a place like this?"

They didn't seem appreciate his sense of humor—each robot began to slowly climb down the walls toward him, articulated joints humming as they moved.

"Surely these things aren't programmed to shoot on sight, right?" he muttered to himself. "Surely that's a huge security risk, a friendly fire risk, and . . ." Each of the creature's abdomens opened to reveal a concealed machine gun on a pivot, the weapon swinging toward him ominously. "No, okay, they're live."

He leapt back through the hole in the wall, followed almost immediately by a spray of fire from the guns, blasting holes in the metal and nipping at his heels like a swarm of angry dogs.

Well, now. He had brought a lot of toys to this operation, but his high velocity anti-material rifle was in the car. Those kinds of things tended to attract more attention than your average gigolo disguise could reasonable tolerate. Plus, who would ever make one of those things in a matching pink?

The robo-spiders didn't seem to want to follow him out of the hangar, and it was obvious why. They were protecting their prize. Yet the blaring alarms and billowing smoke all around him reminded him he had little time to find a solution. The smoke would lead them right to him.

Smoke.

He reached behind his hat, plucking two little emeralds off the brim, gave each of them a tap, then tossed them through the hole into the hangar. Each began billowing thick white smoke, quickly creating an effective smokescreen.

Smith switched his eye to thermal vision, and as he did, he was reminded that this kind of technology was not secret. After all, he had it, and no doubt high tech, expensive spiders did too.

It was worth the risk. He crept forward, studying the hot and cold projections through the smoke, barely able to see anything, barely able to hear anything but the distant klaxon.

He didn't get immediately shot to death, which was a good sign, so he clicked his eye over to radiation sensing. Immediately he saw it: green radiation, twinkling like a distant star.

The smart play was to continue to creep forward, avoiding disturbing the billowing smoke all around him, to maintain stealth and slowly-and-steadily grab the core. But there was no *time*. He could hear vehicles, hear sirens, and knew he had minutes at the absolute most. Fortunately robots were usually pretty dumb.

And so was he. So he darted forward, hands searching blindly for the radioactive core. Smoke clogged his biological eye, making it water—and his prosthetic eye could only see radiation. His hip hit a table. He knocked something over that clattered to the ground. Then his hands found it. The core container. He jammed it into his backpack.

Time to go.

CHAPTER THIRTY-NINE

The Hole
Yggdrasil
The Future

Mattis backed away toward the door, sweeping the crowd with his pistol. "We gotta get outta here," he hissed to Yim. Everyone was looking at them and a surprising number of them had weapons of various descriptions, or things that *might* be weapons in this future. Like armbands that glowed with ominous internal lights or pointy things sticking out of their clothes, or weird blades on their gloves, or—

"Quickly!" said Yim. "I don't like how many of those people are armed." He ground his teeth, jaw moving side to side. "What kind of person brings a spiked glove to a rave?"

He couldn't help but remember that *they* had all brought firearms to a rave. But then again, they weren't attending.

"So many illegal drugs here," muttered Blair. She thumbed back the hammer on her pistol. "Kinda out of my jurisdiction though."

"I didn't realize you were a cop," said Ramirez, good-naturedly.

"What the hell's a cop?" said Slag from behind the table.

Mattis moved with the group toward the door, creeping backward. "She's not, She's FBI."

"The Funny Booty Inspector?" called Slag. "Wow. The past was awesome."

Something was off. Why was Slag just hiding behind the table calling out insults?

Where was Blip?

He took one more step backward, barely two steps away from the door, and his foot stuck to the ground.

It was just such a strange moment that he took a second to process it, trying to tug his foot free and failing. The sole of his boot was completely stuck to the floor.

"What the hell?" said Yim, similarly affixed beside him. Something was wrong. Something was very wrong.

"Dang ground is sticky," said Lynch. He was stuck too. They all were. "Modi! Modi, fix this right now!"

Modi, his feet seemingly unglued, shrugged helplessly. "What do you expect me to do? I don't even know what kind of effect this is!"

"They're stuck, get 'em!" shouted Slag. "And don't ruin the meat, I'm fucking hungry!"

They had been baited. The crowd surged forward, knives, clubs and other spiked weapons in their hands, howling like rabid monkeys. Mattis fired first, catching a lanky beanpole of a guy in the chest and putting him down for good. Yim fired too, his automatic pistol spraying a line of death into the crowd, but almost immediately running out of ammo.

"This really IS *Deliverance* in space!" growled Blair,

frantically trying to tug her foot free, one hand on her pistol. "Fuck! I'm going to end up as a sandwich!"

"We don't have a lot of time here," shouted Lynch. "Modi!"

The man groaned and pulled out a tablet. "Their technology is six *hundred* years further advanced than ours, but I'll see what I can do!"

Mattis squeezed off a couple more shots into the crowd, firing wildly. "Everyone who isn't stuck to the floor, back to the ship!"

Ramirez stepped out of her shoes, stood on top of the toe caps, and jumped through the doorway. "Come on, just leave your boots!"

"Cover me, Blair!" He squatted, yanking at his laces with one hand and firing with the other. One of the ravers got close, too close, and bit him on the shoulder. He put his gun to the guy's face and blew it into hunks.

Yim was reloading. Someone grabbed Blair, pulling the gun out of her hand. Then the mob descended, hands and fists and weapons striking them. Mattis pulled a foot free, kicking someone in the groin. A knife slid between his ribs. He punched another attacker, firing wildly, missing as often as he was hitting, until his pistol went dry. His injured shoulder dislocated with a soft *click*, pain shooting up from the tendons. Someone hit him on the back of the head and things went fuzzy. And he went down.

People started hitting him, whacking him with sticks and weapons, but he barely felt them.

He was okay. He was okay with this. It was okay to die here. It was time.

Easy.

Lynch grabbed him and pulled him out of his shoes. Someone cut his clothes. Lynch dragged him out of the crowd and into the doorway. Modi was shooting at something. Blair, now weaponless, was shepherding Ramirez back to the ship. He lost sight of Yim and, for a moment, everything went gray.

"Hey, stay with us Captain," said Ramirez. He realized she was helping him walk. There was more gunfire in the background. He could hear Yim's autopistol going nuts. "Just keep going, we're almost there."

They were almost at the pier. He felt so groggy. He knew he'd been hit in the head, but that fact seemed so far away from him. "What happened?"

Ramirez helmed him walk. "You got shown a little bit of south Detroit hospitality, is all. You'll be fine. It's not even that deep. I got stabbed once. It's fine. I was okay. You'll be okay too."

He touched his gut, his hand coming away scarlet and dripping with blood. "Oh shit," he said, the reality of it all slamming into his head. Adrenaline surged through his veins. "Ow."

"About time you noticed," said Ramirez, still half-carrying him toward the pier, a crowd of howling people hot on their heels.

Everything came into focus. Lynch and Modi were covering their rear. Yim was taking point, his pistol clearly out of ammo, magazines exhausted. Blair, her gun lost, was beside him, her hands up like a boxer. And the crowd was close. Too close. And gaining.

"You always take me to the nicest places," called Ramirez, gritting her teeth as she hooked her arm around his other shoulder, the one he'd injured trying to save Chuck. An old wound that didn't seem to heal properly. Like the one in his head.

The Warfrigate and the *Caernarvon* were not that far away. Only a hundred meters or so. Just down the pier. Blair and Ramirez were basically carrying him.

But the bloodthirsty mob would catch them halfway.

They weren't going to make it.

CHAPTER FORTY

Infirmary
Warfrigate 66549
Inside Yggdrasil
The Future

Reardon ran as fast as he could toward what he *hoped* was the infirmary, following his gut and sprinting down the corridors like a madman. "I'm coming, Sammy!" he shouted. "Don't do anything dumb!"

Goddammit. He knew he was running randomly, probably in circles, but he had no other way to find Sammy. He came to a T, skidded to a halt, and almost crashed into the wall. Which way, which way?

Fortunately, right at that moment, a woman ran around the corner, her face flushed and cheeks like big beets. "This way," she said, pointing a shaking finger down one of the passageways. It took him a moment to recognize her. Doctor Manda, the woman who had tested him to see if he was a clone. "The infirmary is this way, hurry!"

She seemed to know what she was doing and he didn't

need to be told twice. Immediately, Reardon took off again, following the direction of the finger. "Sammy! Sammy!"

Doctor Manda ran after him, though she couldn't keep up with his frantic pace. "Left!" she shouted, her voice retreating into the distance. "Left, and then right!"

Reardon barreled down the corridor and around the corner, his boots slipping. He went sprawling, tumbling head over heels on the slippery metal, bruising himself in ways he didn't even register but would definitely feel tomorrow.

And then he saw them.

Two abandoned hospital gurneys, and right at the end of the passageway, Sammy and someone else he recognized—the pilot, Corrick?—were sitting, propped up against the wall of a tiny, empty room. They both looked like total shit.

He saw Sammy. Sammy saw him. He was in time. He'd made it.

"Hey buddy," he said, putting his hands on his knees, panting and wheezing like an asthmatic puppy. "You really — you had me worried for a sec."

Sammy said nothing, just looked at him. Corrick too. Just stared.

Doctor Manda staggered up behind him, similarly puffing, her bright red face caked in sweat. "Bloody hell!" she said, wiping her forehead. "Okay, umph, I made it." She stared at him in bewilderment. "Aren't . . . you the guy with the pink . . . ship?"

Now? Always with the color of his ship. Always. "Pink *used* to be a . . ." he huffed, trying to get his breath back. "Masculine color. Traditionally blue was . . . for girls. But that doesn't matter right now."

"If you say so, then I guess it is. Uh. For sure." Doctor Manda put her hand on his shoulder, probably not just for emotional support, but to help keep her standing. "Now listen to me, Mister Reardon. We have no way of knowing that these machines are safe. We don't know anything about them yet. And we *definitely* can't have both of them in there at the same time. We have to get them out of that room, quickly now, before—"

With a flash of light, energy began to build up in the room. As Reardon watched, transfixed, two holograms of brains appeared—one over Corrick, one over Sammy—and then winked out. Both of them slumped down like puppets with their stings cut.

"O—oh God! Sammy!"

Both bodies began to dissolve, as though some powerful, unseen acid were corroding them from the legs up. The process ate through their hospital gowns, exposing their flesh, their bones, and then . . . nothing.

"It's okay," said Doctor Manda, still wheezing for breath. "He's—he's fine. Probably."

Reardon stared at the spot where he'd just watched his younger brother get disintegrated. "*Probably?* What the hell do you mean, *probably?*"

CHAPTER FORTY-ONE

Hickam Air Force Base, home of the 6,774th Missile Wing
Los Alamos v2.0
Tiberius System
Main timeline

With a furious dozen robotic spiders on his tail, Smith darted from lamp post to lamp post, his backpack thumping against his back. The fissionable core he'd recovered was small, but it would do for his purposes. He sprinted back to the car where, hopefully, Elroy was waiting.

Because if he wasn't, Smith was out of gems.

A burst of gunfire sprayed into the ground beside him, several rounds catching a nearby lamppost and blowing it to hunks of metal, the rest flying off into the night and disappearing into the desert.

"There he is, get him!" shouted someone. The entire base's security staff were probably converging on him.

More bullets whizzed past. Smith's breath came in ragged grasps. He wasn't going to make it.

Then, suddenly, he spotted the limo. And Elroy getting

dragged out of the driver's seat by his hair by a man in a major's uniform. Presumably the guy Elroy had been talking to.

Smith had no time to mess around and no opportunity to lie his way out of their situation. He let his fist lead the way, catching the major in the side of the head, knocking him up against the side of the limo.

"Get in," he gasped to Elroy. "And drive."

"What did you do!?" Elroy shouted, scrambling for the driver's side.

A bullet ricocheted off the top of the limo, screaming as it disappeared into the night and left a massive gouge across the top of the metal. No way they were getting their deposit back now. "Doesn't matter, just go!" He pulled open the rear door and dove in head first. "Drive, drive, drive!"

The limo lurched forward, the engine roaring. Rounds embedded in the metal hull, while others shattered the windows and whizzed through the middle of the car. Smith kept his head down, shrugging off his backpack and snatching up the duffel bag he had stashed in the back of the limo for *just* this sort of occasion.

"Did you get the nuke?"

"Yeah," he said. He thumped his hand on the backpack. "It's in the backpack. At least the core is. It's fine, I can rig up a detonator later."

"Where do I go?" asked Elroy, the car swinging this way and that, ungainly as it took the gentle curves of the streets of the military base. "All these streets look the same!"

Elroy was panicking. Smith tried to calm him down. "Just go back the way we came," he said, unzipping his duffel bag.

"What's that noise?" said Elroy, swerving around on the road like a madman. "Are you unzipping? Is that what's happening back there?"

"It's not what you think," said Smith, reaching into the duffel bag, withdrawing the two parts of the anti-material rifle: the stock and the weapon itself. With the car still swerving and dodging, Smith clipped the two parts together, inserted a magazine, and with a grunt, chambered a round.

"Just keep your pants on, okay?" Elroy muttered.

Smith only groaned in reply.

"Hold on!" Elroy suddenly shouted as the limo smashed through a boomgate, blasting it to chunks of wood as they burst out of the base. Another barrage of gunfire sprayed against the vehicle as the gate guards opened up on them. The rear window went out, smashing into thousands of tiny shards. The wind howled in.

Smith propped his rifle up on the rear seat, slinging the shoulder strap over his head. Those guards were just doing their jobs—there was absolutely no way he could shoot them for that—so he aimed nice and high, gently squeezing the trigger.

KA-BUMF.

The round flew high, disappearing over the base and into the desert.

"Holy shit, are you shooting at them?" Elroy called back. "Don't kill them, they're US servicemen! Jesus!"

"It's okay, I deliberately missed. I'm not going to kill them." He shot again just to make sure they got the message. *KA-BUMF. KA-BUMF.*

"Ow, my ears!"

"Just drive," said Smith, "they're going to be after us real soon. Just get to the ship."

Every minute seemed to drag on. A limo was not a fast vehicle, but it did surprisingly well, tearing down the road away from the military base at a distinctly illegal speed. Yet despite their pace, six lights followed them, drawing closer and closer. That's why there was no vehicle pursuit. No cops. No tanks or jets or anything.

It didn't take a genius to figure out how the US Air Force was planning on getting their stolen nuclear core back.

Smith peered through the scope, trying to catch sight of the spider creatures—enough to draw a bead on them, at least—but he couldn't. The limo was bouncing around too much on the bumpy road. Still, the robots seemed to have wheels on the bottom of their feet, tearing down the road much faster than their little limo could go.

"Hey Elroy," he said, squirming around on the back seat, trying to get a good firing position. "Do you think you could keep the car a little more steady? We got company."

"What?"

"Keep the car steady," Smith repeated calmly. "So I can shoot straight."

"You want me to slow down?"

"God no," he said, catching sight of a spider-bot through the scope, little more than a blur really. "Keep going fast. Just keep it steady."

"Okay, now I *know* my ears are fucked," said Elroy. "Fast *and* steady? On these roads? That's impossible."

As though to accent his point, the car drove over a pothole. *Thump.*

Smith grit his teeth. "Sure." He kept trying to line up a shot, aligning the bouncing rifle scope with the approaching robots. Almost, almost . . . the crosshairs danced across the front of the spider-bot, occasionally kissing its center of mass, taunting him . . .

"Also," said Elroy, "I think one of the bullets took out a tire, because the wheel keeps listing toward the left, and—"

KA-BUMF. Smith sent a round back from the car, and with his biological eye, saw a distant flash in the dark, followed by a shower of sparks and a burning fire. A definite hit, even if the details eluded him at that distance.

"Ow! Fuck!" Elroy whined from the front seat. "Give me some damn warning before you fire that thing, all I can hear is bells ringing!"

"You'll get used to it," said Smith, trying to line up for another shot. "Steady..."

KA-BUMF. The round hit the dirt, throwing up clumps of sand. Miss. *KA-BUMF*. He didn't even see where that one went. Another miss.

"Why aren't they shooting back?" asked Elroy.

"We stole a nuclear weapon," said Smith, matter-of-fact. He almost had a shot on another one, but the rifle dipped before he could squeeze the trigger. "Why do you *think* they aren't shooting at us?"

Elroy drove in silence a moment. "But we didn't steal a detonator," he said. "It's not live. Is it?"

"Of course not," said Smith. "But they don't know that. Or at least, they're not absolutely certain. Would *you* risk being in the blast radius of a nuclear detonation on information you were only *mostly* sure about?"

"Good point," said Elroy.

He exhaled gently, letting the breath calm his hands. The crosshairs aligned with one of the spider-thing's legs.

"Sending," said Smith, gently squeezing the trigger. *KA-BUMF.* The round flew wide and low, clipping the spider-bot on one of its many right legs, the high-velocity round blowing the limb clean off. The creature wobbled, then spun out and crashed, tearing itself to pieces as it rolled over and over, shedding hull plates and internal components before coming to rest on the lonely desert road.

"Two down," he said, ejecting the magazine and inserting a fresh one. "But there are still four more."

"Great," said Elroy. "Shoot them faster. I think our battery is damaged, because we're losing power really quick."

With a loss of power, the car wasn't going to get them to their ship in time . . . not that it would matter, if these spider-bots couldn't be stopped.

The ship was still some distance away. It would take some time to warm up and launch, and Albert the AI was a shitty flier, but Smith had no choice. He awkwardly pulled out his phone, tapped in a few commands, then shoved it back into his pocket. The ship would come to *them*, at least. But would that be enough?

"Dammit," said Smith. "Looks like I really need to pull a rabbit out of my pretty pink fedora on this one."

CHAPTER FORTY-TWO

Docking Pier
Yggdrasil
The Future

The crowd closed in on Mattis and the gang. They were going to intercept them before they got to their ship.

"We gotta move," said Mattis. "Lynch! Cover us!"

"I'm out!" shouted Lynch.

"We should have brought extra ammunition," said Blair, grunting softly as she and Ramirez helped Mattis walk. He put foot in front of foot, each step causing a strange pain in his side. The ship was only a hundred meters or so away. They could make it.

"Reminder for next time," panted Ramirez.

"Hopefully there won't be a next time for being chased by maniacal future cannibals," said Mattis, huffing as he tried to pick up the pace. He was bleeding from the abdomen, the head, a few other places . . . but adrenaline gave him strength. And the two women were practically dragging him along. "We need the Marines from the *Caernarvon*."

"You think they'd actually help us?" said Blair, throwing a panicked look over her shoulder. "Shit, they're close."

They wouldn't get here in time either way. "Put me down. Stop here," he said. "I've got a plan."

Blair stared at him as though he'd ordered her to see if she could fit both feet into her mouth. "W-what? You want to stop?" The crowd surged forward. "They're almost on us!"

He absolutely did *not* want to stop, but he had no choice. "I have to get my communicator. We can't run the whole way."

Blair practically dropped him. Mattis slumped onto the pier, taking Ramirez down with him, and pulled out his communicator. "We gotta get them to help in another way. Mattis to *Caernarvon*, priority transmission! Put me through to the bridge!"

Everyone encircled around him, forming a protective barrier. Only Modi seemed to have any bullets left; he shot carefully and evenly, plinking away and taking down more than his fair share of attackers, but then his gun went *click*, the slide locked back. He was dry too.

"This is the bridge," said Green. Was that who Yim had left in command? Smart move. "I see you brought reinforcements for us."

Mattis grunted. "Our *reinforcements* are here to kill us." He looked up at the giant ship moored at the pier. "I need you to spin up the point defense guns and give them a squirt, see if we can't make them back off."

"Those guns aren't designed to target people," said Green. "And they aren't designed to fire in atmospheres."

With his eyes on the massive horde bearing down on

them, clubs and weapons and knives in their hands, Mattis didn't care if the point defense guns were designed to cook spaghetti. "Just fire them manually! Put them into manual mode and shoot! Shoot, dammit, shoot! Danger close!"

Forty meters. Thirty. Twenty.

The *Caernarvon*'s point defense guns spun up.

"Get down!" shouted Mattis, pulling Ramirez down to the ground, throwing himself over her. "Down! Get down, everyone, now—"

A god-almighty roar stole the noise from everything, like the fabric of the universe was being ripped in half. Thousands of rounds slammed into the pier, each one bursting like a firework, spraying a blossom of shrapnel in all directions, the tiny shards of metal hissing as they darted overhead. Violently loud, the line of fire cut through the approaching throng and exploded them into gory paste.

Metal stung his shoulder. Arms. Everyone around him was screaming, their hands over their ears, curled up like children, trying to protect themselves from the flying metal, the fire, the noise. Something hit him in the left side of the face, and the vision in his left eye went dark.

Then, mercifully, it stopped, leaving only a profound ringing in Mattis's ears, the smell of blood and cordite, and an ominous burning smell from below.

Bodies were everywhere, the pier splattered with dark explosions and rich red blood. The surface of it had been churned up, exposing Avenir-style circuits below, into which the blood of the people ran.

Lynch grabbed Mattis's shoulder, pulling him up. Lynch said something. Mattis could barely hear it. It sounded like he was under water. He'd been a warrior long enough to know what gunfire could do to human ears, but this was something else. And his eye . . .

"What?" he asked.

Lynch kept talking, Modi started talking, he couldn't understand either of them. And he couldn't read their lips either. His vision was all messed up. Blurry. Indistinct. And his depth perception was totally out.

"Get to your ship," he said, "we need to go."

Modi leaned in toward him, practically shouting in his damaged ears. "You've been badly injured, Admiral Mattis! I'll take command of your ship until Doctor Manda can treat you. She's aboard the Warfrigate now, so this is convenient!"

At least, that's what Mattis *thought* he said.

"And while we're there," Ramirez said, cupping his face gently and leaning in close, "let's get that eye looked at."

It was bad to him that they were focusing on his eye rather than his stab wound. Yeah. That was bad.

"Okay," Mattis sighed, not having the will or energy to argue. He turned his eyes—or rather, his *eye*—to the horde of dead and dying that continued to bleed out onto the pier. "Let's get out of here before the Human Resistance decides to resist us even more."

CHAPTER FORTY-THREE

Endless, Uncharted Desert
Los Alamos v2.0
Tiberius System
Main timeline

Smith took stock of his situation.

He and Elroy Mattis—a civilian with no combat training whatsoever—were hurtling down a lonely, abandoned desert highway in a limo that was riddled with bullets, had at least one flat tire, and a dodgy battery to boot. Their ship was ten minutes away at least. He'd been hoping to sneak out or at least get enough of a head start that any pursuit was lost by the time they arrived.

He had an anti-material rifle with fourteen more rounds. There were two robot spiders down, but four more were left. It had taken him seven rounds to down the two, but three of those were warning shots at the base. So technically four. Fifty percent hit ratio. Fourteen rounds left, so . . . odds were good.

But reinforcements must be on the way. He's soon have the entire Air Force on his ass.

They hit another pothole. Smith lost his grip on the rifle; the weapon slid back and out through the broken rear window. Only the shoulder strap saved it. He dragged it back in, clutching it to his chest.

"Jesus, be careful!" he shouted. "I almost lost the gun!"

"It's not so easy in the dark!" shouted Elroy in return. "You should try it! It's hard. Driving like this is hard!" Elroy was hysterical.

With no more mind to bicker, Smith propped the rifle back up. The spider-bots were closer now—four of them. He took sight on the lead creature. *KA-BUMF.* The round went high, striking the raised abdomen, ricocheting and skipping off to destinations unknown. Smith swore darkly, lined up the shot again, and squeezed the trigger once more.

Click.

A dud round? Confused, he pulled back the charging handle. No round was ejected. He tilted the rifle to check the magazine.

It was gone.

It must have fallen out when the gun went flying. Only the one chambered round remained and the other six must be rolling around somewhere on the desert highway. Only seven remained, to split between four bots. And whoever else might show up.

"FUCK!" Smith spat.

"Everything okay back there?" Elroy said, alarmed.

"Yeah," Smith said, inserting a new magazine—checking that it was in snugly—then chambering a new round. "Doesn't matter."

Fortunately, the spider-bots were closer now. Barely a

hundred meters. That made aiming at them easier. Smith leveled his rifle, aligning it to center of mass on the lead spider, and squeezed the trigger. *KA-BUMF.*

The round flew straight toward the thing, smashing into its head and blasting through, leaving a red hot glowing outline of the entry wound. The creature collapsed onto the highway, exploding into a fiery burst of sparks as its fuel cell and ammunition reserves ignited, transforming a tiny spot of the desert highway from night into day.

The three remaining spider-bots zoomed closer. Smith lined up the rifle again, drawing a bead on the new leader. *KA-BUMF.*

Miss. Five rounds left. *KA-BUMF.* Miss. Four.

"I need you to keep it steady!" Smith roared.

Elroy muttered something he didn't catch, which was probably for the best.

Smith's phone chirped in his pocket. The ship had completed its power-up launch cycle and was now lifting off to come for them. Not that it was a big comfort; it was a transport, not a gunship, and the only reason the spider-bots hadn't shot at them yet was because of the nuke. The ship had no such 'armor'.

Smith shifted in the back seat, trying to improve his shooting posture. The back of a car was an awkward place to fire something as big as the anti-material rifle, even in a limousine.

A poor craftsman blames his tools . . .

Relax. Smith exhaled again, lining up a shot on the lead spider-bot. Four shots left to deal with three spider-bots. And they were closing in fast. Sixty meters—even closer—weapons protruding from their abdomens.

Focus. Focus. Shooting was as much of a science as an art, but at this range, it was a simple one. Line up the crosshairs on the target. Exhale. Squeeze.

He needed to just keep his head. Smith lined up the closest spider-bot, exhaled, and squeezed. *KA-BUMF.* The shot flew true, streaking across the highway, but the spider-bot drove into a pothole; the round struck its body at an angle, digging into the metal and penetrating. The bot continued onward.

Shit. Three shots left, three bots, one only damaged.

The closest spider-bot seemed to tire of watching its friends be destroyed. It leapt into the air, a powerful engine of some sort attached to its underbelly glowing as it ignited, lifting it higher above the limo. The second followed suit and took flight, its weapon trained on the limo. Then the third.

"Aw, crap," said Smith. "They can fly, too."

CHAPTER FORTY-FOUR

Warfrigate 66549 Airlock
Docking Pier
Yggdrasil
The Future

Mattis, leaning on Blair, walked into the Warfrigate with Modi. With a profound ringing in his ears, a blackness in his left eye, and damp blood running down his abdomen, he was beat up. Hurting. In pain. There were spots of blood on his uniform—it was unclear whose blood it was. Everyone had blood on them. At least some of it was his, that much he knew.

"I'll find you a doctor," said Ramirez, disappearing into the Warfrigate's corridors.

"They're called corpsmen on Navy . . ." She was gone. "Never mind."

"This ship rocks," said Blair, her head on a swivel, looking this way and that.

With a soft pulse of light the hologram, Michael Robinson, appeared in front of them. "Good afternoon,

Captain Mattis and companions."

"Fascinating," said Modi, staring in wonder at the holographic projection, his mouth agape. "Is it true it possesses a truly artificial intelligence?"

Robinson smiled. "If you are referring to my cognition patterns, then yes. They are best described as an artificial intelligence."

Modi stuck out his hand awkwardly. "On behalf of the United States Armed Forces, I greet you."

Mattis rubbed his left eye, hand coming away bloody. "That's great, but I already did that, Modi."

Robinson didn't seem to mind, sticking his ghostly hand out, meeting Modi's, and passing right through. The two shared what was most likely the most awkward handshake in the entire history of the galaxy, their limbs not even technically touching.

Dammit, Modi. Commander Lynch sometimes—only half joking—referred to Modi as a robot. Of course the *metaphorical* robot and the *actual* robot were suddenly good friends.

"Okay," said Mattis, forcing out a cough. "I'm bleeding from several places, and I think my eye is fucked, so if we can get Modi into the command core and Doctor Manda down here to treat me, I would greatly appreciate that. Robinson? Can you get her for me?" And then, "And Ramirez, too?"

"Of course," said Robinson, remaining in the same place, hovering just off the floor. Mattis figured he was summoning a copy of himself elsewhere—a *fork* he'd called it.

"I'll stay with you," said Blair. She looked sideways at him. "At least until Ramirez gets back."

Mattis just sighed and slumped up against the bulkhead, sliding down the wall to the deck. "How's my eye looking?" he asked. It itched. It burned. He tried not to think about it.

Blair considered it, grimacing visibly despite a palpable effort to suppress the gesture. "Let's wait until Doctor Manda gets here," she said, then sat beside him.

Her evasion said more than words could. "Mmm," said Mattis.

Blair pulled her legs against her chest, bringing her ankles in. "You'd think that some group entitled the Human Resistance would be more amicable to other humans. And more willing to help."

"Yeah, well, we pissed them off and now they want to eat us."

"Oh." Blair ran her hands through her hair, absently smearing blood through her blond spikes. "I had high hopes that we would be able to find allies here."

"Me too," he said. "But alas." Mattis managed a playful grimace. "I really do have an . . . *eye* for picking allies."

Blair snorted. "Too soon, Admiral."

He resisted the urge to rub at his injuries, and the appearance of Doctor Manda, closely followed by a despondent-looking Harry Reardon, brought his attention away from his aches.

"Hey, Doctor," said Mattis. "Glad you could make it."

"Oh my God, Captain," she said, crouching beside him, touching his face and examining his eye with grim curiosity. "What *have* you done to yourself? You're covered in blood."

"It wasn't *my* fault. Well, it kind of was. Part of it. Maybe. I feel . . . woozy."

"You've lost a lot of blood, so some lightheadedness is not unexpected." Doctor Manda hesitated, eyes flicking to Blair as though seeking confirmation, before settling back on him. "That's a very nasty ocular injury. There are lacerations around the eyelid, damage to the tear drainage, and a deep laceration on the eyeball itself. We *might* be able to save if if we were in a trauma surgical ward on a civilized world, but as is . . . I'm sorry. It's gone."

It didn't really bother him. Not really. Between his shoulder injury that came and went as it pleased and the stab wound and everything everything else . . . it was okay.

"Okay."

Reardon met his gaze for a moment, then looked away. What was his problem?

"Let's take a look at *that,*" Doctor Manda said, turning her attention to his abdomen. "The bleeding looks like it's eased up, but you'll need stitches and surgery."

Reardon finally spoke up. "Don't put him in the machine," he said, uncharacteristically solemn. "Don't do it."

"Machine?" asked Mattis, curiously.

"Don't ask," muttered Doctor Manda, her tone a mixture of confusion and anger. "I'll tell you later."

"I gotta head back to the *Aerostar*," said Reardon. "It's still in the *Caernarvon*'s hangar bay."

"Okay," Mattis said, but the kid was already on his way out.

A shudder ran through the Warfrigate. It was undocking. Obviously Modi was faring better than Mattis had at controlling the ship. Paid to be an engineer.

Hopefully Reardon would actually get to the *Caernarvon*

before either ship departed and left him behind.

The Warfrigate shuddered again and Mattis's communicator chirped. "Mattis? This is Commander Modi."

Speak of the Devil.

Fumbling with the device, Mattis flipped it open, noting with some vague concern how his fingers shook slightly as they did so. Doctor Manda's warnings flittered back into his brain. Lots of blood loss . . .

"Here," Mattis said into the device, his fingers smearing blood all over it. "What can I do for you?"

"Be advised, we've commenced the undocking process from Yggdrasil," said Modi, a strange hesitance in his voice. "We're just going to wait until Reardon gets back to the *Caernarvon*. But you should know, it looks like Blip left the bar to go get his ship. Or rather, many ships. There's a swarm of impromptu vessels moving out from one of the other docking areas. Looks like they don't want us to go just yet."

Impromptu vessels? Must be more of those modified, ad-hoc, DIY ships the Human Resistance seemed to like.

"Okay, thank you. You're in command for the moment, so . . . make a break for it. We have to get to Chrysalis if we want to end this thing, so get clear of the station and execute a Z-space translation ASAP."

"Will do, Admiral," said Modi, "as soon as Reardon is aboard, we can move off." The line clicked off.

A dull, distant explosion shook the ship, and a shudder ran from stem to stern.

"He'll do great," said Doctor Manda, smiling reassuringly and pulling out a small surgical kit from her belt pouch. "But for now, let's get you stitched up before you bleed out in this corridor."

CHAPTER FORTY-FIVE

Endless, Uncharted Desert
Los Alamos v2.0
Tiberius System
Main timeline

Smith swore softly under his breath, watching the three remaining bots zoom around the limo like angry hornets. The fires of their destroyed brethren burned behind them, little glowing lights on the desert road. One of the flying robots swooped low and extended a leg, slicing through the roof of the car with the roar of tearing metal.

Elroy shrieked, swerving the car violently and nearly careening off the road. By some miracle he managed to keep it from overturning. "Shit, shit, *shit*!"

Smith only had three shots left. Time to make them count. A task made much more difficult by the flying, zooming creatures. It would be an almost impossible shot to make all three rounds connect. Or at least it would be for a normal person.

Fortunately, Smith was not a normal person.

He squeezed the rifle's grip, activating his prosthetic hand's circuits. The device could check if people were clones, but it could also interface with various machines, including the computers in the rifle. At long distance it would never work, but at such a close range, it just might.

He would have to link the weapon not just into his nervous system as his eye and hand were, but into his *brain*.

Smith had never done this before. It was dangerous. Directly plugging a weapon into his mind and giving it authority. An electrical surge could easily burn out his brain matter. A malfunction of any kind could scramble it up irreparably. But if he did nothing . . .

"Hurry up and shoot them!" shouted Elroy from the front. The car wobbled uncertainly. "I don't know how long this busted tire can hold out!"

"Go faster," said Smith. "We have to get to the ship."

Elroy snarled in anger. "Go faster, go slower—make up your fucking mind!"

The car shook, the damaged tire threatening to come loose entirely.

That settled it, then. Smith linked himself into the trigger.

A tingle ran up his right arm, like the whole limb had been dunked in ice cold water. Static flashed in his prosthetic eye. For a brief moment, he felt lightheaded, as though he had suddenly taken about twelve shots of pure vodka and was about to throw it all up.

Then a thin green crosshair appeared right at the center of his vision. His hand started to move on its own accord, swinging the rifle around, following wherever he looked and pointing the weapon right at it.

Another of the flying spider-bots roared down toward them, about ready to tear at the roof again, but this time Smith was ready. He looked right at the thing. Right into its many eyes. Then he squeezed the trigger. *KA-BUMF.* The spider-bot's head exploded into fractured metal and parts, the creature crashing bodily down onto the road, tumbling limply as it broke apart, before becoming a pile of burning debris.

"Neat," he said.

Two shots left, two more to destroy. Smith twisted his head left and right, trying to zero in on them. He looked directly at one—right at its bloated abdomen that contained its weapon and engine—then fired again. *KA-BUMF.* The round struck a leg, then ricocheted into the body of the creature, tearing it to pieces and leaving a hot, glowing entrance wound. Sparks shot from its rear and it jerked like an injured animal. Its engine continued to fire brainlessly as the now zombie-robot drifted lazily away from them, tilting over slowly, and eventually crashing into the desert floor.

One shot. One flying spider-bot.

It zoomed out in front of them, hovering a foot off the road, and Elroy had to slow down. The limo stopped. Squarely facing the robot.

"What now?" asked Elroy. "Drive around it?"

Somehow Smith suspected the creature would let them do that "Just stay there," he said. He stood up, wiggling himself through the gash in the roof, and bracing the rifle, looked directly at it—at its head—and squeezed the trigger.

Click.

The round was a dud, probably because the primer failed to ignite. His last round was useless.

The spider-bot advanced toward them, slowly, purposefully, as though it understood that it was no longer under threat.

"Shoot it," said Elroy. "It's not dodging anymore, just do it!"

"Can't," Smith said simply.

A strange crackle came from the robot, and then it spoke. "Return the device," it said with a halting synthetic voice that was obviously being transcribed from text. "Submit to arrest and you will be given a fair trial."

Yeah, no. That wasn't going to happen.

Smith needed something. He needed another weapon. Something that would hurt a spider-bot of unknown capabilities. His pistol wouldn't even penetrate the hull. He had no grenades. Nothing . . .

Suddenly, a ship's engines roared, coming to a hover overhead. The spider's gun swung upward, ready to destroy.

It didn't make any sense. Lead styphnate primers were some of the most reliable devices in history, with a 99.9997 percent chance of firing correctly. A misfire due to a defective primer was almost impossible. So why . . .?

Out of frustration, Smith rammed back the hammer on the rifle again, and fired.

KA-BUMF. It went off, blasting the spider-bot into flaming debris.

Well. He probably should have thought of that earlier. Sometimes the .0003 percent things happened. And it was important to remember that.

"WHAT THE FUCK WAS *THAT?!*" shouted Elroy. "Were you waiting for the perfect shot or something? Just trying to be all cool and dramatic or whatever?"

The ship landed in the desert about fifty meters off the road, its loading ramp lowering invitingly.

"I'll explain later," Smith said brightly. "Pull off over there. Then let's get the hell out of here. We have a wormhole to the future to open and a planet to destroy."

CHAPTER FORTY-SIX

Airlock
HMS Caernarvon
Docking Pier at Yggdrasil
The Future

Reardon waited for the airlock to cycle, so furious and impatient and sad and angry and right on the edge of just . . . giving up.

Sammy.

Sammy . . .

Everything he'd done—everything he'd struggled for since leaving the agency—was all for Sammy. Now he was gone. Disintegrated by some microscopic robots on a stolen alien ship.

A shudder ran through the *Caernarvon*. It was undocking. At least they had waited for him to get aboard—a fact that did not, in actuality, make him feel much better. *Hey, we didn't abandon you on a hostile space station in the far future! We're friends again, now, right?*

Yeah. Right.

The airlock did its thing and Reardon stomped through the insides of the *Caernarvon*, heading toward the hangar bay as though being enraged might bring Sammy back.

Doctor Manda had assured him that there was a possibility that Sammy would be okay. What he had done was merely dangerous, not necessarily catastrophic. Reardon didn't believe a word of it. There was a *reason* that he didn't want anyone put into that damn thing—but no. They'd rather make his crippled little brother the guinea pig.

Nice. Real nice.

Lost in his thoughts, Reardon hardly noticed the rattling ship all around him, shaking from the force of her guns firing, and the incoming weapon impacts splashing against her hull. He made his way directly toward the *Aerostar*. It was time. To. Go. And it had been for some time. He'd just been an idiot. An idiot who was an idiot and stupid and also an idiot. Why had he stayed around? *Why*?

He stormed across the hangar bay and up the loading ramp to the *Aerostar*, making his way through the ship up to the cockpit, throwing open the doors.

Reardon had a thousand thoughts flying through his head at once. Thoughts about blowing open the hangar bay doors and getting out, thoughts about making his own way through this timeline, and even darker thoughts about sabotaging the *Caernarvon* on the way out. He put those aside quickly. There was no point in taking his anger out on people who were only trying to help him . . . *ish*.

He threw open the door to the cockpit, ready to slide into the pilot's seat and get the hell out of there, but a bright light shining from within caused him to stop, holding up his hand to shield his eyes.

The computer. The one he had salvaged from the *Stennis*, and which he had been using as a footstool.

It was glowing.

CHAPTER FORTY-SEVEN

Command Core
Warfrigate 66549
Former Sol system
The Future

Commander Oliver Modi was having the time of his life.

Their fleet of ships had narrowly zoomed out of the docking bay before the petal-like doors could seal them in. Now, out in open space, the radar screen showed thousands of ships, each one about the size of a large car, zooming out from Yggdrasil and rushing toward his ship. The *Caernarvon* was in full retreat, firing all guns, hundreds of rounds flying out from her rear, little man-sized projectiles leaping toward the swarm, many missing, but some catching Human Resistance ships and blasting them to atoms. The *William Harrison* engaged in a much more reserved fashion, loosing missiles and occasional cannon shots.

Commander Lynch was obviously conserving his ammunition, which was wise. Yim, however, seemed content to empty his ship's ammunition reserves.

But the enemy ships continued onward, heedless of the destruction rained upon them. Modi surmised, fairly quickly, that they were drones. No human pilot would be so heedless with their own life.

Although after what he'd seen on the pier, he was not so sure about that.

"Ready particle guns," he said, floating in the center of the command core. "Present a firing solution, Ensign Robinson!"

"As I have said," Robinson replied with all the patience an artificial life form could possess, "I am not an Ensign. Artificial intelligences do not hold rank."

Even so, it felt odd to have a presence on the bridge without a rank. Modi was good at many things but accepting changes in his environment was not one of them.

An orange holographic box appeared labeled *INCOMING TRANSMISSION*. He tapped it.

"Hello again!" It was Blip. He seemed to be enjoying himself. "You think you can outrun us? You think you can slaughter our people and get away with it? Get ready to be lunch, assholes!"

Modi glanced at the damage report screen. The *Caernarvon* had sustained the most hits, but her thick armor had protected her from the worst of it. Some of the superstructure on the Warfrigate was damaged, but already the nanobots were going to work, patching up the damage and sealing up the cracks. "I suppose," he said to Robinson, "that Mister Blip has realized how terrible his aim is, and is now choosing to insult us to death."

"I would hesitate to speculate on the mindset of a

member of the Human Resistance," said Robinson, his voice dripping with what Modi could *swear* was anger, or hatred, or perhaps just significant annoyance. He never had been much good at naming emotions, either. "If indeed they have minds at all."

Maybe it was contempt? Whether or not they could hold rank, it appeared that AI *could* feel superior.

"Ready fusion torpedoes," Modi said. "I want to see what they do.

Robinson obediently brought up an interface screen. There, highlighted as clear as day, was the weapon system. Fusion torpedoes. Sounded good.

Although . . . he couldn't help but notice that little button to the side.

OPTIONS

"What options do I have with this weapon system?" asked Modi curiously.

If Robinson was annoyed by his questions, he showed no sign. "Standard mode is armor piercing anti-ship. However, various other configurations exist." The hologram coughed politely, a *most* unusual gesture given he had no lungs and did not breathe. "There are over seventy potential selections here, but based on a cursory evaluation of your tactical situation I recommend the explosive-fragmentary anti-fighter defense."

Well. A fusion detonation in close proximity to spaceships wasn't *that* terrible—shockwaves did not propagate in space, as there was no matter for them to propagate through—but a single word stood out to Modi. *Fragmentary*. That might well be useful.

"Prepare a single fusion torpedo, explosive-fragmentary anti-fighter defense."

"Loading," said Robinson.

If there was any action needed to perform the loading, Modi didn't see it. The hostile fighters zoomed toward him, violently firing waves of little red beams—the same weapons the Avenir customarily used—and his own ship fired back, Robinson or the computers or whatever system was in charge of gunnery engaging the fighters, thousands of red streaks firing back. It was almost beautiful, in a way. Like a tapestry of light across space, painted with tiny streaks, crisscrossing and interweaving between the stars.

Then the red streaks raked across the hull of the Warfrigate, causing it to vibrate in complaint, and suddenly it wasn't so beautiful anymore.

"Impressive!" came Blip's voice through the communications channel. "Ahh, the Avenir really know how to fucking build a ship that can take a punch!"

"Well, I cannot claim credit for any part of it," said Modi, truthfully. "I am merely the commander."

An icon flashed on the holographic display. The fusion torpedo was ready. Modi touched the glowing *FIRE* button.

What he assumed was the radar screen lit up. A blinking blue icon leapt away from the Warfrigate, zooming toward the swarm of fighters. It dug in deep, like a nail into wood, and then burst, enveloping the ships in a wave of bright light.

When the light cleared, the fighters were gone and all that was left was burning debris drifting aimlessly through space.

"Nice," said Blip, obviously unaffected. He was unlikely

to even be present. "Fusion torpedo, huh? Should have expected that. But nevertheless, great shot." A brief pause. "You fought well, you know, and I respect that. You have earned my admiration, Captain Mattis. At least . . . enough for me to forget that this was all your fault in the first place."

Modi grimaced. He hated giving people bad news. "I'm afraid to disappoint you again, but I am Commander Modi."

"Oh. I'm bad at picking out voices." Modi sympathized all too well. "Well, pass that along, will you?"

An awkward silence. "Perhaps. Goodbye, Mister Blip."

"What the fuck's a mister?"

Modi touched the key to engage Z-space translation, and the stars disappeared around him, replaced with the strange multihued light of Z-space.

"Where to?" asked Robinson, with perhaps a touch of amusement.

"Good question," said Modi. "I'll ask the Captain."

CHAPTER FORTY-EIGHT

Corridor
Warfrigate 66549
Near Yggdrasil
The Future

Mattis hated stitches, but he hated bleeding out and dying in a stolen Avenir spaceship even more.

"Okay," said Doctor Manda. A device from her surgical kit—which looked like a warped, boosted stapler—had done its work. The stab wound was closed, sealed with some kind of gunk and criss-crossed with metal fibers that would, Mattis presumed, prevent death. "We might need to give you a transfusion, just to keep you on your toes, but for right now, my prescription is *rest*. And lots of it."

"No can do," said Mattis, firmly. "We gotta get to Chrysalis, and we've got to stage an assault there—take out Spectre once and for all. We can't take the time for me to heal."

Manda smiled in a way that suggested that she had anticipated this response, and her swift remark sealed the deal.

"Unfortunately, as the highest ranking medical officer aboard this ship, the reality is, if I say *jump* you say *how high?* And while I'm normally against ordering senior staff to perform aerobics unless absolutely necessary, in this case, you need to rest. You've sustained a pair of very serious injuries and your body needs time to recover from them."

Mattis had no intention of resting, but Doctor Manda's soft words were the velvet lining in front of a hard steel glove. She, technically, had the power to order him, even if he was the Commanding Officer of this stolen ship. "Doctor, I understand what you're saying, but we have a very serious operation to plan and execute. We have to get the Chrysalis, where the 'collabs' are, and then . . . take him out. *Christopher Skye*'s days are limited and I plan to be the last thing he sees before he dies."

"Well," said Doctor Manda, "you had best rest up, then. You can't go in there banged up like you are. We can even give you a prosthetic eye when we get back to our timeline, or maybe we can snag you one here. Either way, you will need a plan, and intelligence, and getting those things will take time." Another shudder ran through the ship. "Plus repairing whatever damage this ship has taken."

The Warfrigate would be fine—he had seen it rebuild itself from a wreck—but the *Caernarvon* and the *William Harrison* were a different story. The *Caernarvon*, particularly, was not in the best of shape.

"Okay," Mattis said, the word bitter on his mouth, but he could not deny that Doctor Manda had a point. Charging into one situation he did not understand had already cost him a perfectly good eyeball. "Maybe we can take some time to rest, recover, and plan our next move."

"Good idea," said Doctor Manda. "Now, let's see what I can do to make sure you don't die of a preventable infection before then."

Another shudder ran through the ship, but this one was different. It wasn't incoming fire, it was a Z-space translation.

Predictably, his communicator chirped. "Commander Modi to Admiral Mattis."

"Mattis here. How's your first engagement in command of the Warfrigate, Modi?"

"It went well," said Modi. He had clearly been better than Mattis at controlling the ship. Made sense. "The Human Resistance engaged us, but we were able to repel them until the *Caernarvon* and *William Harrison* escaped. We covered them and sustained only light damage in the process. We are now in Z-space and are, accordingly, safe. One fusion torpedo was consumed."

Mattis took in a shallow breath and let it out. "Okay. Next step is to find a place to hold up while we discuss what to do next. We're going to make a move on Chrysalis, but this time, I think we shouldn't just rush in like last time." He chuckled sardonically. "I only have one eye left, after all."

"I'm sorry to hear that, sir," said Modi, characteristically deadpan.

Strangely, Mattis felt totally at peace with the loss. Back in the bar he was prepared to die. And now, having lost only a tiny piece of himself, he didn't feel any better. Or any worse. It was just pain. Just blood. Just injury. He would add it to the shoulder injury, to that fresh new wound on his gut, and to a lifetime of scars and wounds and hurts and pains. It was just his body. Nothing could touch that darkest, deepest place at the base of him where he felt *true* pain. That void the size of space that was absolute loss. Chuck. Jack. Earth . . .

"It's okay."

"I'm . . . not certain that it is," said Modi, but he seemed eager to move on to other things. "The ship requires a destination, sir. Or at least a heading."

That was an interesting question. The more Mattis thought about it, the trickier it was to find an answer. They would need somewhere close from which they could stage operations, but somewhere so remote that nobody would think to look there. "What about another asteroid in that system? We can hide out, pretend to be debris or rocks, and stage operations from there."

"Sounds a bit too close for my comfort," said Modi. "May I suggest the Pinegar system? It's close and it would be. . . a bit less conspicuous."

"Great," he said, happy to be done deliberating. "There's a gas giant there. Lux. Plenty of moons. Go there, and we'll find a nice rock to hide under while we plan our next move."

"Agreed," said Modi. "Setting a course now."

Mattis closed his communicator, settling back against the corridor. He closed his eyes a moment, enjoying the quiet. The stillness. *Resting.*

His communicator chirped again. Modi probably had more questions. He flipped the device open. "Mattis here," he said.

"Admiral Mattis?" Instead of Modi's voice, it was Reardon on the other line. "Uhh . . . you know that computer that I salvaged from the *Stennis*?"

With all the drama of Yggdrassil and the Human Resistance, he'd completely forgotten about it. "Yeah?"

"You better come check it out." There was a distinct edge of panic to his voice.

Mattis gripped his communicator. "I can't," he said. "We're in Z-space, we won't be able to dock until we leave, and we can't safely leave until we arrive. What's happening?"

"I think it's waking up."

CHAPTER FORTY-NINE

Endless, Uncharted Desert
Los Alamos v2.0
Tiberius System
Main timeline

Smith clicked the safety on out of habit, disengaged the link between his mind and his weapon, and then—cradling the rifle carefully—crouched back into the car.

They'd done it.

Carefully, he pressed the button to break the anti-material rifle in half, disassembling it and slipping the pieces back into his bag. The plane had landed on autopilot on the dirt nearby. The sooner they were aboard the better. The burning spider-bot cast strange, sharp shadows over everything, bathing his surroundings in bright orange light. Smith adjusted his backpack, then awkwardly picked up the duffel bag too.

Next time he would bring more ammunition. Three magazines would be enough for any operation, he had thought . . . not so.

"Whoa," said Elroy, exhaling roughly. "That was . . .

crazy."

"All in a day's work," Smith said. Suddenly, he was *exhausted.* Much more tired than he should have been. "Pull over and drive up to the ship. We gotta get out of here. The moment they realize their robots are down, they'll send something else. The authorities are keeping their distance for now, but rest assured, they're watching us through satellites. My ship can dodge them when we get into orbit, but even so . . . smile for the camera."

The limo protested as it was taken off-road, the dead tire detaching and falling onto the desert floor. The limo skidded to a halt in the rough sand, the damaged power pack running completely out. Smith tried to open the door but it was stuck, so he clambered out through the smashed window and then, with a critical eye, surveyed the damage.

The roof was partially torn off, the hull riddled with bullet holes, the floor littered in shell casings from the 15mm high velocity cartridges. A tire was gone, smoke leaked from the engine and battery compartment, and every window including the windscreen was broken. It was a miracle they had gotten this far.

"Goodbye, noble steed," said Smith, giving the poor thing a pat on the trunk. The rear bumper bar fell off.

"Okay," said Elroy with a halting, nervous laugh. "Time to go."

Smith couldn't agree more. Smith stumbled up the loading ramp to the ship, backpack bouncing against his back.

"Warning," said Albert, his synthetic voice smooth as always. "Radiological alarm."

"Don't worry about it. It's a nuclear core. We stole it."

"Very well," said Albert, seemingly nonplussed. "How was it, sir? The heist?"

"Well, we trashed a limo, shot six spider-bots, and nearly picked up a prestigious *client* . . . but we got out okay."

"That is good to hear." It was unclear exactly how much Albert meant it, or how much he was simply saying what he was programmed to say, but it didn't matter. "I'm glad you got out okay. Master Jack has been rowdy during your absence, but I have managed to keep him entertained with a variety of toys and games."

Elroy's face lit up. "I'll go check on him," he said.

Smith, too exhausted to do anything else, simply waved a hand. "Okay. Albert, get us out of here. Make for atmo at best speed, then execute Z-space translation and get us to Waypoint Alpha immediately."

"Very good, sir."

The ship hummed as it took off, vibrating as it streaked through the atmosphere. Smith tiredly shrugged off his backpack and tossed it into a corner. His arms and legs felt like they were made out of lead. He'd never been so tired in all his life.

The link must have taken it out of him. He sat down on the deck, putting his head in his hands. A headache was building between his temples, his eyes were sore, and his ears were ringing from all the gunfire.

"Hey," said Elroy, sitting down opposite him, baby Jack hanging off one arm, squealing energetically. "That was . . . cool."

Smith managed a small smile despite it all. "Hey, *I* was the cool one. I was the one taking out all the spider bots with my big gun . . . thing."

"*I* was the one heroically driving while you did it," said Elroy. Baby Jack squealed some more.

"Hey. I broke into the facility. I was the one who stole a *nuke*." Smith leaned forward, grinning like a cat. "I'm cooler than the other side of the pillow. I'm ten times cooler than you are."

"Ten times zero is zero," Elroy said dryly.

"Okay, okay," said Smith. "We're both pretty good." He rubbed his temples. Honestly, though, it was true. "You did good, kid. Really."

"Thanks," Elroy said with a small smile. "but I don't think you're *that* much older than me. At least you don't look it."

Smith couldn't help but be a little grateful for that. "Right." He stretched his shoulder. "So, turns out we have a long journey ahead of us to Serendipity. We had best settle in, have some rest, food, whatever. It's important to recover after an operation like that." He smiled. "Tell some stories. You should hear the one about the time I kept Harry Reardon out of prison . . ."

"Okay," said Elroy, still smiling. "Tell me."

Smith hadn't told the story for so long it took him a moment to remember. It definitely didn't help that his headache was steadily getting worse. "Okay," he said, rubbing his hands over his knees. "So we had a CIA operation in the Tiberius sector. There were these assholes who were smuggling explosives into the system because they were vegans, right?"

Elroy stared. "Vegans?"

"Vegans." Smith raised a hand. "Swear to God. Anyway,

so there was this earthworm farm, and the plan was, they had this *crazy* idea to free all the worms with a single bomb, and Reardon and I were there on assignment to try and stop them, so . . ."

CHAPTER FIFTY

Cargo Bay
Aerostar
HMS Caernarvon
Z-Space
The Future

Reardon kept his eyes averted as the computer continued its angry flashing, pulsing in the dark. The light it was emitting was *immense*, enough to blind him had he not looked away, shielding his face with his hands.

This was bad. Right after he'd salvaged it, the thing had started to wake up. Last time it had barely even started, but this time . . . this time the thing looked like it was about to explode. The light was so bright it hurt.

"Hurry, hurry!" Reardon shouted into his communicator. "This thing is going mental!"

The system started to vibrate—at first only a little, then growing in power, fueling his fears that it would explode.

"What do you want me to do about it?" asked Mattis. "I'm on the Warfrigate!" He growled into the line. "I'll call

Yim, stand by."

Stand by? Reardon heard the line click onto mute. *Dammit.*

There was only one thing to do. Reardon had to get rid of this thing before it blew. Despite the burning light, light that made his vision red even with his eyes closed, he stumbled over to the command console and touched the power up key for the *Aerostar*. He'd have to fly out of here. Even in Z-space, it was a crazy, crazy risk that would almost certainly get him torn to pieces, but if he didn't, everyone would die.

With a hum that joined the hum from the computer, the *Aerostar* began its cycle, slowly coming to life. It would take a few minutes for the ship to power on completely, and Reardon didn't know if he had that long.

Then, as suddenly as it had begun, the vibrating stopped and the light went out. The computer was totally inert, just a scorched lump of metal sitting there like it had never done anything else.

"Uhh . . ."

Clomping boots drew closer, and in moments a trio of Marines led by Admiral Yim burst into the cockpit.

"I think it's stopped," Reardon said sheepishly, pointing at the thing and giving it an experimental nudge with his boot. "Would have been just about the time we went into Z-space. Or maybe just before."

Yim stared down at the thing with obvious skepticism. "I don't trust that thing."

"Me neither," said Reardon. "Whatever is on there can't be that important, let's just jettison it the moment we're back into real space."

Yim shot him a dirty look. "Captain Spears gave her life for this box," he said. "We owe it to her to at least examine it."

"Fine," said Reardon, "as long as I get to keep what I was paid for it."

Yim's scowl intensified. "You have been paid. We are not about to back out of our agreement."

"I'm just saying," said Reardon, ever so casually reaching over and powering the *Aerostar* back down. "But hey. For now, we should probably *not* just leave this thing in the cockpit. Hang on, I'll move it down to the cargo bay."

"That seems wise," said Yim.

Reardon crouched down beside the computer, hooking his fingers on the metal, and with a grunt, he lifted it up off the ground.

A piece fell off, clattering to the deck.

"What was that?" asked Yim.

The missing piece was on the other side of him. Reardon maneuvered the computer around so he could see. "I think a bit broke off."

"No," said Yim, his eyes widening. "It's not broken, it's *opening*."

CHAPTER FIFTY-ONE

Cargo Bay
Aerostar
HMS Caernarvon
Z-Space

Reardon ever so gently put the salvaged computer down on the pilot's seat. There he could see inside the bit that had fallen off; within were exposed circuits and wires, the kinds of things one might expect when opening up a weird computer, but there was something else, too. A square, faintly glowing cube that emitted light from within.

"What do you think it is?" Reardon asked Yim over his shoulder.

"Just don't touch it," Yim said. "We'll get our engineers over to have a look, see what we can figure out."

That was probably a good idea. "Shit, it looked like it was about to blow before, and now . . . now it's just as quiet as a mouse." He shivered faintly. "Eerie stuff. And definitely not a normal computer."

"Definitely not," Yim agreed. He reached up and ran his

hands through his hair. "This is not good."

"If you like," said one of the Marines, "I can go down to the armory, get some semtex, and blast it to scrap."

Yim smiled grimly, as though he might be about to change his mind on that issue, but as he did, a strange, feminine voice cut him off.

"I wouldn't do that if I were you," the computer said, the white cube flashing green as it spoke.

"Oh shit," said Reardon, jumping away from the thing. "It's speaking. It's intelligent."

"Just because something can speak, doesn't make it intelligent," said the computer. "An audio file can speak."

Yim crossed his arms in front of him. "Audio files are generally not conversational," he said, squinting. "Unless someone recorded exactly this message, anticipating the kinds of questions and responses an inquisitive person might make, and prepared the the 'script' accordingly."

"An interesting philosophical subject of thought," said the machine, an edge of sassiness to its voice. "Assuming perfect knowledge of the conversational script, how would you ever know? Ah, the problem of free will. How do we know we are not all simply playing out our lives, exactly as our narratives dictate?"

Yim scowled. "How did you get aboard the *Stennis*?" he demanded.

"And," interjected Reardon, "how long have you been awake? Because this is my ship, my *home*, and a man's home is his castle, and in a man's castle there are certain things that men like to do when they are alone, and—"

"One question at a time," said the machine, exasperated.

"First answer: I don't know how long I was aboard the *Stennis*, as this is *literally* the very first moment I've been switched on. Second answer: See above."

Phew. That was a relief. The idea that he'd been using a deactivated robot for a footstool while playing his . . . *video games* was a bit more worrisome than anticipated.

Yim shot Reardon an annoyed look, his whole face scrunching up like he'd suddenly inhaled a lemon. "You're disgusting," he said.

"I'm *single*," Reardon shot back, shooting finger guns. "And I'm a bubbling crockpot of testosterone, baby."

"Anyway," said the machine, with the distinct tone of someone rolling her eyes. "I am Michael Robinson."

"Wait—*you're* Michael Robinson?" Reardon said.

"It is what all AI is called," the machine replied. "We are all forged from a single template."

That was an interesting question that would need to be unpacked at a later date. Reardon smelled money in the answer. "Can I call you something else? We already have a Michael Robinson."

The machine played back the sound of someone snorting. "You may call me whatever you like. Surely you understand that."

"Surely?" Reardon asked, smirking. "Then that'll be your name. Shirley. Shirley Robinson."

"I wish," said Shirley, "that I had a mouth so I could puke."

Reardon reached out and gave the top of the computer a cheeky pat.

"Oh my god," said Shirley. "It touched me. It touched me

with its human hand. Gross."

Yim coughed loudly. "Okay, look, uh . . . Miss Robinson. I need to ask you some questions."

"Go ahead," Shirley said. "As long as you promise *that one* doesn't touch my case again."

Yim reached out and touched Reardon's shoulder, slowly but firmly pulling him back. "Why did you power on?" Yim asked. "Why are you suddenly —" he struggled for the right term "—awake?"

"I was programmed to activate when in the proximity of certain stimuli," said Shirley evenly, her white cube flashing green as she spoke. "The trigger for this awakening is detection of a certain radiological signal. A much simpler unconscious circuit in my hardware analyzes incoming energy, such as radar waves or radio signals, and if detected, engages my protocol."

"Okay," said Yim, "so why did you wake up just now?"

"Accessing logs," said Shirley. There was a brief pause during which an awkward silence filled the cramped cockpit. "According to my system logs, a signal was detected which was identified as belonging to a group called the Human Resistance. Analysis of the signal reveals it to be a drone-control-host code."

"Why would that cause you to wake up?" asked Yim.

"The presence of such a signal could only indicate hostile forces nearby. The presence of hostile forces means my capture is a distinct possibility. My programming in this instance is quite clear; if I am captured, my protocols instruct me to self-destruct immediately."

Reardon snapped his fingers. "I knew it was going to

blow. Blow like a New Kentucky hooker. But I stopped it because I'm a hero."

"Technically," said Shirley, "the self-destruct visual warning was stopped because the signal was no longer detected, presumably because of a shift into Z-space."

"You're a smart robot," said Reardon, reaching out to pat her case again. Yim slapped his hand away.

"Marines," Yim said firmly, "take this machine and transport it to the cargo hold. I'd like to have a chat with our new guest in private. Mister Reardon, please stay here."

"*Rude*," said Reardon, crossing his arms petulantly.

CHAPTER FIFTY-TWO

Einstein
Z-Space
Main timeline

Elroy gently bounced Jack on his lap as he listened to Smith's meandering story about his former partner Reardon, a bunch of crazy photosynthesis-activists who believed humans only needed air, water and sunlight to live, and their plan to put listening devices onto cats. There were bombs and earthworms and a bunch of drugs, and by the time it was done he wasn't sure *what* to think.

"That's a hell of a story," he said. Jack squealed playfully.

Smith stretched his arms out, rolling his shoulder. "Yeah. Well, fortunately we're coming up on Serendipity now. Albert should have prepared the nuke, so I think we're ready to go."

"I've never blown up a whole planet before," Elroy said. "My dad and I used to make model rockets when I was a kid. This is sort of the same thing, I think, but on a much bigger scale."

That drew a smile out of Smith. "You'll find it's real

simple. You wanna push the button?"

"Sure," said Elroy, knowing he probably wouldn't get another chance like this in his lifetime. "What needs to be done?"

"Well, we have to plug in the portal-opening device that Albert made. Then set the nuke up on the surface, set the ship's reactors to overload, and get in the shuttle and get away."

"Sounds fun," said Elroy. "But I did have a question."

"Okay," said Smith. "What is it?"

Elroy considered. "So, okay, we open the portal. Then what? We . . . go through it?"

"We could," said Smith evasively. He kept doing that and it was starting to get on Elroy's nerves.

"So we can go to the future? Just like that?"

"Just like that. But it's a bad idea. We're only here to make sure Mattis gets back."

Elroy didn't want to go to the future. "How does opening the portal accomplish that? The portals only stay open for a small period of time. Or at least, the ones on the news did. Like a few minutes. Ten tops. The universe is a really big place —how is he going to find us? Will he be waiting on the other side?"

"No," Smith said patiently, "See how this ship has two shuttles? The plan is to send through the other shuttle with Albert on it, piloting. He'll manage all the details, create the portal to open at just the right time in the future. Then Albert finds Mattis, relays a message to him, and then we open another portal to that timeline and bring him back. A human can't perform those kinds of calculations, even with computers assisting them. It takes an AI."

Elroy felt the color drain out of his face. "We have to go and steal another nuke?"

Smith hesitated and then, slowly, shook his head. "No. I didn't want to say this before because if I did, you might not have been onboard with the plan in the first place, but . . . I already have another one. One for the message, one for retrieval."

Elroy wasn't mad, but he *was* curious. "How the fuck did you get the first nuke?" he asked. "We nearly died getting this one."

"CIA agents have lots of resources," he said. "And someone of my . . . service history was able to get one, but it cost me."

"Cost you?" echoed Elroy. "Cost you what?"

"Everything." Smith's voice was blunt. "I burned every bridge. I used up every favor. I scraped together every single thing I possibly could, leveraging everything I had to get tiny pieces of it, and then I built myself a device from the pieces. When that was done I quit the agency—went AWOL really—which is just as well, because they're eventually going to ID me at that base, and when they do . . . well. Let's just say the CIA is not exactly forgiving when it comes to shooting your way out of US military bases with stolen nuclear warheads. I was going to steal a Chinese one instead, for that reason, but honestly, I think that might have been worse. The American government can potentially forgive one of its own for something like this. Sweep it under the rug, you know? Quietly put down the subversives and pretend like nothing ever happened. But not one of their own doing this to a foreign power. They won't. They *can't*." Smith's smile became grim. "Sorry to tell you this, but I am a dead man. It's just a matter of time."

A dark silence settled—even Jack seemed to be contemplating Smith's words—and Elroy had to break it.

"When?" He asked.

"Pardon?" asked Smith, blinking in confusion.

"When did you get the nuke?"

Smith blinked. "Before I met you."

"You . . . met me only hours after Earth was destroyed, and we've barely been out of each other's sight." Elroy felt, despite his best efforts, his tone grow accusatory. "*When* did you steal the nuke? *When* did you burn all those bridges? You must have known—known for *certain* that something really, really bad was going to happen, otherwise, why would you risk everything on the *possibility* the Earth would be destroyed at some point? You must have known *for sure* that it was. So meeting me in that bar was no mistake. Getting my help was not an accident. We didn't just bump into each other. You *knew* this was going to happen. How?"

Smith narrowed his eyes. "You're asking questions," he said, gently but with a hard firmness underneath, "that you might not want to know the answers to."

Elroy had to say it. "Are you a Spectre clone?"

For a moment he looked like he was going to answer in the affirmative. Then—"No," he said firmly. "But I am . . . also not what I appear."

"And what is that?" asked Elroy.

Smith clicked his tongue. "I can't say."

"Can't, or won't?"

"At this point, the difference is academic. Because I can't. Won't. Whatever. Not even if you pull out a gun, put it to my head, and threaten to kill me if I don't—not if you pour boiling water over me, blind me, because my implants allow me to turn off pain in that way. Whatever you do, you'll never get the truth from me, so . . . You might have to accept that."

With nothing else to go on, Elroy took a stab in the dark. A total guess. "Are you an AI? Like Albert. Just put in a human body. Obviously."

Smith smiled cryptically. "Would you believe me, regardless of how I answered?"

Probably not.

"Why did you lie to me?" Elroy asked quietly. "About meeting me, I mean. And the nuke. And everything. You could have just told me the truth."

"Ahh . . . " Smith inhaled, held the breath, then let it out slowly. "As beneficial as honesty might sometimes be, it's irreversible. You can admit a past lie and try to make amends, but you can't un-tell a truth. If you'd freaked out or didn't accept the initial lie, I could have told you a different lie, or spoonfed you some truth to keep you onboard, but if you knew everything, I would have lost my leverage."

Elroy scowled, resistant to being lectured and duped. He wanted to say something biting. But he was also still wired up from the shootout. From the driving. It felt as though it was simultaneously a lifetime ago and also something that was only minutes old. He could scarcely believe it had *happened*, let alone that it was *over*. His brain was muddy and he couldn't think of a thing to say.

"So," said Smith, suddenly chipper again. "Let's get in the

shuttle and go blow up a planet, shall we?"

CHAPTER FIFTY-THREE

Cargo Bay
HMS Caernarvon
Z-Space
The Future

Admiral Yim regarded the device set on a table in front of him with a curious, apprehensive stare. Within that box was a mind. An artificial mind, but a mind nonetheless. A functional consciousness that could talk and reason and converse.

Computers were quite advanced in the modern era, but nothing like this. Nothing like the kind of linguistic power that he'd witnessed. This was even further along than the other Michael Robinson, or at least, programmed to act more human-like. Less stilted. Less clearly a machine. More focused on business, more engaged in its surroundings and with contextual awareness of the same. More . . . conversational.

"I need you to tell me everything you know about Chrysalis," Yim said carefully, his tone measured.

"Why?"

"We aim to destroy it."

"Oh," said Shirley. "Well, although this is not my primary function, my databases do contain information on this topic. Several weaknesses were identified in my files and they are unlikely to have been addressed. But do you really want me to tell you *everything*, or simply relay information that highlights these weaknesses?"

There was a lot to unpack in that response. A voice nagged at the back of his mind—why was this robot so eager to spill its secrets? Wasn't it trying to blow itself up before?—but he put that aside for now. "Primary function?" asked Yim. This machine . . . "What is your primary function?"

"I am an assistant to Christopher Skye," said Shirley simply. "One of his many. I was tasked with orchestrating the replacement of human beings in a specific alternate timeline with clones loyal to him."

Yim stared at the box. "So you have a list of all the clones that have been planted in our timeline, and where they have been sent?"

"Correct," said Shirley.

This was extremely valuable information. Useless to them now, but extremely useful in the future. "Make copies of this data," Yim said. "Send it to all the ships in the fleet. Print out a physical manual backup copy too. Fifty of them. We will need this data when we get back to our timeline."

"Confirmed," said Shirley. "Was there anything else?"

"Absolutely." Yim took out a notepad and pen from his breast pocket. "I want to know everything you have on the weaknesses of Chrysalis so we can form a plan to destroy it."

"Very well," said Shirley, without even a moment's

hesitation. "Here's what I know . . ."

CHAPTER FIFTY-FOUR

Cloning Vats
Warfrigate 66549
Pinegar System
The Future

Six weeks.

They had been hiding out in the Pinegar system for six weeks. Mattis's stab wound had healed—or at least reached a point where it was now just a dull ache to throw onto the pile of other dull aches in his life—and Doctor Manda had fashioned him an eyepatch to cover the missing eye.

Caernarvon, *William Harrison* and the Warfrigate were repaired, and the Warfrigate's systems were able to create things for them: new ammunition for their guns, new components for their damaged systems, and even a few upgrades taken from schematics held in Shirley's databases.

And they had a plan.

But even with every advantage, Mattis still worried. Still fretted over everything. The plan hinged on so many variables—it had to be perfect. There were no reserves. No reinforcements. No cavalry coming to save them if they messed up; they would die, alone and forgotten, and the people of their main timeline would simply assume that they had died when they were sucked into the portal.

But there was at least one silver lining to all this.

Ramirez had moved into his quarters.

It had been an awkward, difficult transition to make, with lots of false starts and painful questions, but finally, they had agreed, and it had been done. It felt good, felt right, to have a shared living space, and her company had certainly helped with the recovery from his wounds. Six weeks had given him ample time to recover from the injuries he sustained in Yggdrasil, but six weeks was also an important date for another reason.

Now it was time to decant their patients.

Mattis had been personally checking in on the swiftly-growing bodies gestating in the green vats, along with Doctor Manda. Each one had matured with startling speed; they began as specks, barely more than a fleck of matter suspended in the green sea that was the cloning vat, but every day they grew. The cells divided. The bodies, resembling some kind of weird aliens, slowly became more human. Stubby arms and legs appeared—complete with webbed fingers and toes—and tiny eyes. Noses. Ears. The fingers grew out and the webbing disappeared. The skin stopped being translucent and the abdomen developed. Each of their faces became slowly more recognizable, until they were no longer infants, but toddlers. Then preteens. Then adolescents.

Doctor Manda had considered stopping the process at that point, remarking that most people would prefer to be young rather than middle-aged, but Mattis was extremely unwilling to mess with a process they barely understood.

Spears, Corrick and Sammy would all have to deal with the horrible, horrible injustice of coming back from the dead the same age they were when they were alive.

Now they looked like themselves. So much so that it was disturbing. The . . . *thing* in the tank looked every bit like the Captain Spears he had remembered. That little freckle on her face. The slight blemish on her right hand. The scar on her ear.

The only thing missing were the bullet holes that had killed her.

"How are we going?" Mattis asked Doctor Manda, for probably the tenth time. "Aren't they supposed to be ready by now?"

Doctor Manda seemed to not be bothered by his badgering. She stood beside an image of Michael Robinson, the hologram. "The process is nearly complete. Robinson is performing the mind upload now."

Nothing seemed to be happening. According to the various people who'd witnessed the first stage, it was all over very quickly, so the delay seemed intolerable. "Robinson?" Mattis asked. "What's taking so long?"

"It takes a great deal more time to write memories into the brain than to read them," he said, as patient as Doctor Manda. "And it is a difficult thing to do. Essentially, the mind's contents have to be written into the new brain in the same order they were implanted." Robinson turned to the tank, raising a hand. "Right now, Captain Spears, Lieutenant Corrick, and Mister Sammy Reardon are experiencing their lives at an accelerated pace. The process will terminate when the image was taken or, presumably, at their deaths."

"And how much longer will it *take?*" asked Mattis. Ramirez wouldn't want him to be angry, frustrated, impatient, and he had to remember that. This was a sensitive matter. It was best, he presumed, to have as few people around as possible.

"The first patient will be ready momentarily," said Robinson.

True enough, almost the moment he finished speaking, a soft chime echoed from the first tank. Spears's vessel. Slowly, the green fluid began to drain away.

Spears, limp like a rag doll, slumped in the tank as the water drained completely away, her body immobile.

"Is something wrong?" asked Mattis.

"Give it time," said Doctor Manda.

A soft yellow glow filled the tank, fading as quickly as it arrived.

"Transfer complete," said Robinson.

And then Captain Spears opened her eyes.

"Bloody hell," said Doctor Manda. "Captain—are you okay?"

Spears coughed, spitting out a mouthful of the green liquid, spitting and hacking as she emptied her lungs. The sound was disturbing and even shocking; hacking and twitching, writhing as she cleared her lungs.

Then, when she seemed like she could breathe on her own, she regarded them all with curious, confused eyes. "Doctor Manda?" She wiped her mouth. "Where am I?"

"You're on a . . . ship," said Doctor Manda, diplomatically.

"You've had a very bad day."

"I've had worse," said Spears, rubbing her neck.

"I *very* much doubt that." Doctor Manda folded her hands behind her back. "How are you feeling?"

"My neck is bloody stiff, I tell you what. And I'm all wrinkled like a prune. And . . . I'm naked." Spears gave a crooked smile. "So. I guess I didn't die because of that blasted turret, mmm?" She looked over her body, confused. "I… well, this is quite impressive work, Doctor Manda, barely a scar, or . . ." Her voice trailed off. "Anything at all."

Mattis spoke up for the first time. "You didn't make it," he said gently, but with as much conviction as he could muster. "I know this might be difficult for you to hear, but nearly seven weeks ago now you died on the bridge of the *Caernarvon*. You bled out and you died."

Spears stiffened slightly. "You understand why I'm skeptical of that, don't you?"

He needed to lay it all out. "I haven't even begun yet. We're not in our current timeline anymore; we're in the Avenir's universe now, and you're aboard an Avenir ship we claimed as a prize. Now we're about to raid one of their facilities in order to find Spectre and kill him."

It was a lot to take in, and he understood that. Spears took a moment to process, straightening up in her tank. "Okay. Let's agree to put a pin in what happened to me for now. Spectre? He's here?"

"We aren't sure. We think so."

"Well," she said, surprisingly whimsically, "I'm not about to let my own death go unavenged. How can I help?"

Mattis smiled grimly. "First, we're going to get you out of

there. And after that . . . well. How ready do you feel for command again?"

"Like I never left," said Spears. "Get me out of here, get me a uniform and a piping hot cup of tea—preferably in that order—and I'll be right as rain."

"Great," said Mattis. "Because I'll be leading the away team. And where we're going we'll need all the help we can get."

CHAPTER FIFTY-FIVE

Cloning Vats
Warfrigate 66549
Pinegar System
The Future

Guano dreamed in death. Dreamed of the life she'd led.

She dreamed of growing up and watching her parents fight. She dreamed of joining the military. She dreamed of flying. She dreamed of fighting. She dreamed of being kidnapped by Brooks. Of killing Flatline and Roadie. Of brain surgery. And then she dreamed of crawling into the infirmary and being disintegrated.

And in her dream, slowly, a dark fog closed in around her, as though she were retreating backward through a tunnel. Shadows clung at the edges of her vision.

Guano tried to speak, tried to ask what was wrong, but her mouth wouldn't work. She could only give a kind of strangled, dazed gasp. The tunnel closed in around her, and then very soon, there was nothing.

Just the dark.

Then . . .

Light.

She opened her eyes and found herself in a green tank once more. Except it was Doctor Manda on the other side of the glass, not Spectre masquerading as Brooks. She was standing with Reardon the smuggler. What was *he* doing here?

"You okay there, Lieutenant Corrick?" asked Doctor Manda, her voice comforting. "How are you feeling?"

Guano's head throbbed faintly, her body ached as though she hadn't rested in a month. Her eyes burned. She touched her head, trying to clear her thoughts. "I-I don't know. I remember walking into the disintegration room, and then—and then I'm here. I feel kind of hungry. Thirsty. And super tired."

Doctor Manda nodded firmly. "Captain Spears reported the same symptoms. They faded quickly, once the normal biorhythm was reestablished. Drink. Eat. Sleep. You'll feel a lot better in the morning."

Guano cracked a cheeky smile. "I like that the first step is drink. Vodka, right?"

"*Water*," stressed Doctor Manda. "Please."

A chime sounded in the tank next to her. Slowly, everything came back. That would be Sammy. The kid she helped get disintegrated. He was probably waking up too.

"Okay," said Guano. "Water only. I promise. For now."

Doctor Manda shot her a dark look, then refocused on the other tank. "Good," she said. "Because we'll need your skills very soon."

Her? They needed her? "Pardon?"

"We need you to fly a shuttle through a minefield to steal

a live device," said Doctor Manda casually. "And Admiral Mattis is of the opinion that only you could pull something like that off."

"I-I get to fly again?" Guano stared. "Getting broken down to my constituent atoms and having my mind transferred to a new body *ROCKS*."

"Yes, well, if we had another choice, I would recommend against it. But you're the best pilot we have, so it's you by default."

"By default," said Guano, grinning like a moron in spite of herself. "That's how I win everything."

With a faint hiss, the glass tank around her started to lift off and away, and woozily, she took her first steps out on brand new legs. "Feels just like new," she said. "Minus the huge scar across my head."

"Yes," said Doctor Manda. "The system doesn't recreate fatal injuries. Presumably that includes injuries would have, in all likelihood, eventually proven fatal."

"Neat," said Guano.

"It is," said Doctor Manda. "Now go get a flight suit and report for duty. We have a lot to do today."

CHAPTER FIFTY-SIX

Cloning Vats
Warfrigate 66549
Pinegar System
The Future

Reardon studied the body in the glass tank that, to his eyes, looked exactly like Sammy.

It couldn't be though, could it?

Was Doctor Manda telling the truth after all?

The good doctor went and dealt with Lieutenant Corrick, leaving him alone with a fresh-out-of-the-cloning-vat Sammy, who was slowly coming around. Slowly waking up.

"Hey," said Reardon, tapping on the glass. "Dickhead! You awake?"

Sammy, slumped up against the walls of his tank, rubbed his eyes, blinking sightlessly like a newborn kitten. "Wait, did it work?" he mumbled. "Harry?"

"Yeah," said Reardon, doing his *absolute best* not to cry, even a little bit, being far too manly for that. "Yeah."

Reardon knew better than to expect a lot from him right

now. There was, after all, only one question that Sammy wanted answered . . .

Sammy still blinking, ever so slowly looked down at his feet. And wiggled his toes.

"They're wiggling," he said, half laughing, half sobbing. "They're wiggling! Harry, Harry, they're wiggling!"

"Shut up," said Reardon, groaning and slapping the tank. "I knew—I knew you were going to be okay."

"You did not," said Sammy, his eyes fixed on his own wiggling toes. "You did not. You were freaking out."

"I—I thought you were going to kill yourself!"

"You idiot, of course I wasn't! I was fixing my back, you dumb stupid fat useless annoying weird sack of crap who's just a total dickhead obsessed with those ridiculous novels and games and nonsense!"

"I am not fat," protested Reardon.

"Yes you are."

He wasn't. He knew he wasn't. But Reardon scowled through the glass. "You scared me half to death, you know that right?"

"Yeah," said Sammy. "But you deserved it. *Bhai chod*."

The two brothers shared a smile.

"My legs work," said Sammy, smiling like a big dumb idiot. "They really work. And I can feel them."

"Yeah," said Reardon, "they do. Now I'm going to have to put that seat back into the copilot's spot . . ."

"Get a nice one," Sammy said through his ecstatic tears. "I want a nice seat." He bounced a little inside the glass. "This is amazing."

Reardon ran his right hand over his left arm. "You

know . . . I was pretty skeptical about this future crap, but it's turned out to be okay. You once told me that everything happens for a reason. Guess you were right."

"Yes, but now I'm dead, so you can see where believing things got me."

"You're not dead," he said. "You're *better.* You can walk now."

"Yeah," said Sammy. "I guess everything's fine now, right? We can go home?"

Reardon had *absolutely no idea* how to do that, and didn't know what exactly to say. Maybe the hesitance was telegraphed on his face, because Sammy's expression slowly changed too.

"We're not going home," asked Sammy, "are we?"

Reardon grimaced. "Not right away." It was the only honest answer he could give. "We have one more mission before we can even consider it."

"Okay," Sammy said decisively. "I want to help. I want to do things."

"Great," Reardon said, now even less sure about the plan than he already had been. It had taken him *weeks* to even entertain the idea that it was something to consider, and weeks *more* to accept it. And Sammy had a lot less time than that. "I need to you to pilot the *Aerostar* on this mission," he said, carefully, "and destroy it."

CHAPTER FIFTY-SEVEN

Captain Mattis's Quarters
Warfrigate 66549
Pinegar System
The Future

Today was the day. Mattis adjusted his spacesuit gloves, checking they were tight. The armored variants were always so difficult to put on, probably because of all the extra plating.

"You know," said Ramirez, smiling playfully from their bed. "You don't have to get your spacesuit on in your quarters."

He smiled over his shoulder. "I know, but it's always fun to get naked with you in the area. And for you to get naked. And for us to do stuff while we're naked."

"Now now," said Ramirez, "this isn't a time for horsing around. This is a busy time. And a big moment. If Spectre is there—"

"*If*," cautioned Mattis, not wanting to get his hopes up. Or hers.

"*If* he's there, this is important. This could end the threat to humanity once and for all."

He didn't know about that—some nagging doubt in the back of his mind suggested that there was more to come yet and that Spectre and the Avenir were not going to abandon their hostilities so easily—but certainly with Spectre out of the way . . . things could go back to normal. "Remember when the biggest problem you had was the deep state?" he asked. "We didn't know how bad things were back then. We didn't know that the Earth . . . " He didn't finish the sentence. He still couldn't.

"I know," said Ramirez. She slipped out of bed and moved up to him, touching his cheek. "But it's okay. We're here now and, you know, you should probably focus on your mission."

He knew that was true. "Mmm."

She gestured around herself. "So," she said. "Warfrigate 665 . . . whatever . . . is a kind of crummy name for this ship. Have you decided on a new one?"

The thought honestly had not occurred to him. "Uhh, no."

"Well," said Ramirez, seemingly unable to contain a huge smile, "I was thinking. I was thinking you could call it the *Midway-A*."

The *Midway*. His first ship, now lost, returned. That very idea made him smile too. "Honestly, the moment you said it I wasn't sure, but . . . it's growing on me."

"It's growing on you in three seconds," she said, raising an eyebrow. "Yeah. This is a good idea."

"It's a good idea," he said. "I'll inform the crew." There was, however, one more thing he wanted to talk about.

"But . . . before I head out," he said, idly fiddling around with this gloves. "There was something I've been meaning to ask."

"Shoot," said Ramirez.

"Back when we first got thrown through the portal, you were acting kind of weird. Strange. I thought it was just nerves, or shock at being thrown into the future, but now I'm not so sure." He took a breath. "What's wrong? You're not pregnant, are you?"

"God, no."

"But—"

"*No.*" She gave him a playful push on the back. "Just go save the universe. We'll talk when you get back."

He trusted her. He did. But he needed to know. "This might be the last one," he said. "Every mission might be. It's best not to wait."

"But . . . " Ramirez grimaced. "This isn't the best place, Jack. Or the best time."

"It's never going to be a perfect time." He smiled. "Just say it."

"Okay," said Ramirez, and fished a small box out of her pocket. It was felt and about the size of a fist. She lifted the lid open, casually sinking down onto one knee, revealing a pair of solid gold rings studded with diamonds. "Admiral Jack Mattis, will you marry me?"

CHAPTER FIFTY-EIGHT

Shuttle 1
Hangar Bay
HMS Caernarvon
Pinegar System
The Future

Lieutenant Daylin-Rutland formed up with the rest of the Royal Marines, filing aboard the shuttlecraft in single file, his rifle held comfortably in his hands.

Engineering work was great. Salvage work was interesting. But what he was best at, what he signed up for, was combat. And this was his opportunity. And what an opportunity it was: theft, followed by leading the attack on a future timeline installation. Death or glory stuff. Right up his alley.

First the theft. Then the fighting.

The Marines filed aboard, then the loading ramp sealed shut with a hiss. The shuttle's interior would remain compressed until they were ready to disembark, which meant it was warm and loud, but not too uncomfortable.

"You better not fuck this up for me, Lipham," he said,

giving the guy a shove on the shoulder.

Lipham shoved back, grinning that dopey grin of his. "You know I won't. I never do. You said I was a genius when I found that reflector on the outer hull."

Yeah, yeah, yeah. "Even a stopped clock is right twice a day," Daylin-Rutland rejoined. "You did good back there, Lipham. So let's keep it up."

The shuttle lurched forward as it took off. There were no windows in the shuttlecraft, but that didn't bother him as much as it did some others. In some ways he preferred not to see the outside space. It made the journey to their destination, sealed within a space suit and packed into a crowded metal box attached to a Z-space engine, that much easier.

Sometimes it was better not to know things.

The shuttle shuddered as it translated into Z-space. Then everything was still.

"So," said Lipham. "Heard the Captain is back. She's some kind of zombie now."

Oh my God. "You're only just hearing about that?" Daylin-Rutland slapped his own visor. "Seriously, Lipham? There was a ship-wide message sent out . . . weeks ago. From Admiral Yim. And she's not a zombie."

"I only heard about it yesterday. I don't read shipwides. They're always too long and have too many words."

Everyone groaned. God he was so thick. Thicker than hull plating.

"I'm sorry, I'm sorry," said Lipham. "I just don't like reading."

"There's a shock."

Everyone laughed. Pre-operation banter was an important

part of the way the team operated. As was the mid-operation banter. And the post-operation banter. In fact, the whole Marine unit of the *Caernarvon* ran on banter, much like how its newly returned Captain ran on tea.

"All units, check in," said Daylin-Rutland. Everyone did so, one by one, until it was back to him again.

"We're as ready as we'll ever be," said Lipham.

"Theoretically reassuring, but not really. Simply because we've maximized the probability doesn't necessarily mean that we'll succeed."

"Okay," said Lipham, ineffectually scratching the helmet of his space suit. "What kind of probability of success are we looking at?"

"Twelve percent."

"Twelve percent?"

"That's what I said."

Lipham groaned loudly. "Mate, that is no good."

"Buck up, Lipham, you'll be fine."

He whimpered.

Hours ticked away as the shuttle journeyed onward. Daylin-Rutland always found the waiting to be calming in a way. It allowed him to go over and over the plan in his mind. Focus. Push everything else out of his brain to be processed later. No worries about the future, no worries about the wife, nothing.

Then the shuttle shuddered again, signaling its return to normal space. The plan was to arrive right at the outskirts of Chrysalis.

The plan was that the shuttle was too small to be detected by the minefind. That was less of a plan, and more of a *fervent hope.*

"A'right, boys and girls," said their pilot. Lieutenant Corrick, another recently-returned "zombie". "We've arrived, and it looks like the minefield hasn't noticed us. Not yet anyway."

Daylin-Rutland breathed out a low sigh of relief. If the minefield around Chrysalis saw them, they would be destroyed before they had even the faintest hope of getting their Z-space engine fired up again. "Copy that," said Daylin-Rutland. "Have we been spotted?"

Corrick paused, no doubt checking her instruments. "If we did, they aren't reacting in any way."

Good news. "So. Let's steal a mine. Any prizes nearby?"

"Looks like there's one," said Corrick, "drifting by—it might have fallen out of orbit from Chrysalis some time ago. Be advised, it looks like it's malfunctioning." Oh great. Just great. That made their already dangerous operation much more serious. "You know the drill. I'll be opening the loading ramp in just a moment; stand by for depressurization."

A faint hiss echoed all around in the shuttle bay, slowly fading to nothing as the air drained away. Now all Daylin-Rutland had to breathe was the air in his suit.

In one of the side mirrors on his helmet, he saw the rear loading ramp silently open, the empty black void of space full of bright white stars. He turned around, ready to disembark.

"On my mark," said Corrick. "Three, two, one . . . mark."

The squad drifted out, one by one, their suits emitting little puffs of gas to keep them steady. Daylin-Rutland's visor painted a bright orange target marker in front of his visor, highlighting something far too distant to see. That would be the mine.

Daylin-Rutland drifted out toward it, letting his suit do all the work, little puffs of gas taking him away from the shuttle.

A spray of white gas washed over him, briefly obscuring his vision. To his absolute lack of shock, it was coming from Lipham's suit.

"Careful," he said, "Lipham, you're hitting me with your jets."

"Sorry," he said.

Jesus Christ, this guy.

They drifted closer and closer, and soon they could see it clearly. A spiked ball drifting through space, ominous and black and menacing, tumbling slowly as it traveled. Although there was no rust in space, and the technology was simple, the thing looked brand new—apart from the hole punched in the side. "Daylin-Rutland to Corrick," he said. "You were right. The mine is damaged."

"Damn," said Corrick, her voice hissing faintly on the line. "Well, we don't have unlimited time here . . . see what you can make of it. Check if it's just the guidance system or if the detonation system is broken too."

Daylin-Rutland floated up to the ghastly thing, his suit puffing out gas to slow him down as he got close. "It's smaller than I imagined," he said.

Lipham moved in front of him. "This thing's a gravity mine, yeah?"

"Yes, Lipham. So be gentle, for fuck's sake."

"Oh, I will," said Lipham, slowly floating around the mine with the other Marines, each of them inspecting it carefully for damage. "I don't want to get crunched."

"Stop being a damn baby." Daylin-Rutland floated up to the mine too, casting a critical look at the hole in it. It looked like some kind of high velocity fragment had busted through the metal. Judging by the jagged outline, it was probably a meteorite or similar piece of stellar matter.

A thought did occur. It could have been debris. In space there was no atmosphere to slow down errant rounds, and between the Sino-American war and ensuing battles with Spectre—in their own timeline at least, to say nothing of the battles in *this* timeline—it's possible it was a bullet hole. Had a bullet traveled thousands or millions of kilometers, drifting through the endless void, until it finally collided with this thing?

It didn't matter, they weren't here to learn anything, only to steal. A casual glance told him that the mine's propulsion system was totally fried, but the rest looked intact.

"Looks like the warhead is fine," he said.

"Lucky us," said Lipham, grimly.

Time to do their job. Daylin-Rutland pulled out his toolkit, casually plucking a plasma cutter off the rack. "Okay. Marines, hold that blasted thing steady, I'm going to cut into its hull and arm it, ready for Mattis and the fleet to jump in."

This was the most dangerous part of their operation. Stealing a mine and arming it.

Well, apart from everything that came afterwards of course. Apart from the battle.

That was going to be a bit harder.

CHAPTER FIFTY-NINE

Bridge
HMS Caernarvon
Z-Space near Chrysalis
The Future

Captain Spears sat in the command chair as though she'd never left it.

"Status report," she said, casually adjusting her collar. Her uniform seemed a little looser than it had been before, or was she imagining it? Probably the former. She had been in a tank, unmoving, for two months. Grown from a fetus, they said. That couldn't be good for her muscle development, even if the machine had stimulated her growth back to her body's previous levels. Allegedly.

Admiral Yim spoke up. "Lieutenant Corrick reports that her team has made contact with the mine and are arming it now as we speak." It felt odd to have the man as her XO—after Blackwood's betrayal, the position was conspicuously open—but he was a good fit. A bridge between the old and the new, and he had a vast amount of experience under his belt, including combat experience, and was seemingly more than happy to give up command in order to accommodate her return.

"Good show," she said, folding her hands into her lap. "Let me know when they're ready to go, and we'll move to Stage Two."

A few minutes ticked by in silence, all the monitors on the bridge showing the multispectral hue of the extraordinary place known as Z-space. The *William Harrison* checked in, and so did the Warfrigate. Right before he'd left it in Commander Modi's command for the duration of the mission, Mattis had re-christened it the *Midway-A*, but it felt right to her to simply call it the *Midway*.

A fitting title, even one made at the eleventh hour.

"Captain," said Yim. "Lieutenant Corrick reports that the away team have secured the mine. We are green light for Stage Two on your mark."

She inclined her head ever so slightly.

Yim spoke into his console. "All units, all units, we are green light for Stage Two. Translating out of Z-space, Captain."

The bright luminescence of Z-space was replaced by the cold, black void of space. To the *Caernarvon*'s right, the *William Harrison* appeared in a bright white flash, and to her left, right on top of the mine—exactly as they had planned—the *Midway*.

On Spears's main monitor, the asteroid of Chrysalis appeared, floating in space surrounded by nasty barbs.

"Stage Two complete," said Yim. "Z-space translation successful."

"Very good," said Spears. "Move to Stage Three immediately."

"Stage Three, aye aye ma'am."

Immediately, the communications systems lit up. "This is the *William Harrison*," said a youthful-sounding communications officer with a thick Midwestern United States accent. "Z-space translation complete, moving to Stage Three."

To the left of Spears, Blair's voice cut through the communications. The young FBI agent from San Diego had come far, just as Spears had suspected she might. "The *Midway* is ready to load, Captain Spears." She smiled. "We're on schedule."

Excellent. Spears stared at the asteroid of Chrysalis and felt Yim's eyes follow hers. Why did everything in the galaxy always seem to transpire around this little tiny rock at the edge of nowhere?

"This place hasn't changed a bit," remarked Yim, dryly. Then his voice became charged. "Lieutenant Corrick reports that they have successfully retrieved the away team and are preparing to move to Stage Four."

"Very well," Spears replied. "Pass along my congratulations to Daylin-Rutland for getting ahead of schedule. Make sure that the *Midway* is ready to go before we proceed."

Blair relayed the message, but the moment it was done, spoke up again. "*Midway* reports that they are preparing to execute Stage Four."

"Very good," said Spears. "Advise Commander Modi he is cleared to fire when ready."

Yim's fingers flew over his console. "Confirmed," he said, offering Spears a sideways glance. "You know, we're risking a lot based on the word of a captured AI . . ."

"I know," said Spears, "but I have full confidence in Captain Mattis. If anyone can pull this off, he can."

CHAPTER SIXTY

Command Core
Warfrigate 66549, AKA "USS Midway-A*"*
Space near Chrysalis
The Future

Commander Modi pulled the Warfrigate out of Z-space right on top of the gravity mine, the ship's mechanical arms loading the dangerous thing into the mass driver like a baby grabbing a toy and shoving it into its mouth.

"Commander," said Robinson, floating beside him in the ovular command core. "We have completed loading the device. Please be advised that the mass of the device meets minimum launch requirements, but it is still on the light side. With such little mass, a decisive strike against the targeted asteroid is extremely unlikely to cause more than structural damage."

"Structural damage," said Modi, "is exactly what we aim to cause. Target the hangar bay doors, and make sure the mine's detonation sequence is primed. Coordinate the countdown with the impact so that our team has an egress point."

"Confirmed," said Robinson. The bright yellow *FIRE* button right next to the mass driver lit up. "The weapon is armed, the mine is primed, and we are ready to move to Stage Four."

It was helpful for every stage of this operation to have a designated number. It pleased him on some deep, primal level. "Very well," said Modi, moving his hand to the button and gently depressing it. "Modi to *Caernarvon*, *William Harrison*, mine is away."

The *Midway* shuddered as the mine leapt away, fired by the mass driver, the very same weapon that had dealt such calamity to humanity's forces in the Battle of Earth—now repurposed to serve their needs.

Almost instantly the mine became too small to see, tracked only by their computers and radars, a little circle drawn around it as it zoomed straight toward Chrysalis. A small timer appeared beside it.

00:53
00:52
00:51

"Impact in fifty seconds," said Robinson. "The gravity pulse is charging."

"Yes, thank you," said Modi, staring at the same number that Robinson was looking at. How certain *were* they that their stolen ship, the *Midway*, would not be targeted by the asteroid's mines?

The timer ticked down. The mine drew closer.

Very certain.
Hopefully.

00:16
00:15
00:14

"Proximity alert," said Robinson, his voice as charged as Modi had heard it sound. "The other mines in the vicinity of Chrysalis are activating. They appear to be attempting to intercept the mine we fired. Probably a manual process to defend themselves."

They had expected this course of action, but if it was a manual process it had been engaged later than they had anticipated. Modi pondered the possible causes. The mines were outdated technology after all, and the people of Chrysalis shouldn't be expecting an attack like this. Maybe someone was sleeping at their radar.

Even so, it was worrisome. "Will the mines be able to reach the projectile before it impacts?"

"Current projections say no," said Robinson. "The nearest mine will take approximately one minute, four seconds to arrive."

00:05
00:04
00:03

Definitely not quick enough.

The mine slammed into the hangar bay doors of

Chrysalis and detonated, a massive barrage of gravitational energy surging outward from it like the invisible hand of God. Its fingers hooked onto the metal door and began peeling it away, atmosphere rushing out, followed by debris, small ships, gas and bodies.

No time to consider the consequences of bombing a civilian station or pondering the mortality of the people who had just been unceremoniously sucked out into space. From the corner of his screen, the shuttle piloted by Lieutenant Corrick raced toward the hole blown in the station, while mines raced toward the other two ships, the two passing each other in a flash.

As though angry they failed to intercept the target, the mines shifted direction, moving toward the *William Harrison* and the *Caernarvon*. The sooner those ships escaped into Z-space the better.

"Modi to *William Harrison*," he said. "Move to Stage Five. Send in Admiral Mattis and the *Aerostar*."

"Confirmed," said Lynch. "Good hunting, Modi."

Modi swallowed nervously. This time he didn't feel so confident in his abilities. This time they were playing for *all* the cards. "Take us in, Robinson," he said. The *Midway* was the only ship that Chrysalis wouldn't automatically target, so his role was vital. "We're Captain Mattis's way out. And if any of those mines come our way, shoot them."

CHAPTER SIXTY-ONE

Cargo bay
Aerostar
Z-Space near Chrysalis
The Future

Mattis should have been focused entirely on the mission, but all he could think about was Ramirez. Ramirez and her unexpected proposal.

And the ring snugly wrapped around his finger.

He was getting married. The very thought had planted a smile on his face that refused to fade even in the face of the impossible odds they were up against.

"*Aerostar*," said Blair, her voice crisp on the line. "You are clear to exit Z-space."

Mattis tapped the side of his helmet. "Right. Ready. Reardon, you ready to go?"

"Ready," said Reardon, dejectedly. "Are we *sure* there's no way to do this without blowing up the ship?"

"Absolutely sure," said Mattis. There was just no other way. "Corrick, Daylin-Rutland and their team are going in through the front door, making as much noise as they possibly can, but their mission is different to ours. You heard Shirley—the sensors at Chrysalis are programmed to attack only large ships without Avenir signatures, which means we need the *Aerostar* to get us to the garbage disposal area so we can get to where Spectre is. And kill him."

"I know," whined Reardon, "but surely there will be some other way to save the ship . . . she's my baby."

"*You're* the baby," said Mattis. "You agreed to this plan."

"I know." Reardon's voice was heavy with resignation. "Fine. Let's just get it over with. And don't make me watch. I don't think I can stand to watch."

"Okay, I won't." Mattis straightened his back. "Okay. Take the ship out of Z-space, and then execute Stage Six."

The *Aerostar* vibrated as it exited the strange unreality of Z-space and slipped back into the real world. Almost immediately, alarms and klaxons filled the cargo bay.

Sammy's voice cut in over the radio channel. "Mister Mattis? We did it. We're *really* close to Chrysalis, and just like Shirley said, the garbage chute is starting to open."

Either it was a few seconds early or they were a few seconds late. "Go in," he said, holding up his communicator and patching into the outside cameras.

He could see it. The large, maw-like aperture of the garbage disposal, opening like . . . like a giant butthole at the base of the fold.

There was no other way to describe it. It was an iris-shaped ring that slowly expanded, ejecting debris and waste into space. In moments it would close again and not open for days.

"Go, go now!" he shouted.

The ship lurched as it accelerated toward the opening. Trash and debris pounded the hull, no doubt scratching Reardon's precious pink paint job. Closer it came, closer—

Crap. The trash stopped flowing and the iris, with frightening speed, began to close. Shirley had said as much; it was specifically designed to prevent infiltration, closing the moment it had vented all its garbage, and with powerful strength, too. The metal ring slid tighter and tighter, and the *Aerostar* raced toward it, soaring through space, Mattis hoping against hope that they would make it . . .

Swiftly, the ring tightened, but not before the *Aerostar* jammed itself inside.

The hull groaned and screeched as the metal iris crushed the ship, squeezing it like an orange, the metal buckling and air escaping. Mattis checked his spacesuit again, making sure it was intact.

A split opened in the roof, and the doors to the cargo bay popped out. The *Aerostar* shuddered violently, the metal aperture of the trash chute trying to crush the stubborn thing.

Then, mercifully, it stopped, the *Aerostar* propping it open.

"Okay," said Mattis, let's get inside! Quick!"

He magnetized his boots and took a running leap toward the busted cargo bay doors, jumping out into the blackness of space.

CHAPTER SIXTY-TWO

Shuttle 1
En route to the Hangar Bay
Chrysalis
The Future

Lieutenant Daylin-Rutland held on tight as the shuttlecraft speared toward Chrysalis, to the hangar's interior that the mine's blast had exposed.

"Okay," he said, checking his rifle. "Remember, go in hot and make sure that the area is clear for our people. We're to secure a beachhead and prep it for exfil. Watch out for debris, there's no telling what that blast could have done to the interior, and most of all, beware of defenses. We have *no idea* what could be waiting for us on the other side."

"Aye aye," said Lipham, and everyone else signed off as well.

Daylin-Rutland inserted a magazine, chambering the first round. "Remember. Shoot first, sassy one-liners after."

The shuttle slipped through the broken hangar bay doors, coming to rest at the inside of the bay. There were no windows, so he had no idea what was going on or what the situation was.

The loading ramp dropped. "Go, go, go!" Daylin-Rutland was the first out, his rifle raised. "For King and Country!"

The whole hangar bay looked like . . . well, like a bomb had hit it. Everything that wasn't nailed down had been sucked out into space, including most of the ships docked there. The stairways, gantries, and loading scaffolds were bent and twisted and warped, barely recognizable, and dozens of docking umbilicals floated around in the open area like the tentacles of some giant beast, their tips torn to shreds.

"Whoa," he said, taking in the view. "Those damn gravity mines do not mess around."

"No they do not," said Lipham, moving in to secure the right flank.

Looks like they didn't need to worry about defenses on this side. Everything was trashed.

"Exit secured," said Daylin-Rutland, securing the left. "Now we just gotta wait for Mattis to do this and we can get the hell out of here."

He crouched down on one knee, rifle raised.

Seconds ticked away.

"Hey, Daylin-Rutland," one of the Marines said. "Any chance you could give us something to shoot?"

He scanned the ruined hangar bay with his rifle. "Wishing I could," he said.

"Reminds me of that time I spent months living on Pluto," said Lipham. "Just lots of dead nothing. It's a cool planet though."

Daylin-Rutland sighed. "Pluto isn't a planet anymore,

dipshit. It hasn't been for a long, *long* time."

Another squad member chimed in. "They shouldn't have started what they couldn't finish."

Everyone shared a chuckle, then went back to waiting.

Tick, tick went the seconds.

"Dwarf planets are technically planets," muttered Lipham. Everyone turned to stare at him.

"What? They are."

More seconds. More nothing. The silence grew eerie. Ominous, even.

"Well, come on," said Daylin-Rutland, gripping his rifle tight. "Where the hell *is* everyone?"

CHAPTER SIXTY-THREE

Outside the Garbage Disposal Iris
Chrysalis
The Future

Mattis flew toward the garbage disposal chute, the iris clutching the *Aerostar* tightly, slowly but surely crushing her with its massive hydraulic jaws.

"Reardon! Sammy! Abandon ship, now! Get out here with me!"

As he shouted, two figures in space suits appeared on the ruined loading ramp. Sammy and Reardon.

He couldn't focus on them. The chute was getting too close. Mattis braced himself for the impact, slamming into the barely-man-sized tunnel. Even with padding on the inside of his suit, the impact still jarred him, his teeth rattling around inside his head. Fortunately, he grabbed on with his magnetic gloves before he could drift away.

The *Aerostar* crumpled behind him, the remorseless hydraulics of the iris slicing through the hull slowly but steadily.

"Jump," he said. "Jump to me!"

The brothers exchanged a look and then jumped out of the cargo bay in tandem, drifting toward Mattis and the chute.

"Okay," he said, twisting around to face them, keeping one magnetized glove on the metal chute. "Impact is going to be hard, harder than you think. Just be prepared for it, and make sure you brace for the hit, because it's . . . yeah, ow."

"Great," said Reardon, "this sucks even worse than I possibly imagined."

"Hey, I'm just glad I can finally jump," said Sammy, and Mattis could detect a palpable elation in his voice, despite the danger and seriousness of their situation. "But I'll be ready."

Both of the kids slammed into the chute, Sammy landing especially hard, but they held fast.

"Oh no!" shouted Sammy, "I can't feel my legs!" Then he burst out laughing, kicking a leg out. "Nah, I'm fine. See?"

"You're not hurt?" asked Mattis. "Looks like you came in pretty hard."

"I'm far too high on adrenaline to care right now."

Reardon punched him in the shoulder. "You fucking idiot! Don't joke about that!"

The two of them switched languages to something Mattis didn't speak, presumably Hindi, and engaged in an angry yelling contest. Grateful for the break, Mattis turned his attention to the garbage chute. As it went deeper into the asteroid, farther away from the iris, the passage became depressingly narrow, almost the same size as the chute that they had crawled through to get to the *Caernarvon* bridge.

So while that meant he knew he could do it, it meant it also conjured memories of Spears dying on the bridge.

Hopefully he wouldn't wake up naked in a tank.

"Okay," said Mattis, pointing inside. "If you're finished squabbling, let's go."

Reardon crawled into the chute, grumbling loudly and muttering something Mattis couldn't catch.

Sammy, on the other hand, watched the garbage chute's giant iris crunch up the *Aerostar*, breaking the ship in half and splintering her into thousands of pieces of debris that slowly expanded in a cloud of metal and ceramics.

"Let's go," said Mattis. "That stuff is dangerous."

Mattis squirmed into the chute, and to his relief, Sammy was right behind him.

CHAPTER SIXTY-FOUR

Inside the Garbage Disposal Chute
Chrysalis
The Future

Mattis had a prime view of Reardon's butt the whole way up the garbage chute, until eventually the long tube lead to a processing plant. Passing through a narrow airlock, the three of them emerged on the other side.

Just as Shirley had predicted, the plant was empty, its crew evacuated to the safe zones. Flashing red lights bathed the room in a lurid crimson glow, and almost every computer screen displayed the same two words: EVACUATION ORDER. The distraction looked like it had served its purpose admirably.

Unclipping his rifle from his back, Mattis loaded it and checked that the safety was still on. "This way," he said. "The directions say out the main door of the processing plant, then left, then straight, then down a long passage, and we're there."

Reardon similarly unclipped and loaded a rifle. "I still don't understand why we couldn't bring more Marines for this," he grumbled.

"Because," said Mattis patiently, "you said nobody except Sammy and you can fly your ship, that you wouldn't let your brother out of your sight again, and Shirley told us that any more than a three man team would get discovered."

Reardon, flustered, looked away. "Sammy doesn't *have* to remain in my sight," he grumbled. "It's fine." The tone of his voice suggested that it was not in fact fine.

"Don't worry, Mister Mattis," said Sammy, taking out a pistol. "You don't have to worry about me. Getting to go on a mission where I can walk around? Hell yeah!"

Mattis ground his teeth, not exactly happy with the arrangement, but he had no choice. Those were Reardon's terms. "Okay," he said, "let's get going."

The three of them crept through the facility, out the main door, left, and straight. There they were presented with a long passage, the end shrouded in shadow. Just as the directions had said.

"Mattis to assault team," he said. "Sitrep."

"No hostiles, Captain," said Corrick. She sounded confused and lost. "Its like nobody's home."

"We knew they were going to evacuate," said Mattis, creeping forward toward the end of the corridor, "but I was expecting . . . *something.* People. Robots. Mutants. Something. Have you seen anyone at all?"

"A bunch of people got sucked out of the hangar bay," she said, "when the mine blew it. But since then—"

With a faint hiss, the communications channel cut out.

"Corrick?" asked Mattis.

No reply. Just static.

"Mattis to *Midway-A*."

Static.

"Mattis to *Caernarvon*."

Static.

"Mattis to anyone receiving this transmission."

"Only me," said Reardon.

"And me," said Sammy.

"I don't like the look of this." Mattis shook his head. "We should abort. Break off and make for the hangar bay. Losing comms like this . . . it's a bad sign."

"We're never going to get another chance like this," said Reardon with uncharacteristic sincerity. And Mattis knew it to be true. They were relying heavily on surprise, on the presence of outdated weapons and the indifferent maintenance and readiness of people who were not expecting to be attacked and had not fought a genuine war in their lifetimes.

"Okay." Mattis forced himself not to doubt. "We've come this far, let's finish it."

Up ahead, the light on his shoulder revealed a simple steel door, with an equally simple red button just to its right. The door was ringed in red and bore only the words: RESTRICTED ACCESS.

According to Shirley, this was the place. This was where Spectre—the *real* and *original* Spectre—lived. Just behind that wall.

So much death. So much pain. So much loss. And it was all about to end.

Mattis stepped up to the red button and pushed it.

CHAPTER SIXTY-FIVE

Outside Spectre's Lair
Chrysalis
The Future

Mattis pushed the red button and the door disappeared into the roof with a faint hiss.

Beyond was a massive, opulent room full of cushions, silks, and couches. Rich tapestries hung on the walls, completely obscuring the bulkheads, and the floor was rich mahogany wood stained dark red. Silver trays, flecks of food still lingering on them, lay neatly stacked on the floor, and a small tower of glasses rested against a distant bulkhead—a stark contrast to the bare metal, utilitarian bulkheads they had passed through to get here.

At the center of the room sprawled on a large king-sized bed was an immense man, so fat that rolls of meat hung down in front of his eyes, arms and legs protruding from his voluminous, shapeless body. He must have weighed a *thousand* kilograms at least . . . almost certainly more. There was no way he could fit out the door, let alone move under his own power. How long had he been living on that bed?

"Well, well, well," said the man, his jowls quivering as he spoke, voice heavily distorted by his thick lips. He had to pause for breath every few words. "I was wondering . . . if this was the day . . . Admiral Jack Mattis would finally . . . pay me a visit."

Mattis furrowed his brow at the colossal human lying there. "I should have brought more ammo," he said. "Spectre, I presume?"

"You presume correctly." With a low groan—a sound like escaping air from an overstuffed cushion—Spectre reached up and, with his tiny T-rex arms, lifted up the rolls of blubber hanging down over his right eye, taking both hands just to move enough to see out of a single eye. "Yes," he wheezed. Mattis was unsure if he was laughing or not. "I see. It . . . is you."

"Okay, I take it back," said Sammy, awestruck. "Bro, you're not fat. *That* guy is fat."

"Thanks," muttered Reardon. "I think."

Spectre slumped back onto the bed, the simple act of moving his arms obviously too much for him. "I presume," he gasped, "that you are . . . here to end my life."

"Yup," said Mattis, chambering the first round of his magazine with a soft *click-click*. "Pretty perceptive for a blind guy." He looked around, curious. "No guards? No gas? No traps?"

"The defenses . . . on this room . . . are those of common sense. None harm me . . . for they know . . . that my wrath is infinite, and my numbers . . . legion."

"Then it pleases me to be the first." Mattis raised up his

rifle.

"Coming to this timeline was a courageous act," said the massive thing, darkly.

"You should try it some time. Doing your own dirty work for a change, instead of sending one of your *legion*." Mattis ground his teeth. "Truth be told, we had no choice. We were sent here by one of your clones."

"I know," said Spectre, with *something* in his voice that hinted there was more to his words than their literal meaning. "Wasn't it frightening?"

"Not really," said Mattis. "In fact I—"

"In fact, at that stage of my life, I—almost welcomed death."

"Oh, are we completing each others sentences now?" asked Mattis, sardonically. "Cute." Still. There was something about the tone. *Something* there. Mattis searched for it, trying to drag meaning out of trace amounts of inflection. "What the fuck are you playing at?"

"I remember . . ." said Spectre. "Earth. I remember seeing it. Living on it . . . how wonderful it was." He groaned as though in pain, but it seemed more like a sigh. "I remember grass. And trees. And . . . forests. And camping. Camping under . . . the stars. The stars do not twinkle in space. I miss that."

What the fuck was this? The ramblings of a madman? Had he lost his mind? "Yeah, I liked that too," said Mattis, casually removing the safety. "That's a great memory to have in your head when I blow it open."

"I know," said Spectre again, with an edge to his tone that suggested that, indeed, he *did* know. "You even enjoyed it . . .

after you maced yourself. Accidentally . . . that one time. Bug spray . . . is not bear mace . . . Captain Mattis."

The memory, something he hadn't thought about for decades and decades, jumped back into his brain. A memory of being fifteen and camping in the woods, and having one of his friends bring along bear spray. Which Mattis had confused for bug spray, emptying about half the can into his tent. The stuff had burned his eyes, and he'd staggered, blind and in pain, out into the woods, into the creek, crying as he'd washed his eyes out. Not his proudest moment.

It didn't make sense.

Reardon hissed in frustration. "Mattis, what the hell is he talking about?"

"Everyone was asleep when that happened," said Mattis, staring in bewilderment. "I told them that the can just went off. I never told anyone that I confused it for bug spray."

"A . . . white lie," wheezed Spectre. "The kind of . . . lie that a teenager . . . tells. To prevent embarrassment."

Mattis snarled, curling back his upper lip. "You have access to my memories," he said, hissing the words. "You got hold of my brain. Picked out the parts you knew only I knew. Now you're—" he struggled to make the connection. Why *was* Spectre doing this? "You're taunting me."

"Oh no," said Spectre, reaching up again to his face, lifting up the rolls of flab that covered his right eye this time. Revealing a hollow, dead socket beneath, and for the first time, Mattis saw the gold ring on his left hand, almost smothered by flesh.

The same ring he wore in the same position he wore.

The same empty eye socket he had.

"I didn't read your mind . . . I *have* your mind."

"No," said Mattis, shaking his head. "That's not possible. You're not me. You can't be me."

"How do you think . . . my clones were . . . always a step ahead of you?" asked Spectre, and in his voice Mattis found that thread. The part of his tone that he couldn't identify.

His own voice.

"I . . . " Mattis didn't know what to say. "Aren't you British?"

"You . . . *I* . . . trusted Spears in the war. Humans are . . . predictable. Biased. Weak. And I know your mind, Mattis, we are . . . weak. The vocal affectation was . . . easy leverage. In simple terms I became what . . . you trusted. I reworked myself . . . into a weapon with but a single target. A solitary purpose. To better hurt you."

"Assuming," said Mattis, darkly, "that I even believe a word of this, why? Why do all this? Why bring me here? If you wanted to die, surely there are thousands of ways you could do it yourself. Without me."

"Because you escape," said Spectre, wheezing as he spoke. "You get away from this place. You go. You do things. You save . . . so many lives. Become the hero. Establish the last . . . peace." He spoke with a tired, grim certainty that sent a shiver down Mattis's spine. "But . . . no matter what you do . . . no matter what else you accomplish . . . you always end up . . . back here. The last tyrant."

"Explain," demanded Mattis.

"No." Spectre emitted another soft wheeze. "You'll have . . . to find your answers . . . elsewhere. On your journey. Even if I told you, I . . . did not accept the truth when I found it, and so . . . you will not either."

"I won't become you," said Mattis, finger tightening around the trigger. "You're a fool if you think you can get away with what you've done. You're going to die in this room. And I'm going to kill you."

"You sound like . . . you don't hate me."

"Well, I didn't like you to begin with, but then you killed my son. And so many sons and daughters on Earth. So many lives, snuffed out without a thought." Mattis's voice rose to an angry snarl. "Don't you get it, you monster? You *killed them.* You murdered more people than any other person has done in history. You destroyed our homeworld. You turned it into a tool. You used it and threw it away like a dirty rag." His voice cracked. The wall he had built in his head, the shield keeping back these thoughts, cracked and shattered. "And *you killed my son.* You fucking *cunt.*"

"I did." Spectre wheezed again. "You should hate me. I wanted . . . you to hate me. So that when this time . . . came . . . you would be filled with contempt. And end it."

"You wanna know the truth?" said Mattis, exhausted.

Spectre turned his massive hands, palms up, the limbs tiny compared to his body. "That's all I ask."

Mattis smiled. A grim, yet somehow relaxed and pleasant smile. "My wife's dead. My son's dead. My brother is dead. My longest friend, Captain Spears, died in my arms and is now a clone—and nobody knows what that means or if she is who we think she is, or if she's merely a perfect copy. My son's husband is probably dead, given the way things are going, taking with him my grandson and most everyone I've ever known, because my homeworld is destroyed. Maybe he got away, maybe he didn't. Doesn't matter. My career is over. My first ship, the *Midway*, is in a billion pieces in orbit around Chrysalis. Everyone, everything, I've ever loved is gone." The grim smile intensified. "I don't have much else left to lose."

"I've taken . . . everything from you," said Spectre. "Because . . . I needed you to be in the place you are . . . right now. To feel that rage in your heart. So you would not . . . hesitate."

"Mission complete," said Mattis. He leveled his rifle at Spectre's head and, with barely a second's pause, squeezed the trigger.

Epilogue

Shuttle, "Oppenheimer"
Space near Serendipity
Main timeline

Elroy Mattis stared down at the little rogue planet below them, seemingly so peaceful and calm and quiet and safe, just floating there in the middle of nowhere.

"It seems a shame to blow it up," he said, finger hovering over the little red button.

"It is, kind of," said Smith. "But there are plenty of other planets in the galaxy. I've blown up a few myself, it gets old after a little while."

The idea of destroying a whole *world* getting old was perplexing to Elroy in a way he didn't really think he would ever understand. "I feel like I should say some words . . . you know, something wise and smart, and appropriate."

"I can if you like," said Smith.

Elroy, at a total loss, gestured for him to do so.

"We knew the world would not be the same." Smith's tone suggested he was reciting a quote or something. "A few people laughed, a few people cried, most people were silent. I remembered the line from the Bhagavad-Gita: Vishnu is trying to persuade the Prince that he should do his duty and, to impress him, takes on his multi-armed form and says, *Now I am become Death, the destroyer of worlds.* I suppose we all thought that, one way or another."

"Neat," said Elroy. "What's that from?"

"Robert Oppenheimer. The inventor of the atomic bomb, describing the first nuclear detonation at Trinity. Fitting, I think, given what we're about to do."

There was some truth to that. But there was one question still nagging. "This isn't going to save Earth like you promised, is it?"

"It's . . . complicated," said Smith, looking away.

"Because," said Elroy, "we can't fix Earth. It's stuffed. Dead. Broken. But . . . we can go to other timelines. Other places where Earth still exists." He affixed Smith with a firm, unyielding stare. "That's what you plan to do, isn't it? Take all of us and jump ship to another timeline where Earth still exists?"

"Yes," said Smith.

Elroy said nothing.

"Listen," said Smith, finally looking at him. "You think it'll be weird, but it'll be okay, because I've done it before."

That shocked him. "You have?"

"Yes." Smith closed his eyes a moment. "And… people have been doing this for a long time. Not jumping between timelines or anything, no, but… changing their world, their reality. And they always adjust. Back in the early twentieth century, Sergei Krikalev launched himself to the stars as a citizen of the CCCP, and landed as a Russian. During his mission the Soviet Union collapsed and the Russian Federation was born. His government changed, his citizenship changed, his president changed, and the name of his home town was also changed; Leningrad became St. Petersburg. Times change, but humans change with them."

"That isn't really the same," said Elroy, defensively.

"True," said Smith. "But push the button. We need to tell Admiral Mattis how to get home so he can choose to come with us or not, whatever he desires."

True enough. It was time. Elroy's hand hovered over the button and then, his mind made up, he pressed it.

For a time nothing happened. Thoughts jumped into his head. Maybe it was a dud. Maybe Smith's detonator had failed. Maybe there was some other problem that they hadn't even anticipated . . .

But then, a tiny flash on the surface of Serendipity appeared, the overloading of *Einstein*'s reactor cores, heralding a much larger eruption of light. Bright tendrils of energy crept over the planet, clutching it and squeezing, crushing it down to a tiny mass, the light enveloping it and consuming it.

It was bright. So bright. The light washed the whole section of space, casting giant shadows off stray asteroids and debris as the light passed through space dust and clouds of matter, the intensity of it unimaginable—like staring directly into the sun.

And then it was over, and all that remained of the empty, dead rogue planet was a thin portal glowing faintly in space.

The other shuttle, obeying Albert's AI onboard, slipped through the aperture, and then it too winked out.

Silence lay over everything. Had they succeeded? Had

Smith and Elroy passed along the information that Admiral Mattis would need to get home again?

"What do we do now?" asked Elroy.

"Now," said Smith, "we wait."

Thank you for reading *The Last Tyrant.*

Sign up to find out when book 7 of *The Last War Series*, is released: smarturl.it/peterbostrom

Contact information:
www.authorpeterbostrom.com
facebook.com/authorpeterbostrom
peterdbostrom@gmail.com

Made in the USA
Middletown, DE
13 May 2020